DAMIEN and DUTTON

TWO JOSEPHS ON MOLOKAI

DAMIEN and DUTTON

TWO JOSEPHS ON MOLOKAI

by

HOWARD E. CROUCH

Published by
The Damien-Dutton Society for Leprosy Aid, Inc.
616 Bedford Avenue, Bellmore, New York 11710
U.S.A.

THIS BOOK IS DEDICATED TO

RHODA VAN DER CLUTE

WHO HAS BEEN RESPONSIBLE FOR THE

EDITING, LAYOUT AND PUBLICATION OF ALL MY BOOKS

INCLUDING OUR NEWSLETTER, "THE CALL."

SHE ALSO SERVES AS CHAIRMAN OF OUR BOARD OF DIRECTORS

GIVING GENEROUSLY OF HER TIME AND TALENTS.

Copyright © 1998 by Howard E. Crouch
International Standard Book Number: 0-9606330-4-9
Library of Congress Catalog Card No. 98-93417
Published by Damien-Dutton Society for Leprosy Aid, Inc.,
616 Bedford Avenue, Bellmore, New York 11710
Printed in the United States of America

ACKNOWLEDGMENT

I wish to acknowledge my gratitude to the wonderful staff at the Damien-Dutton Society headquarters, all of whom have taken on so many extra responsibilities, allowing me the freedom to write this book. They include:

Betty Campbell, my secretary and Vice President of the Society who has been at my side through many crises. She is responsible for much of the historical research.

Betty Lanigan who had the thankless task of transcribing my garbled tapes on to the typewritten page.

Stephanie Albinski, Terry Baldassi, Terry Donnelly, Mary Egolf, Angela Isgro, Marguerite King, Florence Martini, Rose Rampanelli, Edith Rose, Ellen Russo, Eleanor Smutney and Carol Tufano for their dedication to the work of the Society.

I also wish to express my sincere thanks to the professional proofreaders of the manuscript: Clifford Sawkins and Betty Towner.

All profits from the sale of this book will be given to the Damien-Dutton Society for Leprosy Aid, Inc.

BOOKS BY THE AUTHOR

Brother Dutton of Molokai

Damien and Dutton, Two Josephs on Molokai

In collaboration with Sister Mary Augustine

After Damien: Dutton

Two Hearts, One Fire

Once Over and Lightly

NOTES FROM THE AUTHOR

It all began on a Sunday in November 1941. Stationed as an army medic at Fort Simonds, Sandy Gully, a lend-lease base in Jamaica, West Indies, I was invited by the base chaplain to accompany him on a visit to the Spanish Town Leprosarium. The patients there were being cared for by the Marist Missionary Sisters of Massachusetts, U.S.A.

It was for me a horrifying experience but it changed my life forever. This was at a time before the discovery of the sulfones, and victims of leprosy presented a physical appearance of such revulsion they were banished from their homes and torn from their loved ones to live in isolation.

That night, tossing on my cot, I recalled a novel I had read, "Phantom of the Opera." It told the story of Eric, who was born with such a hideous facial disfigurement he was shunned and spent his life hidden in the bowels of the Paris Opera House deprived of companionship and love. His father fashioned a mask to hide his face but he was still angry at a world that ignored him. He wrecked the lives of all who dared to invade his domain, that is, until Christine entered his life and he fell in love.

I was determined to look behind the mask when I next visited the leprosy hospital. I would look into their eyes. When I did, I found the human beings behind the mask starved for friendship and love.

Thus began my crusade to bring some hope and pleasure into their lives. Enlisting the aid of the servicemen and women on the base, the leprosy hospital became the focus of much of our off-duty activities. We brought them entertainment, refreshments, and gifts, but most of all, someone who cared. No wonder they cheered when our fighter planes, returning from a scouting mission, would swoop low over the compound dipping their wings in salute.

It was then that seeds were planted for what would later become the Damien-Dutton Society for Leprosy Aid. For more than 50 years I have tried to bring a glimpse behind the mask, and to tell the story of Father Damien and Brother Dutton to all who would be interested.

On that fateful day in July 1886 when Dutton, dressed in denim, walked down the gangplank at the dock in Kalaupapa to be greeted by an unsuspecting Damien, God had sent Damien a precious gift—a friend.

Damien, shunned by many because of his disease and disfigurement, had faced abject loneliness and misunderstanding. He had certainly not expected this visitor, nor did he know anything about him. With the first handclasp, a bond was formed between them only to be broken by Damien's death in April 1889.

Much has been written about Damien over the years, little of Dutton. Most of the information is in the form of letters, without reference to conversations that took place between the two Josephs.

They spent their days and their nights together. They shared their joys and their sorrows, their accomplishments and their defeats. As anyone knows, a friendship is based on conversation and I set about the task of bringing their story to life with the probable talks they had together. They were two different men in temperament and in likes and dislikes. Perhaps that is why their friendship was bonded in diversity. Many of the events are based on fact, others on figments of my imagination. Nearly all of the dialog is how I believed they would have spoken to each other. Damien was talkative, Dutton taciturn. They both possessed a modicum of humor but there is no denying that they had the greatest mutual respect. As Dutton wrote, "Father and I had great love for each other."

I apologize to those who presently are victims of leprosy for using the odious word "leper" in this book. It was a word widely used during the time of Damien. Hansen's work was relatively unknown then and no one cared how the patient felt about being so labeled. Leprosy is still a viable medical term but Hansen's disease is more widely used to identify the victim.

If, through this book, there is better understanding of the past and a determination to make the future brighter, leading to the eventual conquest of leprosy, then I will have fulfilled my promise to both Damien and Dutton that their story has been well told.

H. E. C.
June 30, 1998

Brother Joseph Dutton

Father Damien

CHAPTER ONE

He is kneeling among a crowd of people. Some are in shining armor. There is a group of wailing women and among them he can make out the Mother of Christ at the foot of the cross. Alongside her is Mary Magdalene. The sky is dark. There are flashes of lightning streaking across the clouds followed by loud claps of thunder, shaking the ground. He is at the foot of the crucified Christ. Suddenly a loud piercing voice shatters the very soul. A voice that seems to come from the depths of loneliness. Eli, Eli, Eli, My God, My God, why have You forsaken me! He sat upright in bed. His heart pounding and sweat pouring from his forehead. Where am I? he thought. Who am I? Slowly regaining consciousness, he looked around to see where he was. Suddenly he realized that it was just a dream.

He was Damien, and here was he in his little bedroom on the second floor of his cottage. He was in his own Golgotha—Molokai.

The sound of a rooster came up from below. "Oh, dear God," he said and blessed himself. "I have overslept and they will be waiting for me at the Church."

The dream—what did it mean? He had been having more of these lately. He glanced at the calendar on the wall, July 29, 1886. It was thirteen years since he had arrived—a voluntary exile—to care for the victims of leprosy. These wretched people were tossed on this God-forsaken spit of land in the Hawaiian archipelago to fend for themselves. He sighed deeply. There was much to be done, as there was every day.

Fumbling for his shoes and putting them on, he felt that they were much tighter then they were the morning before. He ran his hand through his thick dark hair, now streaked with grey. He glanced at his hands, swollen and covered with nodules, some of which were exuding pus. No matter how often he told himself that he did not have the disease, he knew that he was not facing the truth. All the signs were there, others saw them. You could not fool the patients. That he had the disease, there could be no doubt. Why should he not have it, he thought, why should anyone be surprised. Had he not been living with them for more than thirteen years now, sharing their deprivation, comforting the sick, dressing their sores, burying the dead? Shaking his head, he tried to shut out those thoughts. He had too much work to do to have his mind dwell on self-pity.

He finished dressing. His clothes were stained, damp and musty. It was going to be a hot, steamy day. No matter how he tried, the thoughts came tumbling back into his head. For the moment he gave up trying to ignore them.

Maybe if I could have had someone to help me, one who was willing to put up with my stubbornness, it would have been different. Ever honest, he discounted the idea immediately. Don't fool yourself, Damien my man, he chided. The ones who did come to help had good intentions, but they were difficult; wanting to do things their way—always watching every little thing, eternally criticizing. But face it, who could stand a bear like me, he chuckled. Well, soon they will have to send someone but where will they find anyone willing to take up and stay to finish what I have started?

He groped for his breviary, opened it and strained to find his place but gave up as his mind wandered back into the past.

He was a young man, at age thirty-three when he first stepped ashore on the island of Molokai. What tragedy and heartbreaking sights he saw. There was filth and abomination everywhere. He spent much of his time bullying the authorities to get the needed supplies to take care of his flock. No wonder they found him a hard man to deal with. He smiled in grim satisfaction and jammed his battered black hat on his head.

He stepped out on to the small balcony attached to his room. Paul, his faithful helper was waiting below. He called up, "Ready, Father?"

Paul was in his twenties. He had been torn from his family and banished to Molokai when he was but twelve years old. Immediately upon his arrival, Father Damien had taken him under his wing. He was a quiet, diffident lad who seemed ever at Damien's side. He served his Mass, ran his errands, and said little but his eyes spoke volumes. Today, those eyes were full of concern. Damien, noticing Paul's expression, said to himself, "Am I failing so fast? I know I cannot fool Paul." He came down the creaky stairs holding on to the banister. Paul offered his arm to Damien and handed him his sturdy walking stick, for Damien found difficulty at times in keeping his balance. His feet were swollen and painful.

"Is it necessary that you go to Kalaupapa after Mass?" asked the worried Paul. "You look so tired."

"Don't let looks deceive you, my friend," Damien said with a twinkle in his eye, "I can still outrun you!"

They walked the short distance from Damien's house to his church, St. Philomenas. It was originally built as a small chapel by one of the Sacred Hearts Brothers who visited the island prior to Damien's arrival. Damien enlarged it but it still needed further expansion as it could not hold all of the patients cramming into it for daily Mass.

When he entered the sacristy, Damien washed his hands and vested slowly, his fingers awkwardly twisting the cincture which of late was becoming increasingly difficult to manage. He prayed silently, "Gird my loins, O Lord," and he thought wryly of the biblical connotation that "the day will come when another will gird thee and lead thee where thou wouldst not." This is not of my choosing, he thought, yet I have been ready for it over the years. Paul, noticing his abstraction, helped quietly as the priest struggled with the chasuble. Outside, in the eaves overhead, the soft cooing of the mourning doves began their matins. A vagrant breeze wafted in with the fragrance of jasmine and honeysuckle. Imperceptibly and then as irresistibly as the first light of the rising sun on the horizon, a ray of peace flooded his soul. He turned to the waiting Paul.

"Come, my friend," he said, "This is the day the Lord has made. Let us rejoice and be glad therein." Paul pulled the cord and the bell tinkled announcing that Mass was about to begin. They walked slowly to the foot of the altar.

"I will go unto the altar of my God." Then he intoned, "The God who gives joy to my youth."

Damien turned to greet the assembled congregation, each member a part of him. No pastor had ever faced such a congregation. They were lepers, some in the beginning of their disease, others in advanced stages. The air was filled with the nauseous odor of decaying flesh.

This no longer bothered Damien. When he first faced such a congregation, he had difficulty breathing and would leave the altar to go outside to get some air. The congregation consisted of patients of all ages, from small children and teenagers, to young men and women and the elderly. They gave rapt attention to their *Kamiano*, the Hawaiian word for Damien. They sang the hymns beautifully and followed the Mass with piety.

When it came time to receive communion, many tottered to the rail. The blind were helped by the sighted. Damien approached each penitent with the Sacred Host, the Body and Blood of Christ. He had difficulty with some in trying to place the Host between swollen lips. Others had gaping holes where once there were well-formed mouths. In each face he saw the suffering Christ.

Mass over, and the final blessing given, Damien and Paul went back to the sacristy. Damien knelt in humble prayer while Paul cleaned the vessels and stored away the vestments. His prayers finished, Damien staggered to his feet, Paul ever at his side.

"We are late, Paul," Damien said. "We must leave

right away for Kalaupapa."

"But you have had nothing to eat, Father," protested Paul.

"I will get something at Kalaupapa. They will
worry if we don't arrive on time."

Outside the Church, Paul had hitched up the old grey
mare, Daisy, Damien's favorite horse, to a two-wheeled
buggy covered with a canvas canopy. Kalaupapa was
some two miles away on the other side of the peninsula.
Few leprosy patients lived there; most residents were
government workers and homesteaders. In fact, leprosy
patients were forbidden to go there but it was impossible
to keep some of them from travelling the short distance
from Kalawao. A few, from wealthier families, were able
to purchase small tracts of land and build sturdy houses.

Kalaupapa had a better harbor than Kalawao.
There was a wharf jutting out into the water where boats
could tie up and unload their cargo. Being on the lee side
of the peninsula, the weather was milder and less windy.
Vegetation grew in profusion. There were large trees and
plants of many varieties skirting a vast plain covered with
grass where wild pigs rooted, and herds of cattle and
other animals, grazed contentedly.

St. Francis Church, an imposing structure, was
located close to the ocean. Damien travelled there from
Kalawao twice a week to care for the spiritual needs of
the Catholics and to greet incoming patients. The old dirt
road was formerly just trampled-down underbrush making travel very difficult. Damien, with a crew of patients,

had cleared out the brush and removed as many rocks as possible. Now the road was reasonably passable and the patients named it the "Damien Road."

Damien struggled to get up into the seat of the buggy, sat down heavily and turned to Paul who was holding the reins.

"I have a feeling," he said, "that something special will be happening today—perhaps a surprise."

Paul stared at him.

"Don't ask me why I feel this way, I just do."

Jerking the reins, Paul made a clicking sound. Old Daisy did not need any directions. On this morning, she was full of vim. Instead of just clip-clopping with her head down, she tossed her mane about.

"Daisy seems to be full of pep today," Paul laughingly said.

Damien chuckled. "I told you this was going to be a special day and the old girl knows it, too."

Daisy, who knew the road so well, was secure and sure-footed as she trudged along, avoiding the large stones. As they neared the outskirts of Kalaupapa, there was more activity on the road, more people about, obviously from the farmhouses that dotted the landscape. The buggy drew up to the steps of St. Francis Church where a small group was waiting to greet Damien. He gave his blessing. An old man approached him.

"Is everything ready?" Damien asked.

"Yes, Father. I will ring the bell when the ship has docked."

The buggy continued toward the dock. A crowd had gathered and watched as the small steamer came closer to shore. Among them were government workers and patients from Kalawao who would escort the new arrivals back to the settlement. There were extra horses for those who were able to ride and carts for the seriously ill. The rest could walk the two miles from Kalaupapa to Kalawao.

A man in a white suit came over to the buggy to greet Father Damien.

"Good morning, Dr. Mouritz," said Damien. "I see you are here before me today."

Dr. Mouritz had been appointed resident physician for the settlement two years ago by Walter Murray Gibson, President of the Board of Health.

The Doctor laughed as he helped Damien down. "It's not often I can beat you, Father, but I did today."

"Well," said Damien, "I wonder what the boat holds for us. Do you have a list?"

"Yes," the Doctor said, "and we are expecting about fifty new arrivals."

"Is there anyone other than the patients on the list, Doctor?"

"Not that I can tell," the doctor replied. "Are you expecting someone?"

Damien looked disappointed and glanced at Paul who shrugged his shoulders.

The ship had now tied up and the gangplank was being lowered. They walked toward the dock. Damien was determined to greet each new patient as they came ashore. The bell of St. Francis pealed its welcome.

CHAPTER TWO

STANDING MOTIONLESS at the rail of the steamer as it approached the bleak shores of Kalaupapa, Joseph Dutton quietly and soberly scanned the terrain of what was to be his home—his chosen Gethsemane.

It was a far cry from the monastery of the Trappists in Kentucky where he had spent over two years trying to find a place to do penance for his past life. Little did he know then that once he set foot on the shores of this island, he would never leave it for more than forty-four years.

The pale disc of the waning moon still lingered in the silvery sky, barely distinguishable from the molten-colored grey, moving swells of the early morning sea. Tall, bleak, steep cliffs towered menacingly and the raucous gulls broke the stillness, shrieking as they circled and dipped begging for morsels of food. This was the end of a long journey and the end too, of all that went before.

Dutton felt his breast pocket and patted the thick envelope there. It contained the necessary papers from King Kalakaua and from the head of the Board of Health, Walter Murray Gibson, giving him permission to land. He had had a long conversation with the Bishop of Honolulu who also granted his request to offer his services to Father Damien without receiving any salary.

Only a few weeks earlier, Dutton had read about this man, this heroic priest, who had exiled himself on the island of Molokai to care for the victims of leprosy. The word had spread fast throughout the whole world once it was known that Damien himself had contracted the disease. Dutton read this in the papers while visiting a Redemptorist priest friend in New Orleans, and he was positive that at last he had found the answer to his quest.

A tall man, soldierly in appearance, Dutton wore neat, faded blue denims, the only clothing he had brought with him. He ran his hand nervously through his hair as he tried to erase the memory of the sleepless night just spent aboard this little ship.

The night before, standing on the dock at Honolulu, he had witnessed a scene of pandemonium and unrelieved horror. He had hoped to forget the old tragedies of the battlefield, the cries of the bereaved mothers and wives searching the smoldering rubble for the bodies of the dead who had been abandoned in the last frantic days of the War between the States. That was nothing compared with these "living dead" on this voyage from which there could be no return. Fifty protesting victims had been prodded aboard, some hobbling up the gangplank unaided, others borne on canvas stretchers; all herded ruthlessly into crowded, dirty quarters—good enough for those who were considered by the world to be unclean.

For the moment there was a blessed quiet, broken only by the sloshing slap of the waves cresting at the side of the bobbing steamer. The beads of his rosary slipped through his fingers, one by one—the Sorrowful

Mysteries. They took on a deeper meaning as a kaleido-scope of unforgettable scenes of this voyage flashed before his mind's eye. They faded, and then regrouped in a pattern of despair. One scene kept reappearing. At the Honolulu wharf, a poignantly beautiful mother, her flower-like face tight with grief, struggled to keep her five-year-old son who was pulled from her arms and handed over to a withered old woman with disfigured features, leaving no doubt as to the ultimate fate of the child.

Dutton thought of his own mother, long years before, who had tried so determinedly to keep him at her side, and he realized anew what it must have cost her to have to let others guide his growing years. Mother of God, he mused, all mothers share in your loss of the Child in the Temple! As with Mary, he locked this scene in his heart.

"You can come back with me, sir. It's not too late to change your mind."

Dutton, turned to face the gruff, weather-beaten Captain. He had thought the man to be without feeling, hardened against the sufferings of so many.

"No," he replied, "I have come too far to go back now."

The Captain was not convinced.

"I wouldn't blame you, you know. No one would blame you. There's no end to all of this," and he spread his hands in disgust.

Now they were nearing the dock which was tied precariously to the large, heavy rocks that jutted out into the sea. The engines were slowing down. Dutton scanned the waiting crowd, now visible to him. Was Damien there?

Would he accept him or would he turn him back. Shading his eyes, he spotted a two-wheeled buggy with a young man holding the reins of a speckled, white horse. A figure in black with a wide brimmed hat was walking toward the wharf. Dutton turned to the Captain and pointing to the figure asked, "Is that Father Damien?"

The Captain was busy giving orders to the men struggling to secure the boat to the jutting rocks. Without turning his head, he said, "That's the man!"

Some doubts began to creep into Dutton's mind. Am I strong enough? Can I stand it? Will I give away the revulsion on my face for what I shall see?

Dutton was startled by the sound of a bell drifting across the water. He was on his last decade of the rosary now, the Fifth Mystery. Love of God and service, that's what it's all about, he decided, as all his doubts left him. One just can't love God in the abstract, he thought. To love God was to love His creation—all of it, serving all endlessly, the least lovable.

The odyssey which had led him from the drinking halls of Nashville, to the waters of baptism at the Catholic church in Memphis, Tennessee, and to the silent corridors of the Trappist monastery in Kentucky, was now leading him to the end of his journey on Molokai. Peace, which had eluded him in all his undertakings, overpowered him now.

The steamer crunched against the pilings, the lines were secured and the engine shut down. Both Damien and Dr. Mouritz stood at the foot of the gangplank. On board, Dutton stepped aside waiting for the patients to disembark first. As each patient stepped ashore they were greeted with warm handshakes and welcome words by Damien. They all knew who he was without ever having seen him before. He was dressed in his long, black cassock, his black broad-brimmed hat atop his head, similar to the hats they had seen priests wear in the other parts of the islands. Around his neck hung a gleaming cross.

After all the patients had left the ship, Dutton turned to the Captain.

"Thank you, sir, it was a good voyage and your men handled the ship well."

The Captain shook Dutton's hand.

"God be with you and if you change your mind, I will be back here within the week."

He is not convinced that I will last, thought Dutton. He walked down the gangplank with his small canvas bag. Damien had just started to go back to his buggy.

"Father?" Dutton called.

Damien wheeled around and looked at this tall, neatly dressed man standing there with his hand extended. Damien shook his hand.

"Yes, I'm Father Damien, and you?"

"I am Joseph Dutton, I've come from the States to help you."

Pulling the papers from his pocket, he handed them to Damien.

"These are the papers from both the King and Mr. Gibson giving me permission to land. I have also spoken to the Bishop in Honolulu who has approved as well."

Damien said nothing for the moment, scanning the papers through his spectacles. Then he turned to Dr.

Mouritz who was still standing at his side and introduced Dutton to him.

"This is Dr. Mouritz, the resident physician."

Dr. Mouritz put out his hand and greeted Dutton warmly.

"I'm happy you came. Father has been waiting for helpers for a long, long time."

Damien whispered to himself, "So this is the surprise that I knew was about to happen!" As they walked to the buggy Damien seemed lost for words, deeply affected by the turn of events.

Dr. Mouritz scanned Dutton carefully with his practitioner's eye. What he saw was a trim man in a clean denim suit carrying only a small canvas bag. "If this is all of his possessions, then he obviously has little needs." Mouritz's conclusions were right. A denim suit was to be Dutton's uniform for the rest of his life. He never dressed differently.

Dr. Mouritz noticed his slim, lithe body, that he stood about five feet, eight inches tall, had dark brown hair, greyish-blue eyes, a low voice and a pleasant smile. He guessed he was about forty years of age—actually he was forty-three, three years younger than Damien. He appeared to be reserved and thoughtful and said nothing about why he had wanted to come to Molokai. The Doctor liked what he saw, a good companion for Damien, capable of laborious work.

Damien stopped and turned to Dutton.

"I might as well tell you that I cannot pay you." His voice was raspy.

"Even if you could pay me, Father, I could not accept any money. Mr. Gibson and the Bishop both offered me a salary and I turned them down telling them that under no circumstances would I accept money."

Damien was about to ask, why then did you come here, but thought better of it. He would wait until they were alone to ask him all the questions running through his mind.

Damien was leaning heavily on his staff.

"You asked if you could be of some help to me. You have no idea what my thoughts were when I shook your hand," he said laughingly. "If you knew what I have in store for you, you might just turn and walk up that gangplank and go back to Honolulu."

Dr. Mouritz put his hand on Dutton's shoulder. He was smiling.

"I don't know whether to feel happy or sorry for you. I know Father only too well. You will get little rest. He has so many plans, it will take an army to finish them all."

"I'm used to hard work," answered Dutton, "That is why I came here and I take orders very well. The army trained me for that!"

Damien looked quizzically at Dutton.

"That's interesting. You will have to tell me all about it. Right now, I have to see that the new patients are taken care of and are transported to Kalawao."

Dr. Mouritz, realizing the uniqueness of the moment for the ailing priest and his new helper, stopped Damien who had instinctively started to go toward the frightened and weeping patients. He gently restrained the tottering figure and turned him to the waiting buggy.

"Let me take care of them this time and you take Mr. Dutton to the settlement. I'm sure he must be tired after his long journey. And you had better take care of yourself, too," he added.

Damien did not object as he would have under different circumstances, but he was eager to talk more to this man who seemed so sure of himself. Paul jumped down from the rig to assist Damien. Dutton wondered if the young man had leprosy, and would later learn about the special type of leprosy that affected Paul.

Damien introduced Paul to Dutton.

"This is Mr. Dutton from the United States who has come to help me."

Paul hid his claw-like hands but Dutton stretched out his, so he had no choice but to shake hands with this strange man.

"Ah," thought Damien. "A big question has been answered."

Paul helped Damien up on to the seat. Dutton sat next to him. Taking up the reins, Paul turned and whispered to Damien, "Is this the surprise?"

Damien turned to Dutton, chuckling, "This is a little secret we have between us."

He reached out and patted Daisy on the rump.

"Home, old girl, and make it fast."

Daisy switched her tail and slowly pulled the rig. It was as if she said, "I'm in charge and I will get you there in my own time."

CHAPTER THREE

THEY HAD BEEN clip-clopping along for some time now, old Daisy picking her way along the familiar path. Her ears protruded from a battered straw hat perched on the top of her head. Her tail was flicking from right to left, switching at the stinging green flies that clung to her white flanks. There were only occasional breaks in the companionable silence that engulfed them as the blazing sun beat down. Each man was absorbed with his own thoughts. Paul, ever the diplomat, was silent, also aware of what each man must be thinking.

Dutton, with his ability to study the terrain from his experience in the quartermaster corps of the Union Army, took in everything. He noticed that the dirt road was not wide enough for two carriages going in opposite directions to pass each other. One would have to pull off to the side to let the other go by. He saw many gravestones. They dotted the roadway on both sides—no single massing but spaced here and there. So different from the national cemeteries he had helped to create where the graves were lined up in perfect rows.

As they rode farther away from Kalaupapa, he noticed the change in the plants and shrubbery. There were higher bushes, fewer tall trees and lots of tangled undergrowth. The road was hilly and rocky. It has been carved out by amateur builders, he thought, so unlike the efficiency of the army engineers.

Damien turned to Dutton. It was as if he were reading his mind.

"There is so much jostling around, are you uncomfortable?"

"Oh, no, Father, I'm used to this."

"In the early days," Damien explained, "There was no road, not even a trail between Kalawao and Kalaupapa. Those who lived in Kalaupapa had no desire to explore the Kalawao side."

"Why was that, Father?"

"Well," Damien answered, "For one thing they were afraid and for another, as you will see, there is no way that a pier could be built to allow ships to dock."

"It sounds like a pretty forsaken place."

"The coastline is rugged at Kalawao and filled with huge rocks and reefs," Damien explained. "There is little protection from the wind, so vegetation is sparse. The isolation of the place is the main reason the government purchased this part of the peninsula to establish a leprosy settlement. There is very little means of escape, although many have tried it."

Dutton peered at Damien.

He asked, "What happened to them if they tried to escape?"

"They either drowned or if they tried to climb the pali, which we call the cliffs, they fell to their deaths. Several were shot by those guarding the cliffs." Damien shook his head, "It was a veritable hell."

"In the beginning," Damien continued, "I used to travel by horseback between the two villages as there were Catholics at Kalaupapa who needed spiritual guidance. Eventually I built the church, St. Francis, the one you saw when you arrived."

"It is a beautiful structure," Dutton remarked.

Damien took off his hat and wiped his sweaty brow. Paul looked straight ahead, detached, as the two men were becoming acquainted with each other.

"I encouraged the patients to become engaged in work and start growing gardens for food. I taught some of them how to build their own little houses."

Damien was reliving past achievements.

"We had to go often to Kalaupapa for the necessary supplies, so it was evident we needed a road."

He looked at Dutton, eyes smiling.

"I built this road with the help of the patients. I suppose you must think it a very primitive one."

"It is a well built road, Father, and since it serves its purpose, it is a job well done."

Damien liked that. Here was a practical man who saw things the way they were. No flattery, just plain talk.

They both lapsed into silence.

Dutton suddenly looked at Damien.

"I was wondering why we landed at Kalaupapa and not at Kalawao, Father. Now I know!"

Damien swatted at a pesky mosquito.

"No large boat or even a small steamer can get close to the shore. They have to anchor out and launch small dinghies which the waves push toward the rocks, or they have to row. When they are near enough, the patients, or any visitors, have to jump from the boat on to the slippery landing. Many are too weak to make it. Some slip and drown while others fall through deep cracks in the rocks and hope they can be rescued."

"I have landed this way many times," Damien recalled, "And I had difficulty getting ashore, strong as I am. The government confined me to Kalawao and would not permit me to leave to go to Honolulu for confession."

Noticing Dutton's expression of almost disbelief, Damien hurried on to explain.

"A priest would come to the island and the boat would anchor offshore. I would row out to get as close to the steamer as possible. My confessor would then lean over the rail as I shouted my sins to him, and those on board would hear almost every word I spoke. I cannot tell you how I felt confessing my sins this way instead of in the privacy of a confessional."

It was then that Dutton noticed Damien clutching a rosary tied at his waist. He could imagine the pain that the memory of this had caused him.

The only sound was clip-clop, clip-clop, like the beating of the metronome, ticking off the moments between yesterday and tomorrow. A sense of prelude! Dutton was still a little puzzled. Damien had not as yet asked him any questions about his past life or why he had come. On the other hand, Damien's mind was filled with possibilities of tasks to be accomplished, now that the promise of a full-fledged helper seemed to be fulfilled. This man appeared to be able and willing which was more than he could say about some of the others who had come to help.

"Dr. Mouritz," said Dutton, interrupting Damien's thoughts, "seems like a very nice man. Do you work together?"

The priest smiled to himself at some private memory: Should I level with this man, or shall I wait and let him find out for himself.

Damien grunted. "You might as well know from the start, I'm not an easy man to get along with."

Paul nodded his head but Damien took no notice.

"At first, we did not have a resident doctor. A doctor would come once in a while but would stay only a few hours. The Hawaiians do not trust the white man, as you will find out, and they would have nothing to do with the doctors. So the medical care of the patients was left to me."

"That must have been difficult for you, Father."

"I had very little experience except that which I had gained in my other missions before I came to Molokai. But here, there were only a few medical remedies available—mostly salves, and pills for fever. I did the best I could. My poor people trusted only me, which caused a great deal of resentment among some of the government staff."

The buggy swayed as Daisy avoided a large rock. Paul tightened his grip on the reins.

"Dr. Mouritz had heard many tales about me," continued Damien, "before he came here as a resident doctor some two years ago. He was prepared for rebellion on my part. It took a little while but we finally worked it out. After all, that was why I was here, to help my people, so how could I deny them professional assistance? I tried hard to convince them to let Dr. Mouritz treat them but I must be frank with you, not many will have anything to do with him."

"How did Dr. Mouritz take this?"

"Dr. Mouritz has been in the Hawaiian Islands for many years and completely understands the situation. However, there are others, not Hawaiians, who allow him to take care of them. He is a good man," said Damien convincingly.

As they neared Kalawao, Dutton noticed groups of people gathered along the roadside. Some tipped their hats to Damien in greeting, others pulled their scarves over their faces when they saw the stranger riding beside him. Dutton noticed many huts now, and a few neat cottages with small gardens and fences. He also saw long, wooden buildings which he believed might be government buildings. As they passed other groups he saw many on crutches, some leading the blind. It amazed Dutton how quickly he had become accustomed to these sights. Now there were more and more patients visible. Some, who were riding horseback, looked very young and full of life. They were approaching the settlement.

Dutton again waited for Damien to ask him some personal questions. When Damien turned to him, Dutton thought, this is it, when he finds out what my life has been, I wonder if he will send me back on the next boat.

Instead, Damien asked, "Did you know that my name was once Joseph?" Dutton had read only of Father Damien and it had never crossed his mind that he had a Christian name.

But, *Joseph!*

A coincidence surely, but to him a sign, too, that God's providence in all things rules sweetly.

"My name wasn't always Joseph," Dutton went on to explain.

"My given name was Ira, but I took the name of Joseph when I converted to the Catholic faith three years ago."

"Oh," said Damien. With this revelation a little of the mystery was clearing up. "Then what faith did you belong to before your conversion?"

"My parents were Anglican of a sort, and at one time I had considered joining the Anglican priesthood. Then after my conversion I spent some time with the Trappists trying to find out where God wanted me, but. . ." and his voice trailed off. "It's a long story, Father."

"I don't want to pry," Damien said in an understanding way. "We all have a story to tell."

Returning to the original subject, Damien continued, "I was Joseph until I joined my brother, Pamphile, at the seminary at Louvain. His name was Auguste until he joined the Fathers of the Sacred Hearts and took the name of Pamphile. Do you know that, like you, I also had considered joining the Trappists. I was attracted by their rules and wanted to make great sacrifices for God and to do penance."

"That's what I liked about the Trappists, too," commented Dutton.

"But God had other plans for me," Damien went on. "I also applied for permission to enter the Fathers of the Sacred Hearts as Pamphile had done. At first I was not accepted for the priesthood but was allowed to enter as a lay brother and took the name of Damien, the brave physician of Cilicia, Greece, who spent his lifetime in the service of others, dying the death of a martyr."

During the ride, Dutton was struck by the simplicity of this man who had taken the name of the physician and without realizing it, was really describing himself. He wondered again at the workings of Divine Providence which even in the choice of a name seemed to become a bonding between the two of them.

Suddenly, the carriage took a turn in the road and Dutton gasped. Before him was the most magnificent sight he had ever seen. The ocean was now in full view with huge waves crashing against the rocks. The high, somber cliffs of the peninsula were breathtaking. It was a scene he would see every day for the next forty-four years as he walked out of his cottage door. It was a sight he would never tire of, nor ever tire of describing it to his many correspondents. But in all his years to come, he never heard a patient describe it as "beautiful."

Paul started to jump down from the buggy when Damien restrained him. He wanted Dutton to savor the moment. Dutton, realizing the buggy had stopped, got down and offered Damien his arm. As his feet touched the ground, he murmured to himself, "Home, home at last! This is where I belong."

Dutton was so taken by the sight of the cliffs that he had not noticed he was standing near St. Philomenas Church. Turning his head to the left, he saw the gleaming, white-washed building and the tall steeple.

"This is my church," Damien said. "It was only a small chapel when I arrived here, run down and seldom used since few priests came at first. Occasionally Mass would be celebrated but the patients would use it for prayer meetings. Despite all my additions, it still needs further expansion when I get around to it and if I have some help."

He looked at Dutton.

"Are you handy with a hammer?"

"Yes, Father, I'm quite handy with tools and I enjoy building things."

Damien beamed. "Another link in the puzzle," he muttered to himself.

"What did you say, Father?"

"Nothing, I was just talking to myself," he replied. "Would you like to visit the Church before you come up to my house?"

"Yes, I would like that very much."

"Well, go on in then," said Damien. "Paul will take your bag. When you are finished, you will find my house just a bit beyond the back of the Church, next to the pandanus tree."

Dutton saw a two-storied, white-washed frame house adjacent to the tree.

He had been warned that Damien was a careless, slovenly man, but stepping into the Church and assailed by the fragrance of the blossoms, he marveled at the exquisite cleanliness of the place. Everything bespoke the handiwork of a man who not only revered God but loved beauty, balance and orderliness. The brass candlesticks gleamed, and the linens were crisp and snowy-white. The beautiful chandelier hanging over the sanctuary was very impressive. This was not put out just for him, he knew, for no one had been expecting him.

As he entered, an old woman on her hands and knees was industriously plying a coconut husk and bits of tallow to bring the floor to a rich sheen. She arose and tiptoed out, leaving him to enjoy the moment alone. There was a pervasive aroma of incense. He closed his eyes, his soul caught up in a deep peace—thousands of watery miles from his homeland, yet never had he felt so much at home. He opened his eyes to see the sun's rays resting on the golden tabernacle door. Closing his eyes again, he felt closer than ever to Gethsemane, but even closer to God. He knelt there in the pew for a long time and then went over to the statue of St. Joseph. He knelt again and offered prayers of thanks for the journey he had just taken.

Rising, he left the Church, touching his hand into the holy water and blessing himself. He headed toward Damien's house. As he neared, he could see the builder was certainly a professional. The doors and windows were balanced with the rest of the house and perfectly proportioned. A wide, covered veranda surrounded two sides. On the upper floor he could see a small balcony leading into a room.

He knocked on the door and the old woman he had seen cleaning the floor of the Church, greeted him.

"Father Damien asked me to come here," said Dutton.

She stepped aside and asked him to enter. The transition to Damien's house was indescribable. What a man! It was apparent that Damien thought nothing of himself, reserving what beauty he had to offer for the Church.

He entered into a large room which evidently was Damien's office for it contained a few chairs and an old wooden desk in the center. The desk was covered with papers. There was no sense of order to be seen. On the wall was a fading, fly-specked print of the Sacred Heart and a dusty crucifix with the metal parts blackened and rusted in spots. There seemed to be people all about, some sitting on the chairs on the veranda. Looking out the back door he could see them gathered near several small sheds, some of which were covered with wire and others had piles of lumber and stacks of provisions. Then Damien entered the room.

"Well, Brother!"

Dutton was taken aback at the title.

Seeing Dutton's reaction and the expression on his face, Damien explained, "This is what I'm going to call you—*Brother Joseph.* I have waited so long for the Brothers to come."

"Father, I am not worthy to be given such a title."

"Who of us is worthy, Brother? A title only helps to identify you, nothing more. Come, let me show you my place."

He escorted Dutton to the left side of the room where there was a small kitchen, cupboards, a kerosene stove, and a wooden table with several chairs. The old woman was preparing a meal. Damien introduced her.

"This is Malia, she is my housekeeper and cook. Malia came to the island with her husband who had leprosy, but she did not. She was given special permission to stay with her husband until he died and then she came to take care of me."

Passing back through the main room and going to the opposite side, a door led to a fairly large bedroom. Beside the bed was a table with a bowl and pitcher, several chairs, and a prie-Dieu. At one end there was a small closet.

"This is my guest room. It is used by priests who come occasionally to hear my confession and to assist me. It is also used when I have a visitor."

He turned to Dutton.

"My sleeping room and a small study are upstairs. My pride and joy is the balcony which leads from my bedroom to the outside, overlooking the ocean. It is here I say most of my prayers and occasionally, if I have time, just watch the sea. That's when I do my thinking and make plans to improve the conditions under which my poor people live."

He then led Dutton out on to the veranda where Malia had set a small table covered with grass mats.

"Sit down, Brother, and we will have a little lunch. I'm sure you must be hungry."

"Please Father, don't go to any trouble, I am feeling fine."

"You wouldn't want to hurt Malia's feelings now, would you? It gives her such joy to take care of any guest that comes my way. We have some beer, or you can have hot coffee, tea or juices. Which would you prefer? We even have milk!"

"I love milk," said Dutton.

Malia brought out a plate for Dutton on which she had placed several biscuits, pieces of ham and fresh pineapple. There was also a hard boiled egg.

Dutton thought, this is not going to be as difficult as I expected; I had no idea they would have such a variety of food.

Damien, sitting at the other end of the table started to light his pipe.

"I hope you don't mind my smoking, it helps me a great deal. We grow tobacco here and the patients sell it to some of the homesteaders at Kalaupapa. While I used to have a pipe once in a while, it was when I arrived here that I began to smoke more. You see, I was not accustomed to the odors that permeated the air as a result of the festering sores of the patients. The smell of the tobacco helped me overcome this aversion."

Dutton wondered if he were smoking his pipe for him, since Damien, too, had many sores and some of them festering.

Damien only nibbled at a hardtack biscuit.

"I seldom eat much at noon. You will find that with the heat, it is better to have a good breakfast and a good supper and eat lightly at this time of day."

Just then, Dr. Mouritz rode up astride a spirited black horse. Dismounting, he joined Damien and Dutton at the table.

"Would you like something to eat or drink, Doctor?" asked Damien. He expected the negative as Mouritz did not take too kindly to eating with those who had leprosy or even to handling their utensils.

"No thank you, Father. You will be happy to know that all of the new arrivals have been taken care of and many of the patients are already settling into their new quarters."

The Doctor turned to Dutton.

"And how are you, Mr. Dutton? I am sure you are overwhelmed with the activity that you see all about you. There are almost 700 patients scattered around this small area."

"Father has been taking good care of me," Dutton answered.

Damien interrupted, "His name now is *Brother Joseph*, Doctor. It is what I will call him and I hope everyone else will, too."

"That's wonderful," beamed Dr. Mouritz. "I know how you have looked forward to having Brothers with you. So to me, as well, it will be 'Brother Joseph'." He was still smiling as he turned to Dutton.

Damien continued, "There is the matter of where Brother Joseph will be housed for the time being."

Dr. Mouritz spoke up, "I had planned to take him back to Kalaupapa with me and he can stay in one of the government buildings."

"I would prefer to stay here with Father, if possible," Dutton protested.

Damien was quick to acquiesce. "Of course you can. You can stay in the guest room. It certainly won't be as comfortable perhaps as what you are used to, but it will do for the time being and before long we can build a small cottage near here for your own use."

Dr. Mouritz did not seem pleased but he realized that Damien was excited about his new companion.

"Well, it will be alright for a short while, but we must be sure he has a place of his own."

"That will be my number one project," Damien

replied, hoping to appease the Doctor.

"I must get back to Kalaupapa," said Dr. Mouritz, rising. "There are patients waiting for me."

He extended his hand to Dutton.

"I will come by in the morning to show you the hospital."

"I would appreciate that," Dutton replied. "I would like to learn how to do dressings, Doctor, and help Father Damien with some of his chores."

"That's settled, then," said Mouritz. He walked off the veranda, mounted his waiting steed and galloped off at a brisk pace.

Damien, his eyes aglow with pleasure, turned to Dutton.

"Let me show you to your room, Brother. I am so pleased you decided to spend the time here with me."

"Father, that's the only reason I came; to be your helper and do whatever I am capable of doing."

"You must be tired. This is nap time. You will find all of the patients and many of the staff taking a rest during the heat of the day."

Dutton followed as Damien beckoned him toward the guest room.

"I must assure you, that Malia will take good care of you. She will make certain that nothing I handle or eat from will be used by you."

It astonished Dutton that the priest was so frank with him.

"Father, I have no fears and I do not wish to be treated with any deference. It is an honor for me to stay with you and eat at your table."

Again Damien thought: So many things this man says and does are further proof that the surprise I was expecting has indeed come from God.

Dutton smiled as he saw that his canvas bag had been placed on top of the bed. That sly old fox, he said to himself, he knew all along that I would be staying with him.

As Damien left the room, he called back, "Be sure to use the netting hanging from the ceiling. It will save you from many bites." He quietly closed the door behind him.

Dutton opened his bag and took out the picture of his mother. He kissed it and placed it on the stand beside his bed, next to the pitcher. He then noticed a small bouquet of flowers on the windowsill, bright red bougainvillea and small white orchids. "Malia," he said to himself. He removed his personal belongings, his razor, shaving cup and hairbrush, then lay down on the bed still fully clothed, exhausted. He fell into a deep sleep and in a dream, began to relive part of his life.

When the war ended, he accepted a position with the government. One of his duties was to collect the bodies of the unidentified dead still lying on the battlefields and placing them in newly established national cemeteries. Each day was filled with unhappy experiences, and each night with hours of sleepless torture as he tried to erase the scenes of horror and desolation from his mind. One shocking incident in particular haunted him. He had set out one day, trotting along on his big black horse—the air was oppressive, even in the early morning. He approached an open field, mist rising from the bottomlands, and tethering his mount to the stump of a tree, began to pick his way cautiously through the litter of canteens, haversacks, rusting guns, and cannons strewn over the open space. And then it happened.

The field was dotted here and there with rotting bodies of the dead, man and beast. Experience had taught him that there would be bodies also in ditches, behind fences, and even under rocks where wounded men and horses had crawled away to die. Suddenly he stopped, with his foot arrested in mid air. He muttered an oath, jumping back just in time to escape stepping on a big snake unwinding itself from an exposed chest. Death amongst death! He turned blindly and ran back across the field. He was trembling violently, more from the grisly shock than from his encounter with possible death. Reaching his horse, he tore open the saddlebag and pulled out a bottle, which up to this time, he had saved for nights when he was alone. He drank deeply as if trying to forget completely the whole war and all that he had seen. He drank to forget his buddy, Jeb, his body no doubt sprawled on some battlefield. Were snakes crawling out of his chest, he wondered in abhorrence.

Suddenly, he was awakened by a rapping on his door. For a moment he forgot where he was, and then he heard a voice.

"Brother Joseph, are you awake? Father Damien would like you to join him for supper."

It was turning dark outside. Had he slept through the night? He looked at his pocket watch. It was 4:00 p.m. Damien had told him that dusk came quickly on this side of the cliffs. The sun's rays were blocked out by the hovering clouds. A cool breeze carried the salty mist of the sea toward the house.

"I'll be right out, Malia."

He dashed water from the pitcher on his face and straightened his clothing. He entered the kitchen which was lit by the glow of a lamp on the table. Damien was seated and Dutton quickly sat across from him. Malia had prepared a meal of boiled beef, sweet potatoes and greens along with the usual plate of poi.

"Did you have a good sleep, Brother?"

"I'm afraid I fell into a very deep sleep and was dreaming."

"I can see," said Damien, "that you failed to put down the netting."

Dutton looked at his hands covered with bites.

"I forgot," he said sheepishly.

"You will find many companions here in the tropics," Damien said. "You will have to get used to them as you see them skittering all around, here and there, and some flying in and out and up and down. You will not be able to escape from them."

"They don't bother me, Father. Most of my time in the army was spent in the South where there were many flying and crawling insects. They become one's companions."

Damien, blessing himself, offered grace.

Turning to Dutton he asked, "Would you like a

cup of wine with your dinner?"

Dutton, not wanting to hurt his feelings, thought this would be a good time to tell him some of his past.

"I always enjoyed a good glass of wine, Father, but then I wanted more and for many years I drank heavily, eventually becoming an alcoholic. It was one of the reasons for my downfall."

"Oh I'm sorry, Brother, I understand. I will make it a point of not tempting you again."

"No, Father, don't do that. Temptation is good for the soul. How else will I know that I am continuing to carry out my pledge never to have another drop of liquor for the rest of my life."

"Yes, Brother, it is true, the devil tempts us from time to time to see whether or not he can win. We become more worthy of God's love when we resist temptation."

They ate the meal in silence and when they had finished, Damien rose and went out on to the veranda. Dutton followed. A large group of patients had gathered around, some sitting on the ground. Then they began singing. Dutton was enthralled with the beauty of their voices.

"This is my nightly concert," whispered Damien. "They know how much I love to hear them sing."

The two men sat side by side enjoying the sweet sound of the ukuleles and the lilt of the Hawaiian language. Damien had lit his pipe and was puffing away. It was then that Dutton could see that he enjoyed these moments of peace. Suddenly, Damien arose.

"You will excuse me, Brother, but I must go up

and say my Office. Now you just relax and if you wish to wander around be careful where you walk as there are many rocky places and vines that will trip you."

"I think, Father, I would like to visit the Church. Is it open?"

"The Church is never closed. It is open day and night for anyone who wishes to visit."

Damien walked up the staircase to his rooms. Dutton waited a few minutes until the patients had finished their serenade and returned to their quarters.

Entering the Church, he found it full—one of the patients leading the rest in the rosary. Many looked at him as he entered a pew. Some moved farther away muttering *haole*. He took his rosary from his jacket pocket. He carried it with him wherever he went. As he joined the congregation in their prayers, again a sweet sense of peace swept over him. Time passed quickly and when they were finished, it had become completely dark outside. The moon had risen behind the cliffs. He waited until the Church was almost empty then left and walked a few yards toward the ocean. He could see the spray of mist coming from the waves. Not knowing where he was and remembering Damien's warning, he turned and went back to the house.

He sat on the steps of the veranda watching as the moon brought the outline of the steep cliffs into a dark silhouette. No wonder, he thought, that the patients think of this as a prison. The cliffs were a constant reminder that there was no escape. If they did manage to scale the cliffs, the Superintendent and officials who lived on top of the pali would surely stop them.

The perfume of honeysuckle hung heavy on the air, taking his thoughts back to the days he had spent in the old South. Then he smelled tobacco mingling with the fragrances and he knew that Damien was awake.

"Brother Dutton." Damien's voice came from the balcony. "Is that you down there?"

Dutton stood up from the steps walked out a few paces and looked up to the balcony. He saw the shadow of Damien.

Not hearing a reply, Damien asked, "Are you all right?"

"Yes, Father." Dutton called up to him, "I'm just sitting here drinking in all of this beauty."

"Would you like to join me for a few moments?"

"I would like that very much."

Dutton went back to the veranda and climbed the staircase. The moon made it easy to see where he was going. He had not been up to the second floor and saw now how sparsely it was furnished. The small room resembled a chapel with a prie-Dieu next to a table covered with cloth on which stood a statue of the Blessed Mother. The flickering light of the votive candles on each side of the statue cast shadows on the wall on which he saw a large crucifix. Next to it was Father's bedroom and again the contrast between his place of worship and that of his living quarters spoke of where Damien's priorities were. There was a large pallet and a straw pillow on the floor. Again there was a cluttered desk and battered chairs. Three walls were lined with bookcases in which were stacked many books and pamphlets. On the other wall was a large atlas of the world.

Stepping out on to the balcony, Dutton knew why Damien loved this spot. The sea was sparkling like diamonds from the light of the moon and the cliffs looked more inviting than menacing. The honeysuckle vines covered the balcony.

Damien pointed out a new rocking chair and said, "This is my latest accomplishment, I just finished building it." He offered Dutton a chair and asked him if he would like a pipe of tobacco.

"No thank you, Father, I enjoy the smell more than I do the actual smoking."

"I find my tobacco helps to relax me."

"There's nothing wrong, Father, in tobacco or alcohol. It's just that I don't know how to use them in moderation."

Damien sat in his rocking chair next to Dutton.

"I was just thinking of my mother. Is yours still alive?"

"Yes," said Dutton, "she is, and I'm very happy to say that she, too, became a Catholic when I converted."

"I'm so afraid of my mother finding out that I have leprosy," said Damien, tight-lipped. "I have written to my brother, Pamphile, asking him to keep the news from her. But with your arrival and telling me that you read about it in the United States, it must be in the papers in my village, as well. "

Damien paused, resting his chin in his hand.

Dutton respected the silence and waited a few moments before asking, "Where was your home, Father?"

"I was born in a little village called Tremeloo in Belgium. Have you ever heard of it?"

"I'm afraid I haven't kept up with my European history or geography, so I'll have to say no, Father. I was so involved in my own country during its terrible Civil War that all the rest of the world was shut from my mind."

"Well, Tremeloo is the Flemish part of Belgium, a few miles north of Louvain, and it is primarily farming villages. Let me show you the area on the map." Damien pointed to a spot in the northern part of Belgium.

"Tremeloo has several hamlets and about 1,600 people live there. My father, Francis, who was born in 1800, married Anne, my mother, a young peasant girl from a neighboring village. In time there were eight children. Auguste and I became priests. Eugenie and Pauline entered the Ursulines. Leonce, Gerard and Constance married, and my other sister, Mary, died when she was a girl of only fourteen. I am next to the youngest of the De Veuster family.

"It must have been a lot of fun living in a large family," said Dutton.

"Farmers had big families in those days. There were so many chores to be done. Do you have brothers and sisters?" asked Damien.

"No, Father, they died before I was born. I missed having brothers and sisters."

"It is difficult being the only child," sympathized Damien.

He relit his pipe, and seemed to want to recount his early family life.

"We lived in a small, red brick house," he continued. "My mother called me 'Jef'—it was her pronunciation of Joseph. When Eugenie, who was the oldest girl, took her vows with the Ursulines she became a teacher. Mother was very instrumental in the family's religious upbringing. She had a big book written in old Flemish with Gothic type and beautiful pictures of saints. Almost every evening she would read from the book and we would marvel at the stories of the holy martyrs."

"It was those stories, heard at an early age," Damien went on, "that made me want to follow in their footsteps. From then on, without the family knowing, I would practice various forms of sacrifice. I would go into the woods and make believe that I was a hermit living off the plants and herbs. I would tend my father's flock of sheep and pretend I was the Good Shepherd."

Dutton smiled. "That certainly came to be true, for you are a good shepherd to your flock here on Molokai."

Damien seemed pleased.

"You know," he continued, "the Flemish have a reputation for being very frank and often when words flow freely, fists settle the argument. I guess I inherited that trait and I'm sure you've heard of my temper."

Dutton didn't answer. When, in New Orleans, he had read about Damien, he had also heard of a Professor Charles Stoddard at Notre Dame University, South Bend, Indiana, who had visited Damien several times on Molokai. Before making a decision to join Damien, Dutton went to see Stoddard to ask him if he thought he would be of any help to Damien. Stoddard was most enthusiastic and encouraged him to go. He said, "Damien has quite a temper, you know, but you will find a way to get along with him."

Damien continued to reach back into his memories, telling of his First Communion at Tremeloo on Palm Sunday when he was ten.

"I believe God had planted the seed of my vocation at a very early age. At first, I was a fat, roly-poly little boy but then over the years with hard work, my muscles firmed up and I became quite sturdy. I could lift heavy sacks of grain and work long hours in the fields. I particularly enjoyed carpentry as the barn roof often needed repair, and we made most of our own furniture as well. My father thought then that he had a son who could succeed him."

Damien leaned forward.

"Did you come from a farm, Brother?"

Dutton replied, "I was born in a farmhouse in the village of Stowe, Vermont, in the northeastern part of the United States. My father was not a farmer, he was a salesman, and my mother was a teacher."

"Oh," remarked Damien. "How wonderful to have a teacher in your family. I was given little schooling when I was young. Not many in those days went on to higher learning. My father felt I had enough education when I was about eleven and I had to leave school and help him on the farm. Did you finish school, Brother?"

"I was only five," replied Dutton, "when we moved from Stowe to Janesville, Wisconsin. The West was just opening up and my father's brother had established a successful business in this thriving little town. He wanted my father to join him. I can show you where Wisconsin is on your map."

Dutton pointed out Vermont and ran his finger across the country to Wisconsin.

"My," said Damien, "that was a long journey. It always astounds me how vast the United States is."

"My mother," Dutton continued, "kept me home and tutored me until I was twelve."

"Oh, I see," said Damien. "My growing-up years were a little different. My brother, Auguste, was much smarter than me and he soon entered the Minor Seminary. Eugenie died at a relatively young age and Pauline, my other sister took her place with the Ursulines. My parents were giving their share of their children to God's service. They never thought at that time that I would be another."

"They probably thought that you would always be home helping out on the farm," said Dutton.

"It wasn't the hard life on the farm that disturbed me," Damien went on, "it was the fact that I was not doing what I felt I should do—and that was to be in the service of God."

Damien paused, rocked back and forth a little, and puffed on his pipe.

"Since I spent so much of the day tending to the animals and other chores, I never had the opportunity to develop relationships with girls and social activities."

"Although my parents didn't know it," he confided, "I gave up sleeping in my bed and spent the nights on the hard floor."

Dutton observed, "I noticed there was no bed in your room."

"No," said Damien. "I don't like sleeping in beds so it really is not a sacrifice for me to sleep on the floor."

Damien was relishing this opportunity to talk about his early life. "As I matured and developed, my father decided that he would make me an associate in the grain business. He knew that while I could become a good trader, I did not have enough education to find my way in the world of business, so he decided to send me to an upper school nearby. The director liked me. I was eighteen at the time, and he realized that I was deficient in most of the intellectual studies required for advancement. I loved that school and studied real hard to try to catch up to the others."

Damien paused for a while. "When did you enter school, Brother Joseph?"

"After my mother ceased tutoring me," answered Dutton. "I was in my young teens when I first entered formal school. My mother objected somewhat, but my father put his foot down because, he said, I should be with others and learn how to get along with them. He took me to the local school and when I saw all the books in the headmaster's office, I was fascinated. They gave me a test and came to the conclusion that I had enough education to enter the higher grades. It was a challenge to me and I excelled after that."

"It is true what you say, Brother. Not only is it important to be educated but also to know how to get along with others. In my school, religion was an important part of our studies and I knew that if I were ever going to join Auguste—who was now called Pamphile, his name in religion—I must study very hard and I did. Often I would stay up at night reading and poring over my books while others were asleep."

"I know just what you mean," agreed Dutton.

"My father was having a difficult time handling

his business and travelling to Antwerp so often," said Damien. "However, I was just as determined to enter the priesthood, hoping I could join Pamphile. When I visited home during school breaks, my mother began to realize that something was going on with her 'little Jef.'"

Dutton broke in, "Mothers have great intuition."

"Yes, and they always seem to be right," Damien admitted with a nod. "My mother talked to my father and told him she thought I was leaning toward the religious life. He was disappointed, but a good man, and realized that if God wanted me, then he could not say no. One day a Redemptorist priest came to the school to give a missionary talk. I was most taken by what he said and this strengthened my resolve more than ever."

Damien noticed that Dutton quickly sat upright in his chair.

"It was a Redemptorist friend of mine," Dutton said, "whom I was visiting in New Orleans when I read about you in the papers."

Dutton was struck by the fact that it was a Redemptorist who played such an important role in the decisions made by both of them, eventually leading to their meeting on the shores of Kalaupapa.

"After I finished my schooling," Damien said, "I thought at first I would join the Trappists. I liked their rules and the fact that I could make great sacrifices."

Shaking his head in disbelief—Dutton blinked. He was stunned as all of these coincidences cropped up. "How strange. As I told you in the buggy on the ride over from Kalaupapa, I entered the Trappists. I, too, was attracted by their life, and felt it was the best place for me to work out my penance."

"You didn't tell me why you left," said Damien.

"I stayed for over two years but it was evident to me that God was not calling me to the priesthood. The Abbot came to the same conclusion. Finally, I departed on good terms, and he gave me a letter of recommendation.

"I, too, changed my mind about the Trappists," said Damien. "I decided that I wanted to follow Pamphile and become a Father of the Sacred Hearts."

Damien was obviously enjoying this conversation and wanted to continue.

"One day my father had business in Louvain and he took me with him to visit Pamphile. He left me at the seminary and told me he would return later to take me back to Tremeloo. But I had other plans and asked to see the Superior. After a long talk, during which I told him of my desire to study for the priesthood, he told me that I didn't have the necessary studies. However, he said, he could enter me as a postulant to study as a Choir Brother. I asked him what that meant. He explained that the regular Brothers did many manual chores but a Choir Brother would take care of the chapels, work in the infirmary or even be a secretary. This relieves the priests from menial tasks and administrative problems, so that they can concentrate on the spiritual needs of the people."

"Yes," said Dutton, "The Trappists have the same arrangement."

"The Superior saw that I was disappointed. He told me later he sensed I had a vocation and didn't want to lose me. So he was quick to assure me that if I would study hard to make up the requirements, he would again consider me. At least, I thought, my foot would be in the door and I accepted. When my father came back to take me home, the Superior, Pamphile and I gave him the news. It shocked him! He was to lose his dream of 'little Jef' becoming his successor. He then realized that he had no alternative but to give his permission. He went home without me."

"We are both lucky, Father, to have had such loving and understanding parents," said Dutton. "They allowed us to follow the paths we have chosen. They may be disappointed that we did not take all their advice, they still loved us enough to let us pursue our own dreams. Not many children are that fortunate. Parents can only guide us, they cannot live our lives for us."

"That's right," Damien agreed. "So many of my boys here at Kalawao have never had the love that parents would give them."

There was a long, reflective pause.

"Am I boring you, Brother? It is seldom I have anyone I can talk to this way. I know you must be very tired."

"Oh no, Father," Dutton protested. "I want to learn all I can. I remember my mother once telling me, 'Ira,' she said, 'if you wish to have knowledge you must learn to listen.' "

Damien was encouraged to continue his story. "I knew very little of the necessary basics, including Latin, but I was determined to work hard. When I eventually became a postulant, I took the name of Damien and was now known as Brother Damien."

Dutton smiled. "If you had not taken the name of

Damien, then you would be known as Brother Joseph, the name you have bestowed upon me."

"How interesting—two Brother Josephs!" said Damien laughing.

His pipe had grown cold. He stood up, strolled over to the railing and knocked the dead ashes into the earth below.

Looking at Dutton, he asked, "Are you sure you wish to hear the rest of this now? It can wait until another day."

"Father, if you don't finish I will be thinking about it all night. I'm not tired at all."

"Well then, how about a cup of hot tea. I would like one, will you join me?"

"Of course, Father. Let me get it for you."

"Do you know where Malia keeps everything?"

Dutton didn't wait to answer, he was already halfway down the stairs. It was dark at the bottom. The light of the moon was hidden. He jumped as a figure darted out. It was Paul.

"You frightened me," breathed Dutton.

Paul put a finger to his lips as if to say don't talk too loud. "Is everything all right?" he whispered.

"Yes," said Dutton. It's just that we were having a long conversation and forgot the time. I am going to get Father a cup of tea. You go on to bed, Paul. I'm here and I will take good care of him."

Paul turned and quietly left the veranda.

Dutton thought, they love him, they worry about him. All day long Dutton had been struck by a paradox: if Damien's reputation is so bad, why do so many love him.

He went into the kitchen, lit the kerosene stove, put on a pot of water and brewed the tea. He took the steaming cups back up to the balcony, not bothering to determine which cup was his or Damien's.

Damien had relit his pipe and was rocking in his chair. They both sipped their tea in silence.

"Well, where did I leave off?"

"You have just entered the seminary."

"Oh, yes." said Damien. "I was very disappointed that they did not accept me to study for the priesthood, but deep down I knew that eventually I would become a priest. I worked very hard, spending hours and hours on Latin and the other required subjects. In six months I was able to read a fifth year Latin text."

"That's remarkable," exclaimed Dutton. "I remember the difficulty I had with languages."

"My Superior," Damien said, "was aware of my determination and my progress and he told me that there was no doubt God was calling me and I could enter the seminary to prepare for Holy Orders. I was overjoyed and wrote my parents about the good news."

"I learned the rules and prescriptions of the Congregation. Soon I was able to take my first vow. They then sent me to Issy, France, with other novices where I took my final vows. I had no difficulty with the rules and regulations, though at times, inwardly, I would argue over something that I did not quite agree with."

"My mother," said Dutton, "told me as a teacher, she enjoyed a student who questioned her. It gave her an opening better to explain what she was teaching and often she learned something from her pupils."

"I can relate to that," agreed Damien. "I enjoyed the night adoration and would extend the hours assigned to me, often lasting until daybreak. It was good preparation for the hard work that was to come and fortunately, I was able to get by with just a few hours of sleep."

Damien finished his tea. "After my novitiate at Issy, I went to the motherhouse in Paris, located on the Rue du Picpus. The Sacred Hearts Fathers are often called the Picpus Fathers because of that location. Finally, there I was, in the same House as Pamphile. My studies included philosophy, theology, Greek and Latin. I was able to adapt easily to any new surroundings. I kept copious notes in class, jotting down every idea I had, even though it might not agree with the ideas of the professor. It was a trait that would get me in trouble all too often in the years to come."

"At this time my grandmother died," Damien said sadly. "We were very close and I felt it keenly. When I was a young boy, she would often use an old Flemish saying, 'You are as busy as rabbits'. Memories of her often flood my mind."

"During recreation, the students were allowed to go into the streets of Paris, or to the woods located near the seminary. I did not appreciate the hustle and bustle of the city but did enjoy the silence of the woods. France was caught up in its well-being, bathed in brilliant luxury and finery. One thing I liked was watching the activity everywhere but after a while, I longed to get back to the seminary. From behind its iron gates the Tuileries could be seen and I would watch the Zouaves marching in their colorful uniforms. They were fierce warriors and if called into battle, would usually emerge victorious."

Dutton said to himself, "This is too much!" Then he spoke up.

"I can't help but tell you, Father, that I belonged to the Zouaves in my home town. It was more like a social group of young men instead of warriors. While we drilled and marched, it was the uniform that brought us much admiration from the ladies."

Damien laughed. "I can see why. If ever there were a colorful bird of paradise, that uniform certainly resembled one."

Damien then told Dutton how he was finally selected to serve in the Hawaiian Islands. One day the Bishop of Tahiti, who was a Sacred Hearts Father, came to the Motherhouse to give a conference about the mission field, after which he was to return to Tahiti taking several Fathers with him. He had been Vicar Apostolic of Tahiti for over thirteen years and was in Paris for a few months. He told the seminarians of his work with the Polynesians whom, he said, were pagans and had to be brought to God. He also described the beauty of Tahiti— the tall palms, white beaches and coral reefs.

Damien could not get enough of his tales and could picture himself in such a place. He was hoping he would be chosen by the Bishop to go back to Tahiti with him, but he was not yet ordained.

Later, word came from the Hawaiian Islands asking for more priests for the missions there. Damien's brother, Pamphile, was among those chosen. At that time there was an epidemic of typhus in Europe and Pamphile, working in the suburbs of Paris, was stricken with the disease. He was devastated when he was taken off the list of priests going to the Hawaiian Islands.

Damien just knew then that God was calling him but he wondered how he would be able to get the Superiors to accept him. He knew his local Superior would not consider it, so he skirted around it by taking advantage of one of the rules that allowed anyone to write to the Superior General—which he did.

About a week later he was eating in the refectory when the local Superior came in and threw an envelope by his plate. Damien trembled as the Superior just stood there. The letter stated that the Superior General had given his permission for Damien to replace Pamphile. The local Superior remarked to him that he was acting with foolish recklessness. Damien kept quiet but he later related, "I was full of gratitude to God and my heart was ready to burst."

Damien pushed his empty cup and saucer away and leaned his elbow on the table, deep in thought.

Dutton had listened intently and was impressed with Damien's ingenuity in using the rules to attain his goal. "That's a good example of how important it is to know the rules and regulations, otherwise how could you find ways to skirt them. If you had not done that, you might never have come to Molokai."

"So right," answered Damien. "Of course I went immediately to Pamphile to tell him the good news. Although he was disappointed that he was not going, he was happy at my being accepted."

"I had little time to say good-bye to anyone," said Damien, "but I was able to spend a day with my mother and family. She was silent all day but I could see she was proud. I left without looking back."

He stood up abruptly.

"Well, Brother Joseph, I think that's enough for one night. It's time for bed and I have some prayers still to be said."

Dutton arose also, stretching his arms.

"Thank you, Father, for having such confidence in me and for revealing so much of your life. I feel more welcome than ever. Before I turn in, what time is Mass in the morning?"

"Mass is at 5:30 but don't worry if you do not get up in time. I know how tired you must be."

Dutton hesitantly placed his hand on Damien's shoulder saying, "Good night, Father, include me in your prayers."

He went down the stairs and into his room which was bathed in moonlight. He fell on his knees at the bed-side and said the evening prayers he had learned while in the Trappists. Finishing, he removed his suit and lay on the bed—the end of his first day on Molokai. Thoughtfully Malia had provided a light blanket as the evenings were cool. He covered himself and was about to doze off when he remembered, and reaching up, pulled down the mosquito netting, frustrating the flying and crawling critters which had hoped for a good drink of his blood.

CHAPTER FOUR

THE RITUAL CROW of the rooster first echoed in the distance, then became louder and more important. Dutton, midway between sleep and dreams, stirred uneasily. His mind was still in the half-real world of the Wisconsin hills where he had spent his childhood.

As he turned his head on the pillow, a prism of light streaked across his face and he sat up with a start. He glanced hastily at his timepiece—5:00 a.m. He surveyed the unfamiliar room, then remembered he was at Kalawao on Molokai. Today he was to begin a new life!

He arose abruptly, knelt beside the bed, blessed himself and prayed, "Father in heaven, help me to do your will. Thank you, dear Lord, for showing me the way. Dear Blessed Mother, keep me ever close to you. At long last I feel strong and sure of what my life is to be. Dear Saint Joseph be ever at my side. I am counting on you to help me in all the days to come. Amen."

Dutton dressed hurriedly, quietly left the room and went out on to the veranda. Fully awake now, he was aware of the strange smells of the tropics. The air was heavy with morning dampness rising up to a new day. The odor of burnt-out fires mingled with the tangy salt of the sea. The all-pervasive scent from tropical flowers combined with the odor of rotting flesh and decay.

Walking briskly over to the Church, Dutton found it filled almost to overflowing. He entered the sacristy. Damien was kneeling to the side, deep in prayer. After a few minutes, he looked up and saw Brother Joseph.

"Good morning, Brother, you're just in time. Will you serve my Mass?"

"I would be honored, Father," and he looked toward Paul.

"It was Paul's suggestion," said Damien, whispering. "He told me last night that he was very happy that you had come to help me."

Dutton had served many times at Mass when he was with the Trappists, and had helped the priest to vest. Serving Father Damien was to become one of his cherished duties.

When it came time for Communion, nearly all the congregation filed to receive. Dutton, holding the paten under each chin, watched as Damien placed the Sacred Host on the outstretched tongues. The mercy of God seemed very close. Each patient bore the marks of Christ's suffering and each time the priest brought the Host to their swollen lips, it reminded Dutton of Christ's coming to the suffering ones to give them strength. He, himself, felt a new wave of devotion when the Host was placed on his own tongue. He vowed again he would work here for as long as God would permit him. "Dear Lord," he whispered, "give me strength to serve these poor people and Father Damien."

Mass finished, he waited until Father had completed his prayers and together they walked back to the house. In the distance, Dutton could see new fires being started in front of the huts as the patients prepared their food for the day.

Entering the small kitchen, they found that Malia had prepared breakfast and the strong aroma of coffee filled the air. Damien said grace. Their plates were full of poi, scrambled eggs and bits of fried fat. Dutton had not yet acquired a taste for poi, but would not embarrass Malia, so he ate it.

"This is my favorite meal of the day," said Damien. It gives me strength so that I can tackle my many tasks."

"Malia is a very good cook," Dutton said loudly enough for Malia to hear. She smiled.

Breakfast over, Damien said, "And now I must feed my flock."

Rising, he beckoned the puzzled Dutton to follow. They went out the back door into the yard. Damien entered one of the sheds, returning with a pan filled with grain. He made a strange sound and immediately the air darkened with chickens flying from everywhere. They lit upon his arms and shoulders, even on his head, as he fed them out of his hands. He stood knee-deep in chickens as they pecked away at the feed. He was clucking to them happily, even talking to them it seemed. There was one perched precariously on his shoulder, flapping its wings for balance, and squawking. Damien raised his hand with seed just for her. Dutton heard the name Gretchen. This must be his pet, he thought.

It was a gentle Damien he saw, a lonely man among his friends. This was a side of Damien his critics could not see. Christ, who railed at the Pharisees, and with knotted cord, drove the money changers from the Temple, could also melt with tenderness to cry out: "Jerusalem, Jerusalem, how I have longed to save you as a mother hen would her chicks." It was the same with Damien, Dutton decided. The gruffness and belligerence was for those who would neglect the needs of his people; like the angry goose, Dutton recalled, who had flailed at him with her wings when, as a child, he had attempted to pick up her gosling.

Damien was making sure that the timid chickens on the fringe of the flock received their share. Finally, evidently in pain, he picked up his staff, brushed off his stained cassock, leaving the chickens still pecking industriously at what was left. He looked over at Dutton, smiling.

"Now do you know what I meant by feeding my flock? I have two flocks, you know."

As he reentered the house, Damien said, "Well, Brother, I know that Dr. Mouritz is supposed to take you to see the infirmary and the hospital, but off I am. If we do not get an early start then the heat becomes too oppressive later on in the day for us to do much work. I will see you, perhaps, for supper?"

"I will be here, Father," Dutton answered.

When Damien left, he went out on to the front veranda and sat on the steps, waiting for the arrival of the Doctor. There was activity as the settlement came to life. Several patients came close to the veranda but seeing him sitting there, backed off. Over by the tree he saw two women gesturing to one another and pointing at him. He acted as if he did not see them. Finally one came over.

"Sir, is Father Damien here?"

"No," Brother Dutton replied. "He went off with Paul in the buggy. He said he had duties to perform."

"Thank you, sir." She ran back to her companion, giggling.

Just then, Dr. Mouritz rode up on his horse. Dutton saw he was wearing his familiar white suit and broad-brimmed white hat. Dismounting, he strode over to the veranda where Dutton was waiting for him.

"Good morning, Brother. I hope you had a good evening."

"It was fantastic, Doctor, better than I had ever expected. Father talked at length and we didn't get to bed until quite late."

"I am pleased," the Doctor answered. "He needs someone to talk to and I'm sure you are a good listener."

Just then Malia came out onto the porch with a cup of pineapple juice which she handed to Brother Dutton. He looked at the Doctor.

"Will you have some?"

Malia scowled and went back into the house. Dr. Mouritz laughed.

"Malia knows that I would not accept any food here. I know it may seem cruel. I have great compassion but I must also exercise caution. I'm afraid she does not like me very much but who can blame her."

"Why is that?"

"I'm sure," answered the Doctor, " she has overheard my many arguments with Father Damien and you know, no one dare say anything against their *Kamiano.*"

"Kamiano?"

"Yes, that's Hawaiian for Damien. He is adored by the patients and woe betide anyone who speaks ill of him in their presence. Do you know much of Hawaiian history?"

"I'm afraid I don't." said Dutton. "I never was interested in other than my own country and its problems. I'm afraid I have much to learn."

"We did the same thing with all our problems here in the islands," the Doctor replied. "We thought little of anything else. That's what happens when we become so isolated and pay no attention to one another. It would be helpful to you if you learn something of the history of Hawaii. It is fascinating and it will give you a better understanding of what you are to deal with here."

"I will do that." Dutton agreed. "I have always been involved in government and politics since I was a student and also after I left school."

"I will set aside some time when we get our regular routine done, and I can fill you in," offered Dr. Mouritz. "I know the patients here are waiting for me but I would like to speak to you. There is someone in Kalaupapa you should meet who knows the history better than anyone."

Dutton pulled out a chair so that they could sit at the table.

"We have a major problem." The Doctor looked around to see if they were being overheard. "Anyone who has heard of Father Damien thinks he runs the place and that he is in charge of the settlement, but that is not so. This is government-owned property and the superintendent and his staff are in complete charge. Admittedly from the beginning the settlement had been poorly run.

Damien was sent here not by the government but by his Bishop to take care of the spiritual needs of the Catholics."

"Yes, the Bishop told me about that when I was in Honolulu".

"Mr. Meyer, the government superintendent, is a good man and a friend of the King," the Doctor continued.

"In fact, he not only oversees his own land holdings on top of the pali but the King's as well. This leaves him little time to pay attention to the operation of the settlement. Over the years he appointed assistants who live in the settlement but not many were effective. Some had leprosy themselves and the patients paid no attention to them. We know the kind of man Damien is. When he saw the conditions, he was not about to ignore the situation."

"That sounds like something Father would concern himself with," said Dutton.

"King Kamehameha IV was being pressured by the white Protestant businessmen in his cabinet who were getting frightened with the growing number of leprosy cases in the Islands. They forced him to write an edict banishing anyone with leprosy to the settlement at Kalawao. This is one of the reasons the Hawaiians do not like the white man. They call us *haloes.*"

Dutton interrupted, "What does that word mean? I heard someone say it last night when I was in church."

"It means an evil white man," the Doctor replied.

"Oh, now I understand," said Dutton.

"The government foolishly thought that by giving the outcasts some clothing and a few tools, they would grow their own food and take care of themselves," explained the Doctor.

"Instead, the unfortunate people took the law into their own hands and created a society in which the strong dominated the weak. Some of the weak were even treated as slaves."

"I know that well, Doctor. If there is no leadership there will be mutiny," said Dutton, drawing on his experience. "I've seen this happen many times in the army. If we had a weak general or officer who did not know how to lead his troops, not only was he resented, but many times he would be removed from his command. He would soon be replaced, for the government knew that if there were no one to lead, there would be chaos."

The Doctor nodded. "That is what happened here without a strong leader. Then Damien stepped in. He brought not only spiritual solace but discipline. In time the patients came to respect him and after that no government worker had a chance. When the newspapers began to write stories about Damien's heroic sacrifices, it put the government in a bad light which resulted in much resentment against Damien. His personality did not help matters. Not knowing how to work his way around the authorities, he bullied them, was belligerent and stubborn."

"I have not seen that side of his character, yet," said Dutton.

"Of course, everything he did was for the sake of his patients," the Doctor continued. "But the government did not see it that way. They felt he was trying to take charge. Mr. Meyer was happy that Damien was taking control. It gave him more time to run his own affairs on his plantation. At one time he even offered him the job of resident superintendent."

The Doctor looked thoughtful. "As long as Damien is here, there will be divided responsibility."

Dutton nodded in agreement. "That must make your job difficult, Doctor."

"Father and I have had many battles, but we have reached an understanding. As a doctor, I am appalled at the way he handles himself with the patients. He even eats from their utensils and I have seen them smoking his pipe."

Dutton kept quiet. He did not want Dr. Mouritz to know that Damien had talked about this just yesterday, giving a much better understanding than the Doctor had, of the difficulties between them.

Dutton changed the subject. "It's strange that yesterday when I saw Father he seemed so ill and feeble, yet today, I watched him with the chickens and he was like a newborn man."

"He can bewilder you," said Dr. Mouritz. "One moment I'm ready to declare him dead, and within hours he's back on his feet, hard at work doing manual labor. He has great resilience. It probably comes from his youth and his hard work on the farm."

"There's truth in that," Dutton agreed, "for much of what we do later in life depends on what we learned during our youth."

"I was serving on the island of Maui, the next island from here, when Mr. Gibson asked me to be resident physician. That was about two years ago. Damien was then forty-four. He was active and vigorous and he had a good physique, upright in his carriage and about five feet eight inches tall, weighing about two hundred pounds. He had a wide chest, his hands and feet were shapely and although his fingers were stubbed and calloused from toil, he did not give me any appearance that he had leprosy, except I could see some changes in the skin color of his forehead. His voice was clear and ringing—he was a powerful baritone and an accomplished singer." Dr. Mouritz paused. It was as if he were seeing Father Damien standing in front of him.

"Looking at him full-face," the Doctor went on, "you got the impression of great harshness and determination due in part to the squareness of his chin and lower jaw. His profile was handsome, much softer and more in harmony with the entire cast of his other features."

Dutton was listening attentively. "Very few of the photographs of Father Damien do justice to him—your description fits mine, now that I have met him face to face."

The Doctor continued, "He has a wealth of hair and usually roams around bareheaded so his face has become very bronzed by exposure to the sun. Most of the time he wears his gold-rimmed glasses."

It surprised Dutton how accurately the Doctor described what Damien looked like two years ago.

"I am shocked," the Doctor said, "how rapidly he has deteriorated in such a short span of time. It is one of the many puzzling aspects of this baffling disease. It may take a long time, as much as ten years, before you show any symptoms although the germs are in you. Then it may take many more years before you die from leprosy.

Most of the time, death comes from some other complication. Rarely does the patient die within a short time
from the first onset of the disease. We have so much to
learn."

"Does anyone know how you really get leprosy?"
Dutton asked.

"Scientifically, no," replied the Doctor. "But it is
assumed that it comes from having direct contact with
the patient or his utensils. Again that is a big question
since we have cases of those with close contact within
the same family and not all the family members get the
disease."

"I guess this accounts for the fear which often
comes from the unknown."

Dr. Mouritz was impressed with Dutton's grasp of
the situation. "That brings me to my main point, Brother,
one I want to discuss with you while Father is not here. I
would prefer that you not live in the same house with
him nor eat from his utensils."

Dutton looked surprised. "Is this an order?"

"No, no, not an order. I cannot tell you what to do
for you are a volunteer in the Church and I have no juris-
diction over you. I am only concerned with your health."

"Don't worry, Doctor, I'm not afraid. Malia does
not give me food on any plate that Father has used. I
would not have come here if I were afraid of catching
leprosy."

"Well, Brother, I can only advise you."

Dutton looked at him gratefully. "Thank you, Doctor, for your concern. I really appreciate that."

"We'd better be on our way to see the patients

who are waiting for me. Do you mind a short walk? We only have to go across the road to the hospital, it's the long building over on the far side."

"I enjoy walking, Doctor."

"Do you have something for your head?"

Dutton laughed. "The only time I wore a hat was when I was forced to in the army. My mother was ever after me when I was a youngster, but I just hated hats."

"You, too, have a good head of hair and that will give you some protection, but the sun can be very strong here and you can burn quickly."

They strolled across the road and approached the long wooden building.

"Did Father Damien build the hospital as well as the houses?"

The Doctor smiled. "While many of the buildings you see were constructed by Damien or with his help, the government had also erected some buildings before any patients arrived."

The Doctor told Dutton of the early years:

The plans that the Board of Health had made prior to the first boatload of patients, were made in haste with little thought of what was needed. Their main concern was to get the sick off the mainland and away from the healthy population. They thought little of what to do with them once they were isolated in Kalawao. There were no plans for any individual housing. It was decided the patients would build their own houses. However, some wooden structures were provided for hospital facilities to take care of the more seriously ill. In those days, they were taken care of by their families who were permitted to accompany them. The government also believed they would be able to hire well-qualified medical workers to help out, but few were available, so eventually the government paid some of the more able-bodied patients to take care of the helpless. The Hawaiians have strong family ties, which the government should have known, but most of the officials were not Hawaiian.

When they started to round up those with leprosy to be shipped to Kalawao, the families would hide them, often going deep into the hills to avoid the officers from bringing them in. The government finally hired armed guards to hunt them down, but still no one would turn their own over to them even when threatened with a gun. If they were found, they were bound, shackled and taken to the holding area on the docks in Honolulu until the next ship was available.

It was a tense and explosive situation. That is the reason the government gave in and allowed family members to go with them.

Dutton shuddered as he recalled the scene at the dock the night he boarded the steamer—the shrieks and cries as some were literally torn from the grasp of their families and shoved on board. He could still hear the wailing echoing across the water as the steamer headed out to sea. It chilled him to the bone. It was different, Dutton thought, during the Civil War. Families were torn apart but it was because of patriotism and a desire to help their country. Young boys left their homes to join the army. Almost every citizen was affected in some way or another. Despite the hatred that had developed between the States, there were many stories of southern families caring for a wounded Yankee, and northerners caring for a Rebel. While one of the reasons for the war was to abolish slavery in the South, many slaves refused to leave their masters, hiding from the troops of the North. Mothers, wives and sisters worked in the hospitals. Often a member of the family would go searching for a husband or brother on the battlefield.

Strange, how the least sight, sound or smell would bring back such vivid memories, thought Dutton. As time passed, he realized more and more how terrible that war was. Brother against brother, American against American. It is a wonder the nation is now so unified.

Dr. Mouritz's voice broke into his reverie. "Of course, Brother, there have been many changes. Families are not allowed to come here if they do not have leprosy and children born of leprosy patients are immediately removed and sent back to their families to be taken care of or they are placed in orphanages. There is an effort now being made to remove some of the girls in Damien's Girls Home at Kalawao and send them back to the mainland to a home being prepared for them by Mother Marianne's Sisters. It is causing a lot of anguish among the girls."

"It's strange, Doctor, that you came here. You seem very sensitive to patients and it must be difficult to be working among so much misery. I wonder if there is any progress toward answering the baffling questions about leprosy."

"I must confess, Brother, that perhaps some of it is selfishness on my part. I have always been interested in leprosy and am involved in my own research. I am not getting many answers, but I must not give up."

"There was a doctor in our brigade," said Dutton, "who once told me that the answers to all of our questions are already out there somewhere. We do not create the answers, what we need to do is to ask the right questions. He also said that medicine was always operating in the dark ages."

"How is that?"

"Once we find an answer," Dutton went on, "we change the course of treatment, and on looking back realize that we were practicing primitive medicine."

"Those are very wise thoughts," said Dr. Mouritz. "I must remember what that doctor said and concentrate on posing the right questions instead of just seeking answers. Thank you, Brother."

"One more thing," Dutton continued. "He said that once we find an answer we shall undoubtedly have more questions. It seems we shall never know it all."

They reached the steps of the hospital where a few patients were waiting in line. Dutton noticed that they greeted the Doctor with reserve and remembering what the Doctor had said about their resenting the white man, Dutton felt he could better understand their attitude.

Entering the hospital corridor, the Doctor led Dutton to a dressing room. One of the patient-helpers was waiting. The Doctor introduced her. "This is Irene," and turning to Irene, he said, "This is Brother Dutton, Father Damien's new helper."

"Is Father Damien coming today?"

"No, Irene, he is busy visiting the homebound. He asked Brother to come with me to learn how to change bandages."

As word seemed to filter down the line that Damien was not coming, several of the patients left.

Dr. Mouritz donned a long, white gown over his suit and gave one to Dutton. The first patient had many sores on his leg and Dutton noticed that the Doctor took great pains not to touch the skin. He used instruments to peel off the old bandage. Using a holder he took several sponges and bathed the sores with an antiseptic solution which he told Dutton was a weak mixture containing carbolic acid. After applying a salve with a tongue depressor, he fixed the new dressing into place then he wrapped the leg in a bandage made from long strips of cloth. The patient thanked him and Dr. Mouritz turned to Dutton.

"As you see, we have to use what we have available, and it is not always the best. We cannot attach the bandage to the skin as it is too sensitive, but we keep the dressing in place by wrapping the long strips of cloth around the leg."

Dutton noticed that the Doctor washed his hands thoroughly after every patient. When several of them had been treated, the Doctor asked Dutton if he would like to try his hand with the next one who had only a few sores.

Dutton felt nervous but after watching the Doctor, he was sure he knew what to do. He took his time, was very gentle and when finished, the bandage was neat and well secured.

"Well done," said the Doctor. "It didn't take you long to get the hang of it."

Dutton was humbly satisfied.

They then entered the main hospital room. Cots were lined up along each wall and there were screens on wheels which could be used to surround a bed, giving some privacy. The cots were occupied by patients in all stages of the disease. Many were suffering from fever, sweating profusely and shivering.

"At certain times," explained Dr. Mouritz, "the patient goes through these bouts of fever and seems to be in a great deal of distress. It is probable that as the bacilli multiply they overwhelm the body."

Damien wanted to ask what he meant by bacilli but held back. He would leave that for later.

At the rear of the room was a kitchen and a small dining room. Patients who could walk ate their meals there. Others were fed at their bedside. Continuing on through the kitchen they came to the pharmacy where the shelves were neatly filled with bottles of every size and color. Finally, they entered the operating room.

"Here is where we do most of the amputations."

"Amputations, Doctor?"

"Yes. Sometimes it becomes necessary to amputate a limb especially when the sores are so extensive that they may cause gangrene. It even occurs in those patients who have the neural type of leprosy. The only difference is that we can operate without giving them ether as they feel no pain."

"That must be gruesome for you," said Dutton.

"Not really, you get used to it and it's easier when you know there is no pain involved. Father Damien did this before I arrived."

"Father Damien did amputations?" Dutton was surprised.

"Yes, " answered Dr. Mouritz. "He had to—there

was no doctor. A patient, a trained nurse, taught him. But then you see, there is so very little we can do for the patients, any well-trained person can handle it. Of course, a professional doctor is needed when the patient has some other ailment or complication. So many outsiders believe that when a person has leprosy, that that is all they suffer from. They do not realize the victims of leprosy are also susceptible to other medical problems such as appendicitis, sore throat, measles, heart disease, and the same ailments that affect all of us. A major part of my practice here is taking care of those problems—I don't just have to change bandages. And this is where you will be so helpful."

"I'm learning more every minute," said Dutton.

"You did very well today, Brother. Now I must get back to Kalaupapa. I have some duties to perform there. I'll walk you back to the house and get my horse."

As they approached Damien's house, they met Paul.

"Where is Father?" asked Dutton.

"Come, I will show you."

The two men followed Paul to the back of the Church. There they found Damien measuring a plot of ground. At each corner was a large stone. Damien, greeting them, explained that these stones would be the corners on which Brother's house would rest. Dutton was ecstatic but Damien saw that Mouritz looked displeased. "What do you think, Doctor?" he asked diplomatically.

"To tell you the truth," said Mouritz, "I am not happy with the location. It is surrounded by graves. I think it would be better if it were built across the road closer to the hospital. . ."

Dutton interrupted, "Being close to Father Damien is more important to me."

Damien liked that remark. "As you can see, the front door will open to this beautiful view of the ocean and the cliffs which, when he arrived yesterday, Brother said was so breathtaking ."

"I'm outnumbered," said Mouritz. "You have won again Father, as you usually do."

"Not all of the time," replied Damien, grinning, "but often enough, I guess."

"I must get back," said Mouritz as he started toward his horse. "I will see you when you come to Kalaupapa and thanks again, Brother, you did just fine today. You were a big help." And he rode off.

After he left, Damien told Dutton that he would not only overlook the sea but that one door would open up directly to the Church and that a pathway could be built from his house to the sacristy.

"Come now," he said, taking Dutton by the arm, "Malia will be waiting for us."

After supper, when they were on their second cup of coffee, Damien asked, "How did things turn out for you at the hospital? The Doctor said you were a great help."

"I think I did all right. The Doctor was very kind and most patient. He even let me change some bandages and also introduced me to Irene."

"Yes, she is a good woman. She knows every patient and all their needs. She is an invaluable worker." He paused. "Did it upset you to see some of the horrible sores and deformities?"

"At first it did," replied Dutton, "but once you re-alize that you are caring for a human being and not a piece of flesh, it makes it easier. The Doctor warned me I might find maggots in some of the sores. He said the flies eat the flesh and deposit their eggs. Fortunately, I didn't see any today."

"Sometimes you may find more than maggots," said Damien. "One day when I unwrapped one of the pa-tient's dressings, I found she had hidden her money in the open sores."

Dutton shuddered.

"She told me it was safe there for no one would dare go near her leg. I soon talked her out of that hiding place." Damien laughed.

"Now, about your house."

"I don't need a house, Father, a small cabin will do."

"A cabin?" questioned Damien.

"Yes, in our country, cabins are common struc-tures in which to live. They are easy to build and very sturdy. Shall I sketch what I mean?"

They went over to the desk and with a few swift strokes of the pen, Dutton sketched a cabin.

"That design looks simple enough. I thought you may wish a fancier house—I mean 'cabin'. You draw well, Brother. You mentioned you were in the Quartermaster Corps, I believe that's what you said. Just what does a Quartermaster do?"

"They play a very important role in the operation of an army. They estimate it takes about ten men behind the lines to supply one man to fight at the front."

"My Superior told me the same thing," said Damien. "He said it takes a lot of people at home to keep a missionary supplied in the field."

Dutton continued. "We have to determine what supplies are needed, such as ammunition, horses, medical equipment, food, clothing, you name it, whatever the soldier requires. Then we have to figure out the best way to get the supplies to where they will do the most good, trying at all times to avoid attacks by the enemy. They would like nothing better than to capture our supplies. We have to move by train, boat, horse, mule, whatever is available. If bridges are destroyed, we have to find the alternative route or rebuild the bridge. There are times we are right behind the enemy lines."

"My, my," said Damien, "no wonder you are so efficient. Speaking of supplies, I must make out the lists of our needs and see that they get to the Board of Health in Honolulu by the next steamer. Will you help me?"

"Of course. I can also write letters for you. I noticed your desk. How do you find anything?"

"Most of the time, Brother, I don't and that is the problem."

"When I met with Mr. Gibson," said Dutton, "he wanted to pay me and when I refused, he told me that if there were anything I needed, I could just ask him and he would try to get it for me."

"That was kind of him," said Damien.

"Do you think I could put some of the things on your supply lists?"

Damien replied quickly, "Yes, what do you want?"

"You could see, Father, by the small canvas bag I came ashore with, I did not bring very much. I would like to have a change of clothes, similar to the ones I am wearing, some shaving bars of soap, and also, if possible, pens, ink and paper. I like to write and I have many friends in the United States from whom I could ask for things we need. They will send me what they can, especially for the children."

An expression of relief flitted across Damien's face. "You know, Brother, with every word you speak, you bring a great joy to me. For you are so perceptive. You know that my greatest concern is for the children."

He gave Dutton a piece of paper and a pen. "Put down all your requests and we can add them to my requisitions. The next boat is due in two days and I want to be sure my lists are on it. They take our mail and bring mail to us from the mainland."

Dutton was about to work on the list when Damien stopped him abruptly.

"Before you do that, Brother, I'd like to discuss your house further. I see you have sketched only one large room. Won't you need a separate bedroom?"

"No, one large room will be sufficient. All I need is a place to sleep and a place to write. What I like most about your plan, Father, is that my front door will open on to the magnificent scene I saw yesterday and as you said before, one can't get enough of it."

They had long finished their coffee and Dutton had concluded his list. Damien pushed back his chair, "Would you like to take a walk with me, Brother, and we can return to the site of your new cabin, as you call it."

Malia cleared the table and set about washing the dishes. They left the veranda, nodding to patients who were always surrounding Damien's house and who were now staring at Brother Dutton.

Damien lowered his voice. "As you can see, they are very curious about you. I thought I would give them a day or so before I formally introduce you which I plan to do after Mass tomorrow."

Damien did not walk directly to the spot for the new cabin but rather went farther on toward the ocean. Dutton was a bit confused but said nothing. Damien found a large, smooth rock and beckoned Dutton to sit near him. They sat in silence. Damien lit his pipe and puffed away. It had been a long day for the priest, too. He was struggling with the maze of plans going through his mind of what he now could accomplish before he would meet God Himself.

There was a breeze blowing in from the sea. The air was sweet and filled with the strange cluckings and warblings of the birds, mingled with the ceaseless boom of the surf. It was a peaceful, satisfying moment with each man deep in his own thoughts.

Dutton was the first to break the silence.

"I won't pretend that what I saw today, Father, was easy for me. But then that's what I want to do, to help you as much as I can and to do penance."

He looked at Damien. Should he tell him everything or should he wait for another time, perhaps after he had proven himself.

Damien, puffing on his pipe, blew a few smoke rings. "I know, Brother, you are anxious to tell me about your past but please do not distress yourself. There is no hurry to do this. You have closed the book on all that went before. There is no one, least of all myself, with any right to know anything except that you want to serve God and His afflicted. God knows, my friend, and that is all that matters."

He was quiet for a moment. "Which brings me to the real reason I wanted to speak to you with no one around." He breathed a sigh, groping for the right words. "I want you to know, Brother, that I am not breaking any confidence between you and Malia or Dr. Mouritz for that matter. Nothing is kept secret here. You will find there is no way that you can escape to be by yourself, nor can you say anything that will not be overheard."

He looked at Dutton. "I am sure you were able to detect the coldness between Malia and the Doctor."

"Yes," Dutton replied. "I would be dishonest to say otherwise."

"She told me this morning of the conversation you had with the Doctor."

"Oh," said Dutton. "I guess I should have told you before she did."

"No, no, Brother, do not put yourself in the middle. Everything will turn out the way it is supposed to. Remember, I told you yesterday that Dr. Mouritz and I had a difficult time at first, and I understand his concern about me and now you. He has that right, for he is a good man and although we do not agree on everything, I am pleased that he is here to help my people."

"Malia told me he was greatly concerned about your eating with me and sharing utensils."

"I told him," said Dutton, "that the dishes Malia gave me to eat from were not used by you and that she had special ones for me."

"I must admit, Joseph, that I was rash when I came here but I had a good reason."

Conditions in Damien's earlier days were quite different from those that were evident at the time of Dutton's arrival. When the first patients were sent to Kalawao and for some time after, there was no priest to attend to their spiritual needs. Of course, not all were Catholics. The Bishop, however, could not spare anyone to stay there permanently and, as a matter of fact, was unwilling to assign anyone to this difficult mission. Priests would come only occasionally, at most for a day at a time. The patients were not happy with that and after a few years, the Bishop could no longer ignore their pleas.

Damien was stationed on another island when the Bishop arrived there to dedicate a new church. After the dedication, he gathered the priests in attendance and discussed his predicament. Every one volunteered when he asked who would go to Molokai. He thought it best to set up a rotating system and chose Damien to be first. Damien was to accompany him back on the boat to Honolulu where he would stay for a few days to make preparations for his new assignment.

The steamer that arrived was headed first for Molokai with a group of patients. Rather than waste time waiting for another boat, the Bishop and Damien asked the captain if they could board and he agreed to take them.

During the voyage Damien told the Bishop that it would save time if he could go ashore with the patients. But the Bishop pointed out that he had no supplies, no clothing, no material with which to celebrate Mass. But Damien said he didn't need anything, that he would be able to get along with what he had and would make improvisations, until the Bishop could send necessary requisites to set up the mission. At first the Bishop did not agree but as the steamer neared the island, he relented. As the pier had not yet been built at Kalaupapa, the patients were transferred into small boats and were rowed ashore. What a sight they were!

The captain allowed the Bishop to escort Damien to the settlement while he delayed the boat's departure, but cautioned the Bishop that he could not wait too long.

As the small boats approached the shore, a group gathered to welcome the new arrivals. When the Bishop and Damien stepped ashore, they were greeted by a swarm of patients. Damien had seen isolated cases of leprosy but never in his life a large group all together in every stage of the disease. Many were dressed in tatters, some more hideously disfigured than others, and the stench was terrible. But the Bishop showed exceptional kindliness toward them with no sign of fear or disgust. He set a good example for Damien.

The Bishop addressed the patients and assured them that they would no longer be on their own, that at last, they would have someone to stay with them. He introduced Damien and the crowd burst into applause.

A shrill whistle from the steamer indicated that the captain was ready to leave. The Bishop took Damien aside and told him how anguished he felt at leaving him there, alone. He made it clear that the moment Damien felt that it was beyond his ability to withstand this, he should take the next steamer back to Honolulu.

The Bishop said he would understand in spite of the fact that they were short of priests. There were so many needs and so few to fill them. But the Bishop promised that as soon as he could he would get someone to join Damien. He said there was no rectory and showed concern as to where Damien would stay. But Damien said he would be fine and not to worry about anything.

Damien knelt at the Bishop's feet as he received his blessing. There was a deep concern on the Bishop's face and tears in his eyes. Bishop Maigret was a saintly man, not only acutely aware of the needs of his people but also for his priests.

The boat's whistle sounded again, this time more urgently. The Bishop hastened to the row boat, boarded the steamer and stood at the rail. Damien watched him until he was out of sight.

Later Damien remarked when Bishop Maigret died, things were never the same between him and his Superiors.

Damien relit his pipe and took a deep breath. He shifted his position on the rock and stared out to sea. Dutton knew that he was reliving that frightful moment which changed his life forever.

Looking at Dutton he recalled, "As I turned from watching the Bishop's departure, and saw the patients still standing there waiting, I knew I had to say something. I raised my hand in blessing. Some made the sign of the cross and others just stared at me."

"I am Father Damien," I said, "and I am your new priest. I have come to stay with you. I know the main settlement is at Kalawao but how can I get there?"

A young man brought him a horse and said, "You can ride with me, Father."

Damien had just finished telling him he would be able to walk when another man came up with a cart. He was to take some of the new patients to the Kalawao settlement, so Damien got up into the cart. The young man rode off on his horse to announce Damien's arrival to the patients at Kalawao. It was very rough going in those days. There was no road, just some beaten down bushes and patches of dirt strewn with rocks. The cart bounced along, many of the patients huddling together in fear and some were crying.

They arrived at the clearing which was Kalawao.

"I saw the same sight that you did, Brother, of the cliffs and the ocean. I saw the small chapel of St. Philomena and several hundred patients who had heard of my arrival, had gathered to greet me. I gave them my blessing and again introduced myself. They were aloof but one or two knelt."

"I had to get away from the stench. I felt nauseated, so I told them I wanted to say my prayers in the chapel. They cleared a path for me and I almost ran inside."

Damien took out his handkerchief and wiped his brow. He was sweating and his hands trembled.

Dutton never spoke a word. He knew that Damien

was going through his personal agony, and realized, although he had volunteered, he had not really known what he had got himself into. What if Damien couldn't stand it, and had to leave and go back to Honolulu in defeat.

Finally Damien turned to Dutton. "I suppose you are shocked at what I just said, after reading about me being a hero."

Dutton, taken up with Father's obvious emotion said, "You did what any normal person would do. That was a long time ago and you are still here!"

"It was the Blessed Mother who came to my rescue, Brother, as she always does. When I entered the small chapel, I fell on my knees before her statue. I poured out my heart to her. I've even forgotten what I said but I did not pray, I just talked as a son to his mother."

"After a while when I had calmed down and my heart had returned to its normal beat, I felt a hand on my arm. I turned to see an old woman with grey hair matted against her head. Her face was half covered with a shawl through which I heard her hoarse voice whisper: 'Father, please come with me. My husband is dying and needs a priest.' I got up and followed her to a small, run-down hut with a thatched roof. Her husband was lying on the floor on a straw pallet wrapped in a stained and tattered blanket. He was an old man covered with open sores. He was not conscious and I heard the death rattle in his throat."

"All my priestly training came back to me. I had no oils but I knew the Sacrament of Extreme Unction, having performed it many times. I took some water and blessed it, then I anointed him. I was not afraid to touch his sores. He was burning with fever and shaking with chills. As I anointed his forehead, he gave a deep sigh and was gone. I had done what I was trained to do, to prepare the soul for its entrance into heaven. The old woman let out a wail and started to chant, which I had heard many Hawaiians do at a death bed. Then I knew why God had brought me here. I had found my place."

Damien took out his rosary and began saying the prayers silently.

"What happened then?" Dutton finally asked.

"After a few minutes, as I tried to comfort the wife, some men came to take the body to the cemetery. I followed. I had nothing with which to celebrate Mass so I planned to say prayers at the grave. As we approached the cemetery I was shocked to see so many graves. Most of them were shallow and I saw several wild pigs tearing at a body that they had dug up from the earth with their snouts. I chased them off. The grave for the woman's husband was only about one foot deep. Before they could put the body into it, I took the shovel and dug furiously, making it deeper and deeper. The men were astonished at what I was doing. I knew then that not only would I say the prayers for the dead, I would actually build the coffins and bury the bodies. I cannot tell you how many coffins I have made since. No longer do any wild animals dig up bodies."

He looked at Dutton. "This must sound hideous to you."

"No, Father. After the war, I was assigned by the government to dig up the bodies of young boys and men who were buried where they fell. The government set aside plots of land in all the states to rebury the dead and care for their graves. At first the sights bothered me but I soon got used to it. I knew I was burying heroes, those who had given their lives for their country."

There was a pause, then Dutton asked, "What did you do after burying the poor man?"

"I again prayed over the grave. His wife, kneeling at my feet, kissed my hand. I did not pull it away and it was then I realized that I had crossed the first barrier to being accepted. The woman offered me her hut, but I had made up my mind that I would not dwell where a leper had lived. I thanked her and told her that I would like to return to St. Philomenas chapel which was next to the cemetery. She seemed to understand me and nodded her head. I decided in my mind that I would do nothing to hurt their feelings, but I would do nothing rash that would bring on any illness to myself."

"Leaving the chapel, I came to the large pandanus tree outside. My problem as to where I would stay was solved for the moment. I would sleep under it."

"The tree next to the Church is the one that I slept under. It has exceptionally large, wide, spreading branches with broad, flat leaves which offered some protection. The gnarled, exposed roots however, did not make for a smooth bed. I had many companions that shared the tree with me."

Dutton looked puzzled. "Do you mean that the patients came to keep you company?"

"No, no, I had company of the four-legged kind, tree rats. And then there were millions of ants and a few scorpions and I knew their sting could be fatal. By the way, I think it would be a good idea when you arise in the morning, to shake out your shoes. The scorpions like to crawl up into the toes where it is damp and warm, to take a snooze."

Dutton looked concerned. "Do they really kill you, Father?"

"No, not usually, but their sting would make you wish they did. They have been known to kill children. Needless to say I did not sleep well that night. I heard so many noises. Those of the animals did not bother me but the piercing cries of some of the patients writhing in pain and the raucous laughter of the insane was very disturbing. More troubling were the sounds of drunken revelers, the angry cries of some engaged in fighting, and the taunting voices of the prostitutes calling out their wares. I was chilled to my very soul."

My work was cut out for me," Damien continued. "Not only did I have to take care of their spiritual needs but their material needs were of paramount importance as well. My mind was filled with many plans to be fulfilled. Progress is slow here. I am in constant battle with the authorities to get needed supplies, but I understand the government has its own problems as it is not in a good financial situation. The royal family is not very strong, as you will find out."

"Yes," said Dutton. "Dr. Mouritz told me I should study up on the history of the islands. Do you have any books available, even school books?"

"I'm afraid not, Brother, but I'm sure Dr. Mouritz can give you a lot of information."

Damien shivered. "It's getting chilly and the hour is late. Enough, Brother, we will save it for another day."

He struggled to his feet. Dutton was quick to help him as they slowly walked back over the rocks to Damien's house.

"I hope you can better understand now, Brother, why I was so careless with myself. I had to be accepted by these, my people. I could not refuse the food they offered, I could not pull my hand away when they extended theirs, I could not live in any luxury that was denied them. I had to be one of them. If I have leprosy because of that, then I am grateful to God for giving it to me."

"I appreciate that, Father, and I am sure that Christ would have done the same thing. I, too, want to be accepted and would not knowingly hurt anyone by my actions."

"I must get to my breviary," said Damien as they reached the veranda. "But before I go, do you know that I have not stopped talking since you came here two days ago?" He laughed.

"All of this has been bottled up inside of me and you seem to be the one, Brother, to have pulled the cork. I'm sorry for burdening you with my problems."

"Conversation is the basis of all friendships. How can I be of help to you if I do not know what your needs are, Father, and where I can fit into the life of this place. Taking me into your confidence gives me even more assurance that I have made the right decision in coming here."

"Prayers are powerful, Joseph and I prayed for a Brother who would come and help me. God sent me you. Never underestimate the power of prayer, dear friend. Good night and thank you for listening." He turned and went up the stairs.

Dutton entered his room. The oil lamp was lit—Malia, ever thoughtful, was looking after him.

Removing his clothes, he lay back on the bed. He was exhausted. God would forgive him for not saying his prayers. He could not sleep. He kept thinking of what Damien faced in his first hours on Molokai. What would he have done were he in Damien's shoes. There was no doubt he would have fled back to Honolulu. What a transformation he found when he arrived—neat cottages, a good road, running water, happy and laughing children at play, a doctor to care for them, and on and on. He listed the improvements Damien had made. No one who would come after Damien would have to face the hardships that he did. There was still isolation, but there were also comforts and those who cared. Few would ever walk in Damien's footsteps.

With that thought, Dutton fell into a sound sleep.

He felt the warmth of the sun on his face and suddenly he picked up a myriad of sounds. There was low murmuring, laughter, and the voice of Damien talking to his chickens. A sense of dread came over him as he realized he had overslept. He had missed Mass and remembered that Damien was going to present him to his congregation. He quickly arose, dressed and washed his face. Still in the last throes of sleep, he hurried to Damien's backyard. Damien stopped throwing feed to the chickens, and looked at him with much amusement.

"Well, you have finally awakened from the dead!"

Dutton, ashamed, apologized. "Father, I am so sorry. I cannot believe I overslept. I missed Mass, and I know that you were making preparations to present me to your people." He shook his head. "It has been such a long time since I had a solid sleep, I must have blocked out all the sounds around me."

Damien put down the pan of feed and crossed over to him putting his hands on his shoulders. "Don't fret, Brother. It is I who am at fault, keeping you up so late last night with my long-windedness."

He took Dutton's arm. "The body needs sleep as much as the soul needs prayer. Come now, Malia has fixed us a good breakfast."

"I still can't believe what I have just done."

"Brother Joseph, you have had a long journey, not a physical one, but an emotional one, and a spiritual one as well. It is only natural that your body had to catch up with your mind."

As they entered the kitchen, Malia smiled.

"She's been warning everyone not to disturb you. I'm famished, let's eat." Damien pulled his chair up to the table and Dutton joined him.

"What are your plans for me today, Father?"

"I had originally planned to take you with me on my rounds, but before that, I do want to introduce you first, which I will do after Mass tomorrow."

He looked questionably at Dutton.

"Don't worry, Father, I'll be there. You can bet on that."

"The steamer is coming in a couple of days and as you know, I would like to get my requisition lists to the

Board as soon as possible. You said you would help me with that, and also with a few letters that must be written. So, while you're straightening out my desk, I will start building your cabin."

"There's no hurry, Father. I am perfectly content to stay with you."

"I'd just as soon not tangle with Dr. Mouritz and the sooner we get you settled the sooner I can take advantage of your muscles to help me finish some projects I have in mind."

He beckoned Dutton over to his desk. "There is nothing on this desk, or in it, that you cannot look at. In fact, the only thing I am hiding is my favorite hardtack biscuits in one of the drawers. Now you go right ahead and act as if it were your desk—as a matter of fact it is, since you have volunteered to keep my books."

Damien went outside and in no time there were the sounds of saw and hammer.

Dutton sat down at the desk and wondered just where he would start. He picked up pieces of paper from here and there but his orderly mind took over and he gradually categorized everything into proper piles. When he had finished he went out to join Damien and was stunned at how much he had done in such a short time.

"Can I help you Father?"

"Yes, when I get it framed, you can finish it. I hardly ever finish what I start anymore. I am the carpenter and you will be the joiner. But first we had better get my requisition lists written."

Damien brushed his hands on his cassock and they entered the house. He was pleased at the sight of his desk; neat little piles of paper weighed down by small stones.

"My," he said, "I can even see some of the wood!"

Dutton sat down, took the pen and opened the bottle of ink. Damien began to recite all the things he needed. Dutton wrote on a straight line, dipping the pen in the ink bottle from time to time.

"I need more poi, nails, blankets, a new hammer, bandages, cornmeal, carbolic acid, oil for the lamps, hardtack biscuits," and he grinned, "canned food," and on he went.

Dutton wrote it all down and added his own list.

"It looks like a lot of supplies, doesn't it. But remember, I have almost 700 patients. Besides, I learned that if I want a hundred pounds of something I will ask for two hundred, knowing they will cut it in half."

Dutton laughed. "Just like I used to do with my supplies for the army." He then took more paper and rearranged all of the requisitions into their categories: food, medical supplies, equipment, and so forth.

Damien, looking at the finished list, said, "This makes sense now. No wonder the Board had a hard time figuring out what I needed. Won't they be surprised to receive this. They will surely know that I did not prepare it! I also have to write to my Bishop and order church supplies—the government does not give me those. I will use the same technique and give my Bishop a heart attack when he sees how orderly it is."

The two now had another peg on which to build their friendship: a sense of humor and the ability to laugh at and with each other.

Dutton was sitting with his chin cupped in his hand. Damien looked at him.

"Is there something wrong, Brother?"

Dutton hesitated. "I wonder if I could ask you a question."

"Of course, go ahead."

"In looking over the list, I am confused that you are responsible for so many things: food and clothing for the patients, medical supplies for the doctors. How do you do it all?"

Damien, nodding his head, said, "You are very astute, Brother. No, I'm not legally responsible for anything except caring for the spiritual needs of my people. When I first arrived here, as I said last night, there was chaos, no law, no discipline. Mr. Meyer, the superintendent of the settlement, who lives on his vast estate at the top of the pali trusted my judgment. There was no one else to whom he could turn and he seldom visited the settlement. He would submit my list to the Board and while they would cut it somewhat, I would get most of what I wanted. When the Board lost their faith in me, due to reports in the press that if it weren't for Father Damien, nothing would be done, this put the Board in a poor light and they pressured Mr. Meyer to take authority away from me. While I have nothing to do with the newspapers since I have no control over what they write, I saw no reason why I couldn't use the power of the press to get what I needed for my people. Now, the resident doctor and resident superintendent are responsible for my supplies, but I still submit my list to let them know my viewpoint. They usually ignore the list except when it includes building supplies. Where else can they get a carpenter who works for nothing!"

Dutton said, "That clears things up for me now."

"I receive a lot of supplies as well from the good Sisters of the Sacred Hearts with whom I came to Hawaii originally. They are now engaged in teaching and other social work on several of the islands. And there are other generous people who read about our situation and want to help," Damien said.

Just then there was a flapping of wings and some loud squawks. "Those boys," Damien shouted, banging his fist on the table, "are at my chickens again." He rose heavily.

Dutton was up on his feet, half curious, half anxious. When Damien appeared at the door, the boys scampered in all directions. Damien used his deep baritone voice when he wanted to strike fear.

"You scamps," he bellowed, "come back here."

The boys stopped in their tracks and sheepishly came back to stand near Damien.

"How many times do I have to tell you to leave my chickens alone?"

One boy muttered, "I'm sorry, Father, we did not know you were home."

"What difference does that make," scolded Damien. "In fact that makes it worse. You are doing mischief behind my back. Come closer."

Seeing the fear in their faces, Damien relented. His voice changed dramatically. "Look at you, look how dirty you are."

He started to brush the dirt from their clothing.

Turning to Brother Dutton who was standing by his side, he pointed and said, "This is Brother Joseph Dutton. He has come to help me. What must he be thinking of you?"

Dutton was about to speak but catching Damien's wink, kept quiet.

"What have you got to say for yourselves and to Brother?"

James, the bolder of the group spoke up, putting out his hand he said, "Aloha, Brother."

Dutton quickly grabbed the boy's hand, "And Aloha to you." He patted the boy on the head.

Damien eyed Dutton carefully, "You seem to like children."

"Oh, yes, Father, very much. Even if I did not have any of my own." And his voice trailed off.

"Well, boys, " Damien said. "Off with you. Get cleaned up and I will soon bring Brother Joseph to the Home to inspect your quarters. Woe to any of you if there is a mess."

Going back into the house, Damien remarked, "The children are and always have been my greatest concern, ever since I came here. I was shocked, on my arrival, when I saw how many there were and they were all miserable. They had been abandoned and were abused by the lusts of the adults in a most revolting fashion. I managed to get them together for their own protection, and built two houses, dormitories rather, one for the girls and the other for the boys. I have a non-patient, a wonderful woman, in charge of the girls. I try as best I can to care for the boys but being away so much with so many other chores, I'm afraid I neglect them."

"I'm sure you do the best you can," said Dutton.

"The dormitory also houses some older men," Damien continued, "who are either blind or cannot take care of themselves, but they do whatever is possible to take care of each other. I pray night and day for Sisters for the girls, and Brothers for the boys. They need guidance, love, and firm discipline. They are getting out of hand. Rough as I am, when it comes to the children I'm afraid I am too indulgent.

Dutton spoke up. "I know, Father, and I also know what you are up to. You want me to help."

Damien nodded. "I can't fool you. Would you be willing?"

"Definitely," said Dutton. "When I was a young man, I opened up a gymnasium. What the children need is activity and to develop strong bodies. I can teach them how to march and I know many games. Baseball is catching on in the United States and I think I can get some equipment."

Damien was delighted and in his usual way of making quick decisions, he said, "I will put you in full charge, right now."

"Father," protested Dutton, "I don't want to be in charge of anything. I just want to help."

"What I said before about titles, they are meaningless, but they do establish who will make the decisions."

Dutton was not about to argue. He pulled out his watch. "My goodness, it is already four o'clock. Where did the time go."

"You were told by Dr. Mouritz that I would give you little time to rest."

Malia appeared and put their supper on the table.

"Perhaps you would like to wash up first?"

Dutton was grateful. He went to his room and washed. As he was scrubbing his face he said to himself, "and you thought you would not have anything to do. Now your problem is, how will you find the time to do it all. Oh, well, God has taken care of everything up to now, so I'm sure He will find a way."

After supper, they went together to inspect the boys dormitory as Damien had promised the boys, and that he would bring Brother Dutton with him.

He knew that the boys would scamper about trying to clean up things. When they entered the dormitory, the boys were still sweeping and straightening their beds. Damien made a big show of inspecting every corner. He smiled to himself when he saw clothes shoved under the cots and dirt swept into the corners. At least they tried, he thought, as he complimented them. He showed Dutton the small recreation room. There were a few long tables with broken parts of games scattered about and several books on the shelves. A blackboard stood at one end of the room and tacked to the wall was a faded map of the world.

Damien introduced Dutton to each of the residents and they chatted for a while.

"I'm pleased that you presented Brother Dutton with a clean room," Father said glancing at Joseph.

"Well, what do you think?" asked Damien as they left the dormitory.

"It certainly needs a lot of improvement, Father, but I agree with you they need more guidance and I already have many ideas."

"I was hoping you would accept the challenge. I have great faith in you, Brother, and if anyone can make the Home more like home, I know you will. I noticed how easily the boys accepted you. That's a good start."

They walked toward Dutton's new house. Yesterday, they had worked on the cabin until darkness fell. Since it was to be a simple structure, they had made rapid progress, and Dutton had jumped into the project with intense earnest. It would be the first house he ever owned! And thus, he thought, I have concluded my second day at Kalawao on the island of Molokai. Upon entering his room at Damien's house, he set about writing letters long into the night.

CHAPTER FIVE

DUTTON AWOKE BEFORE he heard the rooster's crow. There was the sound of footsteps above him. Damien must be awake and stirring about. He had noticed how it pleased Damien when he would be the first to arrive anywhere, so he lay there until he heard Damien come down the stairs and step off the veranda.

He arose quickly, bathed, shaved, then walked briskly to the church. Dawn was breaking and the congregation was arriving. He entered the sacristy. Damien, at his prie-Dieu, looked up, and he nodded. Paul was spreading out the vestments.

After Mass, Damien faced the congregation and putting up his hands for silence, said, "I want to introduce you to my new helper."

He turned to Dutton and asked him to stand. "This is Brother Joseph Dutton, who has come from the United States. You may call him Brother Joseph and I know you will give him a big welcome."

Those who could, clapped their hands, while others called out a strong "Aloha."

Outside the church, Damien and Dutton stood together as the congregation filed out. Dutton clasped their hands strongly though many did not offer to do so. They

were shy, but when they saw Dutton shaking hands without any fear, they relaxed.

Introducing Dutton was really anticlimactic. As
soon as he arrived, word had spread throughout the settlement that a stranger from America was sleeping in
Damien's house. Of course, Malia had told her group of
women friends all about Dutton, what he ate, how he
overslept and how polite he was. It was true, as Damien
had said, nothing was hidden here. Every action was observed by someone. There was little privacy.

At breakfast, Damien said, "I've been told the boat
is coming today and I received a message from Dr. Mouritz that no patients are aboard, just supplies."

He paused between sips of his coffee. "I have so
many chores I want to do. Would you mind, Brother, riding to Kalaupapa with the requisition list we prepared? "

"Of course, Father," replied Dutton, putting aside
his plate. "I wrote a few letters late last night that I would
like to get off on that boat as well."

"Do you want to take the rig?"

"It would be quicker if I had a horse. Do you
think I could borrow one?"

"Paul will get you one," said Damien.

He called out to Paul who, thinking Damien was
going, was getting the rig ready. "Get Brother Dutton a
good horse. I am not going to Kalaupapa today, he will go
by himself."

Paul had mischief up his sleeve and he brought
back the most spirited horse available.

Dutton gathered the mail and said it would be the
first time that he would be alone at Kalaupapa and won-

dered if he would have trouble with the boat captain.

"Not at all," said Damien. "When you get there you will find Dr. Mouritz. He is always present when supplies come in. He checks them thoroughly to see if they sent what he wanted. He will take care of the captain. Perhaps you may want to visit with the Doctor awhile. You are not needed here today."

Paul offered his cupped hand to assist Dutton as he started to mount the restless steed. To Paul's surprise, Dutton swung up into the saddle with no effort. Adjusting the reins he dug his heels into the horse's side and gave a little clicking sound. The horse took off, galloping at full speed. Paul was now frightened and ashamed. Suppose Dutton had a fall. He went directly to Damien and told him what he had done.

Damien just laughed. "Don't worry, that horse will soon find out who is his master." Paul was relieved.

Dutton felt good sitting astride the spirited horse. It had been a long time since he had ridden. He knew immediately that the horse sensed he had a stranger on his back and for a few minutes it was a contest between man and beast. People on the road quickly jumped aside as the horse came galloping toward them. At first they were startled and then looked with admiration as they saw the virile young man, with his head flung back, laughing as he let the horse have its way. It did not take long for the animal to know that he had someone in control on his back and he soon calmed down to a trot as Dutton tightened the reins.

Dutton kept his eyes on the road and in what seemed like a few minutes, actually about fifteen, he wheeled the horse to the wharf where the steamer had already docked.

When he heard the sound of hoofbeats, Dr. Mouritz looked up from checking the supplies. Seeing Dutton, he went over to him as he dismounted. The horse was sweating.

"It looks as though you had a fast ride."

"Yes." Dutton patted the horse's neck. "He gave me a great workout but I think we understand each other now."

Dutton handed the Doctor the packet of letters and the list of supplies. Mouritz scanned the list and looked at Dutton with raised eyebrows.

"This was not made by Father, I can see that. It's so neat and well organized." Then pointing his finger at Dutton, "so he's already got you working on his papers." Dutton just nodded. "I'm glad you came, Brother. When I have finished here I have someone I want you to meet."

Dutton watched the steamer as it was being unloaded. There were boxes of tinned goods, lumber, barrels, and crates of all sorts. The dock was piled high and workers were sorting and loading the cargo into wheelbarrows and carts to be taken to the warehouse. When finished, Mouritz signed the manifest.

Dutton asked, "Where is the Captain?"

"He is visiting a friend of his, a retired sea captain, the man I want you to meet. He knows more about the history of the islands than anyone I know. He lives not far from here."

They walked together down a narrow path skirting the shoreline. "Do you want something to eat or drink? My house is just a short distance."

"Thank you Doctor, but I had a hearty breakfast. Father feeds me well."

"That I know, Brother. He loves his breakfast. I think it is his favorite meal for he eats little for the rest of the day. With a good breakfast under your belt, you really don't need much until supper."

While he doesn't eat with Damien, he seems to know what his dietary habits are, thought Dutton, just like a good doctor concerned for his patient.

In no time they came upon a scene that any artist would love to paint. In the distance two men were sitting on the rocks, one smartly dressed in a uniform wearing a captain's hat, the other, barefoot in wrinkled overalls, a large, straw hat covering his long, white hair, with a full white beard to match. Beside them were two fishing poles standing straight up, anchored between the rocks, the lines leading out to the sea. Both men had tin cups in their hands and were engaged in conversation. Silhouetted behind them were the cliffs of the pali. As they approached, the Captain arose. Dr. Mouritz introduced him as Captain Joshua. They immediately recognized each other.

"Of course," said the Captain, "you were on my ship when I tried to persuade you to come back with me. I see you finally came to your senses. I have room for you."

"No," protested Dutton. "I have not changed my mind. In fact, I'm firmer than ever. I am staying."

The Captain looked puzzled.

"I brought Brother Dutton here to meet Captain

Caleb," said Mouritz.

"Oh, I see," said Captain Joshua. "Why didn't you tell me you were a Brother, it would have made more sense to me why you came here."

The Doctor was quick to explain, "Joseph is not a religious Brother, it is Father Damien who has given him that name."

The older man was still sitting on the rocks. He made no move to stand up or to offer his hand. Mouritz turned to Dutton, "This is Captain Caleb, Joseph." When Dutton extended his hand the old man just grunted.

"Don't worry about him, Brother," said the Doctor. "His bark is worse than his bite." Turning to Caleb, he said, "I wonder if you would spend some time with Brother Joseph. He wants to know about the islands. I think it would be important for him to have this knowledge so that he can come to know the heritage of the patients he is working with."

"Aye," the old man finally said. "If he has come to work with that good priest who is constantly after me trying to change my ways, I will be happy to tell what I know." Looking at Dutton he motioned him to a place on the rocks next to him.

Captain Joshua spoke up, "Well, I'd better be getting back to the ship. We'll be sailing soon. Thanks for the whiskey, Caleb, I'll see you on the next trip."

Walking after the Captain, Dr. Mouritz said, "Wait, I'll go with you." Then turning to Brother Joseph, "I will come back in a few hours. In the meantime, your horse will be taken care of, so don't fret.

"I think Father may be concerned if I do not return soon."

Mouritz laughed. "Don't worry, he is probably so absorbed in a project he doesn't even realize that you have gone." Bending over Captain Caleb, he patted him on the top of his straw hat. "Take good care of Brother, now. No cussing and no booze," and catching up with Captain Joshua, went back down the path.

When they had disappeared, Caleb looked Dutton over. "So you're the man Captain Joshua told me about. He said he tried to get you to go back with him but you refused. Why do you want to stay in this God-forsaken place?"

Dutton looked him squarely in the face, "I could ask you the same question. Why are you here?"

"Simple. This is my adopted country."

"I hope it will be mine also," said Dutton. "Why did you settle in Kalaupapa?"

"It's a long story, son," the old man said. "I live on the big island and only come over here for a while during the good fishing season. There is so much activity back there, that I have to get away once in a while to put my mind in order."

"We all have to do that from time to time," agreed Dutton. "But don't let me interrupt you. You were beginning to tell me why you came to the islands."

Caleb leaned back, spreading himself on the rocks. "I was born in New Bedford, Massachusetts. Did you ever hear of it?"

"Oh yes," said Dutton. "I was born in Stowe, Vermont, not too far from there. When I was a young boy, we moved to Janesville, Wisconsin, so I did not have the chance to visit, but around the dinner table I heard my parents speak often of New Bedford. They said it was a large fishing village. "Yes," said Caleb, "it was and still is."

Caleb's father owned a fishing fleet and Caleb practically grew up on the boats. He never really liked fishing and dreamed about exploring the world. At the age of seventeen he saw a notice posted on a piling down at the wharf that a whaling ship was in the harbor and was looking for a crew. It was scheduled to go to the Hawaiian Islands. Caleb's heart raced. This is just what he had been looking for. It took many hours for him to convince his parents to let him sign on board. They knew that he would be gone for at least a year, but since there were four older boys in the family to help his father, they finally gave in.

Caleb had never been on a whaling ship. Whaling was big business then, as oil was needed in huge quantities to light the lamps of the world. The ship set sail and hugging the coast of the two Americas finally rounded the Horn into the Pacific Ocean. Arriving at the port of Lahaina in Maui, they found sixty whaling vessels from many countries, including England, Japan and Russia. The whales migrated in huge numbers off the coast to spawn and the whalers were waiting for the right time. The town was teeming with sailors. It was all new to Caleb at his tender age—drunken brawls in the streets and of course, easy women.

Finally the day came for their first hunt. Caleb was excited but nervous. During the long voyage from New Bedford there had been many lessons given by the captain and his officers on how to use the harpoon gun and especially how to prepare the ropes attached to the harpoon so that they wouldn't tangle, and the way to man the small boats to give chase. They put out to sea. It was not long before they sighted a pod of whales. The Captain put his sights on a huge sperm whale. It was thrilling to see this giant beast rise up out of the water and dive down again, leaving a large wake and a huge spout rising up from his blow hole.

As the sailing ship neared, the crew shot off the first harpoon. It arched through the air and came down striking the fleeing creature. Instead of being thrilled, Caleb was horrified to hear the squeals of terror as the great whale plunged, trying to rid himself of the harpoon. Blood squirted into the water and the sea turned red. A small boat pursued him and the whaler shot off a second harpoon with another small boat taking up the chase, hooked on to the harpoon rope. Sitting in that small boat as it was pulled along at breakneck speed, Caleb was frightened that they would be tossed into the boiling sea. He was heartsick while the other men were screaming and yelling with glee. Exhausted, the poor animal finally gave up as the men threw their spears into its body. They could hear the labored breathing as the winches on the whaler started pulling it toward the ship. Eventually a geyser of bright red blood shot from the blow hole and the tethered whale floated motionless alongside.

That night Caleb dreamed he was covered in blood and awoke completely drenched in sweat. He had signed on for a year and knew there was no way he could get out of that contract unless he could escape somehow.

The next day, in one of the bars, he struck up a conversation with a member of the crew of a Japanese trading vessel. They were leaving on the tide that evening for Tonga and Tahiti in the Marquesas. Caleb bribed him to smuggle him aboard. After they left the harbor, Caleb showed himself to the Japanese captain. He was understanding and since he saw before him a strapping young lad he said he surely could use an extra hand. Once they reached the Tongan Islands, Caleb escaped once again and hid in the hills. The Japanese made no effort to locate him.

For the next twenty years Caleb signed on various traders going from island to island in the Pacific. It was there that he picked up all the stories and legends about how the Hawaiian Island chain was discovered.

Caleb sat upright on the rocks and turned toward Dutton. "I finally arrived on Hawaii which is called the big island. I had saved my money over all the years and had enough to start a small business. At first I began with sugar cane and as my business grew, I added tobacco and pineapples. I was sixty-seven when I gave up my business. I now have a nice piece of property and a comfortable home."

"How did you come to know about Kalaupapa?" asked Dutton.

"I became acquainted with Captain Joshua and accompanied him on several trips. I loved the isolation and the quiet at Kalaupapa and I staked out a small piece of land where I built my shack. This is my paradise when I want to escape."

"Have you ever gone back to New Bedford?"

"No," said Caleb, "It has been over fifty years since I left New Bedford and I haven't been back." He stood up brushing off his pants. "My throat is dry, I've got some whiskey in my shack, would you care to join me? Captain Joshua keeps me supplied with rum and whiskey but you'd better not be telling the good Father that the Captain brings whiskey here. It's bad enough that he is after me. He is a tough man, that Father. The stories of his courage are known far and wide."

"I'm more aware of that every minute I have been here," said Dutton, standing.

"I don't ever want to tangle with him," Caleb said firmly. "When he first came here there was no law and order. It was the survival of the fittest. The poor people had no hope so what did they have to lose! They knew how to make potent drinks from the roots of plants. Even the root of the sweet potato can be brewed into some God-awful tasting stuff. But it does the trick, it makes them forget everything."

"I know what drink can do," muttered Dutton.

"The worst was what was happening to the children. Some of them were treated as slaves, especially the girls who were abused sexually."

Dutton shook his head.

"The good Father would have none of that," continued Caleb. "Many a night he would appear at the doors of the huts where all this carousing was going on. He cut a scary figure with his long, black cassock, his flying black cape and that funny hat on his head. He had a big stick and brandished it about while yelling at the top of his voice. Scared them half out of their wits he did. They fled the drinking houses like a bat out of hell." He giggled. "Some of them thought the gods had come back."

Dutton laughed. He remembered how he had almost jumped out of his skin when he heard Damien yelling at the boys who were tossing rocks at his chickens.

"Not all of them gave up their ways," said Caleb, "but enough did and he took the children away from the criminals. I steer clear of him when I see him coming. As I said before, he wants to convert me. I'm not a religious man and I'm not having anything to do with those papists. I can't help but admire him though, for what he has done to help his people. I don't know anyone who could do what he has achieved."

He checked the fishing poles. "It's getting pretty hot here with the sun beating down. Let's go over to my house."

Dutton started to follow but stopped. "What will you do about the fishing poles?"

"Oh, we've got all that settled here. You can leave your pole and if anyone should come by and see there's a catch on the line, he hauls it in and leaves the fish by the pole."

"That's wonderful. It shows they can be trusted."

"Oh " cackled Caleb, "anyone can get a fish but I wouldn't leave my money there."

The walked across the slippery rocks and arrived at Caleb's thatched-roof hut.

What Dutton saw was not a house, not even a cottage, and barely a hut. It was, in fact, an old fishing shack just thrown together without a door and with holes for windows. Dutton wondered how it could stand a stiff breeze let alone a strong wind. Then he noticed the old man had driven iron pegs into the rocks and anchored the roof firmly with strong ropes. Stepping inside he was shocked at the mess. If he thought Damien's house was unkempt, this was so much worse. It was a shambles. A rusty old steel cot with a stained mattress and a pillow filled with straw was in one corner and clothes were strewn everywhere. There was a tiny sink filled with dirty dishes and a row of bottles on the shelf above. The place reeked with the smell of fish.

"Sorry for the appearance," Caleb said. "It's the maid's day off." And he laughed. Throwing off a pile of clothes draped over the only chair, he offered Dutton a place to sit.

"Will you join me in a glass of whiskey?"

"No, thank you, but if you have water, I'll take a cup."

"What about coffee, I don't know a seaman who can't make a good cup of coffee."

"That would be great," said Dutton.

Boiling the water on a small kerosene stove, Caleb poured it into a pot containing crushed coffee beans. They soon dissolved and he reheated the pot, letting it come to a boil. Dutton tasted it. It was strong, yes, but well brewed.

Caleb sat on a little stool by the open doorway. "So it's the history of the Islands you'd be wanting. Not much has been written but it has been handed down from generation to generation, most of it based on legends. These I picked up along with a lot of stories from the natives of the many islands I visited."

He scratched his chin. "Where to begin?"

Caleb pursed his lips and thought for a while. Then he proceeded to tell Brother Dutton the story of Hawaii as he knew it.

CHAPTER SIX

MILLIONS OF YEARS AGO in the middle of the Pacific, there was a great upheaval of the ocean floor and from it volcanoes arose, spewing molten lava, building layers and layers of solid rock. Some piled on top of others, tall cliffs emerged and a chain of islands was formed, later to become known as the Hawaiian Islands. Some of the volcanoes have remained active to this day.

Hundreds of years later, seeds borne by winds and birds, dropped on the islands and took root. Mosses and lichens grew on the rocks. As the plants and birds evolved over the centuries, new species arose, some not seen on any of the other islands. There were no reptiles, very few insects, no flies or lice. Some animals from the sea crawled up on to land and adapted to the new environment. The islands remained unknown to man for millions of years.

Other islands farther to the south soon became inhabited and it was from these islands, principally the Polynesian group, including Samoa and Tahiti that the first settlers arrived in the Hawaiian chain. As legend tells it, there was a great upheaval of tribal warfare in some of the Polynesian islands. Two classes of people made up the population; the chieftains and their families, and the commoners. The commoners, having no power, were being persecuted so they decided to flee and find a land of their own.

In secret, they built the most powerful canoes ever known. Some were large enough to carry up to forty people as well as animals which included pigs and chickens. Food supplies and plants consisted of breadfruit and bananas and taro roots which when mashed formed the staple of their diet called "poi" that contained much needed proteins. Sails were made from the leaves of the pandanus tree, and ropes from vines and coconut husks. Nothing was wasted—everything had its purpose. They made long spears for catching fish, and hollowed out bamboo stalks enabling them to catch rainwater. They took with them large women, prized for their stamina. Females were treated as slaves, doing most of the physical labor. Only the strongest men were picked to paddle the canoes.

In plotting their escape they had slim knowledge of navigation except that which had been passed down to them over the years by observance of the moon, the birds, the sea and the position of the stars. They did not know that the Hawaiian chain was 2,000 miles from any piece of land. Twelve islands made up the chain, approximately 1,500 miles long forming an archipelago, but only eight were habitable.

The escapees had no idea how long it would take them to find a new land, and nobody knows the time it took them or how many were lost at sea. They were constantly on the lookout for birds that could not land on water which would tell them that an island was nearby.

After months at sea, they finally spotted land. Rising in front of them was a huge mountain surrounded by a white cloud that did not move with the wind. As they neared, they saw fire spewing from the top. They had arrived on the southern shore of the biggest island, now called Hawaii. Beaching their canoes, they tentatively set out to explore.

They could hardly believe what they had found. There was lush vegetation everywhere with streams filled with fish. Since they were all commoners with no classes or chiefs, they shared everything they found with one another. They were now working for themselves and soon built makeshift shelters. They were very industrious and innovative. Finding pools of water nestled between the cliffs and fed by beautiful waterfalls, they laboriously strung makeshift ropes across the entrances. Then they hung netting with openings of many sizes so that small fish would swim into the pond from the sea. They cultivated the growth of algae and plants upon which the fish would feed. Growing fat and big, the fish could not get back out of the holes from which they entered and thus were trapped. This added up to a plentiful supply of fish. The commoners lived in peace and harmony with nature for almost 500 years.

Then came the second wave of settlers. They, too, were Polynesians but mainly from Tahiti. They brought their food, their plants and animals. However, they also brought their chiefs, kings and gods, who controlled every aspect of life. Once again the caste system was established bringing conflict with the original settlers who were eventually conquered.

When the new settlers thought the gods were angry, they would make human sacrifices to appease them and usually the victims were female slaves. They had also brought with them their kahunas (witch doctors) who were thought to be descended from the gods and who wielded great power. The chief goddess was Pele and she ruled their realm. They believed that she made her home in the pit of the volcano and when she was angry she would cause it to erupt, spewing the hot lava that destroyed everything in its path. They threw the slaves into the pit hoping to satisfy the goddess.

Pele had a sister, the Goddess of the Sea. They were enemies who fought each other constantly. When Pele's fire was intense, the sea goddess would cause the sea to swell and put it out. The natives feared mostly the kapu (taboo) established by the kahunas. These taboos were usually against women and anyone who broke a kapu would be put to death.

Women were not allowed to eat bananas or shark meat, nor could they eat with the men. The only power a woman had was in raising the family. She had no power at all in the running of the tribe.

The Polynesians brought with them their dances and their music. Most of the dances were based on legends and old stories. The commoners, working now for the chiefs, worked only when they were forced to. They contented themselves with pleasurable activities when they rested from their labors.

Many of the new arrivals had landed on the island of Kuahi. The islanders were not aware of what was going on in other parts of the world. This was changed with the arrival of one of the greatest explorers of all time, Captain James Cook.

Cook had enlisted as an able bodied seaman in the British Royal Navy and soon rose in rank. He made many voyages to the Pacific, always taking with him map-makers and anthropologists who were also artists and sketched the unusual plants and animals.

After sailing around New Zealand, he put ashore and it was there he met the savage Maoris who practiced cannibalism. He did not stay long! He also explored part of the east coast of Australia which he named New South Wales. He returned to England several times and on other voyages went south of Africa, farther south than anyone had ever been, dodging enormous blocks of ice. He also crossed the Indian Ocean and then went back to New Zealand, where he rested briefly. He took off again, sailing halfway across the Pacific to discover Tahiti and Tonga which he named the Society Islands. Later he charted the Easter Islands and the Marquesas. Seeking a northwest passage to the Pacific was the objective of his next trip and he sailed again from England in July 1776.

When his ships approached the Hawaiian Islands they frightened all the natives who, seeing the ships coming with their tall masts thought they were trees. Cook did not land at that time but circled Maui.

In January 1778, he sailed into the harbor of the big island of Hawaii, the home of the gods. One of the gods had left the island, promising to return. When Cook's ship sailed into the harbor, the natives thought it was the returning god and they treated the Captain as if he were that god. They gave him anything he wanted. The crew, however, brought with them what was to be the downfall of the Hawaiian people. Cook had forbidden his men to associate with the women but he was not able to control them. When they left they had infected them with venereal diseases, scurvy, measles and many other sicknesses.

Sailing out of the harbor, Cook ran into a storm that damaged some of his ships. He had to turn back, and when the natives saw the ships returning they realized that he was just a mere mortal who was afraid of a storm. They stopped treating him as a god and regarded him as a foreigner. There followed a fierce battle on the beach and Cook was murdered. He was only fifty years old.

The natives buried him on the beach but later removed his bones, holding them in great awe. They knew that he was not a god, but certainly a great navigator.

The islands were now open to invaders: British, French, Russians and finally the Americans. The British kept the other nations from conquering the islands, their big guns making them more powerful.

Now, there were three kingdoms on three separate islands. The three kings chosen by their chiefs rivaled each other and soon warfare broke out between them. The islands became fractured. Not being able to stand together, they were vulnerable to foreign forces.

At that time a son was born to a high chief and his chief priestess who knew in their hearts that he was destined to become king and was in danger of being murdered by the other kings. They took him into the hills and kept him in hiding. He possessed many natural talents, was very athletic, fearless and intelligent. When he grew into manhood, it was determined that he should leave his hiding place and go back to his people.

At the age of fourteen he took the name of Kamehameha I. He made friends with the British who helped him build canoes and vessels mounted with guns which could be used for battle. When he had enough knowledge, he declared war on the other kings and set out to conquer them. His purpose was to create one kingdom. He fashioned new weapons never seen before, including longer spears. His men learned how to shoot the guns. When conflict began, he was very successful, eventually conquering the other kings. Once, when the enemy was trapped on the side of a mountain, the volcano erupted and the flowing lava forced them to jump to their deaths. The natives believed that the gods were on his side.

While he was away, another king invaded his island so Kamehameha I had to return to oust the invader. Through his wise efforts, the three kingdoms were eventually united and he created a single monarchy. It was from Kamehameha I that all the succeeding monarchs were descended.

Peace reigned for many years but the natives continued to practice the kapu. The king was intelligent enough to know that he could control his people through the kapu. There was no doubt that he was the greatest warrior and leader the Hawaiian people had ever known. In gratitude to the British for helping him, he incorporated the Union Jack into the flag of Hawaii. In 1819 he died and his body was secretly buried. No one knows, even to this day, exactly where his body lies.

His eldest son, Liholiho, became King Kamehameha II and ruled for only five years on the island of Oahu. The seat of the kingdom was then moved to Honolulu. Now that they had more contact with people of different cultures, who were arriving in ever increasing numbers, the people became disillusioned with old beliefs and particularly with the strict laws of kapu.

King Kamehameha's mother, who had been his father's favorite wife, held the title of an important minister in his government. She had great powers behind the throne but could not express them because of the taboo against women. She encouraged her son to eliminate this strict rule. He was willing to do so and at a large banquet he got up from the men's table and went over to the women's table to eat, thus breaking the kapu. Following that he issued orders to break other kapu restrictions.

People were confused. Temples were destroyed and the gods were banned. The kingdom was without a religion. Fortuitously, a group of New England Protestant missionaries set sail from the United States for the Hawaiian Islands to convert those they called heathens. The king agreed to meet with the missionaries and was persuaded to allow them to preach Christianity to the islanders. He did not realize the changes that were to come about as a result of his decision.

When they landed, these proper New Englanders were stunned at what they saw. The natives wore very little clothing and the women danced the hula, which to their eyes was obscene and sinful. The missionaries were successful in converting many of the Hawaiians to Christianity and they set out to change most of the practices of the island women, particularly their garb. They made long dresses, covering the women, who did not object, from head to toe. It wasn't long before nakedness was banned.

King Kamehameha and his queen decided to visit England on an invitation from King George IV. Shortly after they arrived, they both contracted measles and died. The King's younger brother, Kauikeaouli, was crowned Kamehameha III. He was only ten years old and his grandmother, the Queen Regent assumed the real power. She, too, was converted to Christianity.

Many more missionaries had arrived and they built additional churches and schools. They created a written alphabet for the Hawaiians and published bibles and textbooks. There were separate schools for the children of the royal family and with this close association, they assumed political power. The Queen appointed several to advisory posts which led to the restructuring of the Hawaiian way of life. In less than ten years, Protestantism was established as the official religion of Hawaii. The small number of Catholic missionaries who had arrived were forced to leave the island and their teachings were forbidden. Anyone who converted to Catholicism was imprisoned.

With their need for funds to run their programs, the Protestants began to invest in sugar mills and local businesses. The royal government was gradually falling into the hands of these American missionaries. A new constitution was established creating two Houses. The upper House which included members of royalty while the lower House was elected by the common people.

Other foreign governments, too, had their eye on

the Hawaiian Islands, including France. Under great pressure the king ceded Hawaii to Great Britain. The Hawaiian flag was lowered and the British Union Jack was hoisted.

In a few months Hawaiian rule was restored with special guarantees for British citizens. Both England and France officially recognized the Hawaiian independence. The king appointed more and more foreigners to important government posts as he wanted his country to adopt the ways of the western world. In 1848 at the urging of the sugar planters, the king made another change in the traditional organization of Hawaiian society.

All of the land belonged to the King and his royal court. Under the new law, it was to be divided into three parts: one portion for the King and his heirs, another to the government, and the third distributed to the chiefs. The laws greatly benefited the foreigners who were now permitted to buy land. They acquired much land from the royal family who needed the money to buy imported goods and to maintain their status. Commoners were allowed to obtain small tracts they had lived on and cultivated. They did not fully understand the concept of ownership and many failed to file land claims. As a result, numerous claims for land ownership were refused. Without the opportunity to continue farming, they had to find work in port towns. Those whose land claims were honored often sold their tracts to foreigners.

King Kamehameha III died in 1854. His nephew and grandson of Kamehameha the Great, Liholiho, was designated to ascend the throne as Kamehameha IV. His reign lasted less than nine years.

He had travelled to both England and the United States before being named King and he felt he had been treated with more respect in England than the United States where he had experienced prejudice against his race. The Anglican Church of England impressed him and he donated land and money to build an Anglican church in Hawaii. His boyhood sweetheart, Emma, now queen, joined this church. She was loved by all the people.

With the acquisition of huge parcels of land, the businessmen developed plantations of sugar cane and pineapples. They were desperately in need of workers as the native Hawaiian population had been decimated. It was believed that when Cook arrived there were at least 400,000 Hawaiians on the islands but by now it had tumbled to 35,000.

Workers were imported from China and Japan as well as from the Philippines. It was believed that leprosy, which was spreading at such a rapid rate, came from the Chinese and it was called "ma'i Páké," the Chinese disease. The foreign workers usually signed a contract to work on the plantations for at least a year. The Chinese were hard workers and saved their money. When their contracts expired, they did not renew but flocked to Honolulu and started many business enterprises. This resulted in the need for the importation of more foreigners to work the fields.

King Kamehameha IV had a son, Prince Albert, who died at the age of four. The King was terribly grief-stricken and quickly declined in health. He died at age twenty-nine.

At the death of the King, his younger brother, Lot,

ascended the throne in 1863 as Kamehameha V. He was more interested in preserving traditional values and customs than his brother. He called for a new constitution returning more power to the throne. He borrowed a great deal of money at high interest rates to build a number of important public buildings, but the national debt rose to a dangerous level.

In the meantime, under the threat of war by the French, the Catholics were able to return to the islands. Many had escaped into the hills when they were banished and had practiced their religion in secret.

The King's attempt to bring more power back to the royal throne infuriated the Americans and the British, who had assumed control of the government.

The scourge of leprosy continued to attack the Hawaiians. The natives were very susceptible to the disease and became infected by the thousands, reaching epidemic proportions. Leprosy greatly concerned the white men on the King's council. They forced the King and his Board of Health to issue an edict banning all victims of leprosy from the mainland.

Anyone showing signs of leprosy had to present themselves to the authorities. The government purchased a piece of land on the tip of the island of Molokai. It was a perfectly natural prison, surrounded by tall inaccessible cliffs on three sides which led down to the tumultuous sea. It was known as Kalawao. On the north side, another strip of land, Kalaupapa, was inhabited by homesteaders.

Victims of leprosy were rounded up and sent to Kalawao by the hundreds. When the Hawaiians heard of this new law, they hid themselves, knowing that it was the white man who forced the King to issue the edict.

The King never married and died in 1872 without an heir to the throne. Thus ended the direct descendants of Kamehameha the Great. One of the major candidates for the throne was Prince William Lumalilo, a cousin of the late king, well educated and liked by the people. He wanted to assume the throne by a popular election and won by a large margin. The legislature then confirmed him as King.

He had little experience in political matters and was sympathetic to the Americans living in Hawaii. He named several able Americans to his cabinet but his reign was a short one. He died a little over a year after taking office. He had not married and left no heir.

David Kalakaua who was a descendant of Hawaiian chiefs was then elected to be the new King at the age of thirty-eight, but he reigned for only seven years.

He enjoyed the pomp and ceremony of the royal court and was impressed by the Europeans more than he was with the Americans. However, the Americans were uneasy about his election and were even more distrustful of his major opponent, Queen Emma, widow of Kamehameha IV, who was very open about her love of the British. His election set off a short-lived riot staged by Queen Emma's supporters. The new King asked for help from the Americans to put down the rebellion and American troops, along with some English, dispersed the unruly crowd.

In 1874 King Kalakaua went to Washington, D.C. He was received by President Ulysses S. Grant and addressed a joint session of Congress. He was the first reigning monarch of any nation to visit the United States and his main objective was to negotiate a trade agreement between the United States and Hawaii.

In 1875, the two countries did sign a treaty which removed the U. S. tariff on sugar. It made the Hawaiian sugar cheaper for American buyers. It also assured the Hawaiian sugar growers a secure market for their product. In return, the King gave exclusive rights to the United States to use Hawaii's ports and harbors, including Pearl Harbor. The King built a new royal palace and planned a grand coronation ceremony similar to those he had seen in Europe. This, along with other expenditures put the King deeply in debt.

CHAPTER SEVEN

"WELL," SAID CAPTAIN CALEB, "that brings us up to the present." He got up from the stool, pushed it aside and walked stiffly to the kitchen sink where he poured himself a glass of whiskey.

"I guess, my good man, that I've wearied you. I'm surprised you are still awake."

"My goodness," answered Dutton, taking out his watch. "I must get back to Kalawao. Father Damien will be wondering what has happened to me. How can I thank you, Caleb, for that wonderful history lesson. I now have a much better understanding of the situation here and it will help me greatly."

Just then, Dr. Mouritz appeared at the door.

"I'm afraid I was so interested in what Caleb was telling me," said Dutton, "I forgot to look at the time. I can't believe the hours have passed so quickly. I wonder what Father is thinking."

"Relax Brother, I have handled all that," said the Doctor. "I knew you would be absorbed in Caleb's tales so I sent word ahead with the supplies that you would be back with the mail in the morning, and that you would be staying with me tonight."

"That makes me feel better, Doctor, but are you

sure I will not be imposing on you. I can get back in no time at all riding that frisky horse."

"Oh, no, Brother. I have plenty of room and besides I would like to show you the laboratory and some other things. Between Caleb here, and me, we will have your head spinning."

They both laughed. Dutton shook Caleb's hand and Dr. Mouritz thanked him as well. As they left the shack and stood outside, the wind picked up and dark clouds were passing overhead.

"I smell rain," said Caleb.

They followed Caleb to his fishing pole and sure enough, there was a big fat fish wriggling on the rocks.

Dutton said, "You are right. There are good Samaritans here." He again put his hand out to Caleb saying, "I am so impressed with your knowledge of Hawaii. I will never forget today."

"I can't believe that I enjoyed it so much myself," replied Caleb. "It brought back many memories, and it was good talking to someone from my home country."

"Once a Yankee, always a Yankee," quipped Dutton. "I hope I will have the chance to see you again."

Caleb cackled in amusement. "The door is always open." He waved his hand and went inside.

As they walked away, Dutton said to the Doctor, "He is certainly a character."

"That he is," came the answer.

Arriving at the Doctor's cottage, Dutton noticed how nicely located it was, a few yards off the "Damien Road" but within walking distance of St. Francis Church. Just beyond were the wharves and the docks. It was a one-story cottage resting on cement footings surrounded by a white picket fence with plantings of many strikingly-colored, flowered bushes. A wide veranda extended from the front around to both sides on which were two white rattan armchairs, a table and several flower boxes. The view of the open sea was spectacular from this vantage point. The serene fields of grass contrasted with the jagged rocks and stark cliffs.

The house was whitewashed while the shutters at the windows were painted a contrasting dark green. The windows were covered with fine mosquito netting. How clever, Dutton thought. The Doctor seemed pleased to show him around. The front door opened into a wide living room, with highly polished wooden floors and several straw-matted rugs.

On one side of the living room, two doors opened into more rooms—two adjoining bedrooms separated by a common bathroom. The front bedroom was larger, the big bed draped with a colorful spread. There were night tables on each side of the bed, on one of which was a tall oil lamp. Several comfortable chairs were conveniently placed, and again straw mats covered most of the floor. The smaller room, Dutton surmised, was used by guests. It, too, was comfortably furnished and both rooms contained ample clothes closets. In the bathroom was a long, wooden bathtub standing on four legs and a large mirror over the sink.

On the other side of the living room was another door which was closed. At the end of the living room was an open alcove which Dutton could see was a dining area. It had a long, wooden table covered with a colorful cloth, surrounded by six chairs. A large oil lamp hung from the ceiling.

At the rear of the house was a kitchen, the floor protected with linoleum, and a door leading to the back veranda. There were wooden counters along the wall, separated by a double sink. Standing to one side was a cast iron stove with four openings on the top and an oven below. The stove pipe ran up to an opening in the ceiling. There was a small table and two chairs and a walk-in pantry which was well-stocked with tins and other food containers. Before Dutton could say anything, Dr. Mouritz told him that Damien had built this house after he built St. Francis Church.

"At the time," said Mouritz, "Damien thought that this would be an ideal place for another priest he was hoping the Bishop would send. That did not happen, so the cottage was used by guests, including a visiting priest, doctor, or a member of the government's administrative staff. Other doctors, who came for short periods of time, did not wish to live at Kalawao and when I was appointed as the first resident doctor, this became my cottage."

Dr. Mouritz, taking Dutton to the small bedroom, said "This will be your resting place for the night." There were clean towels and soap on the bedstand and Mouritz told Dutton to make himself at home and that he would meet him on the front veranda.

It had been a long day at Captain Caleb's shack and Dutton was grateful for the chance to refresh himself. He heard movement in the back kitchen and as he left the bedroom for the veranda, he noticed two women busily engaged in preparing food.

He joined Mouritz who was seated in one of the rattan chairs. The two women, Mouritz explained, were his housekeepers. They were the wives of some home-steaders and they came each day to clean and prepare his meals, returning to their homes at night.

"You must be very tired, Brother, after spending all that time with Caleb."

"I was, but washing up really refreshed me. Caleb was so interesting I never noticed the hours passing." Dutton looked around. "This house is beautiful and so well constructed. You said Father had built it. Isn't it just like him to build a beautiful house for someone else and for himself, such an ordinary place."

"Yes, it is typical of him. He denies himself so that he can give to others."

"Your bathtub is unusual. He does not have one in his house neither does he have shutters on the windows."

"His house is always filled with patients," Mouritz said. "He told me he wants them to see that he does not have any more than they do."

"He has no privacy, and I must admit that is one of the drawbacks living there with him." Dutton went on, "I have always been a private person. I think he realized that, for he wasted no time in starting to build a cabin for me, as you know."

"Yes," said Mouritz, "and I repeat, I am not in favor of the location but he will have his way. Once he makes up his mind, nothing can change it."

Just then one of the women came to the door and said that supper was ready. Dusk was descending and the lamps throughout the house were lit.

The dining room table was set with real china and sparkling glassware. A gleaming white tablecloth had replaced the floral one and an attractive bowl of mixed flowers was in the center surrounded by six tall candlesticks. It brought back memories to Dutton of the dinners he had attended in the beautiful southern homes of Tennessee. Once again he was struck by the comparison of this table with Damien's. There was no china in Damien's house. The plates were made out of hammered tin, the cups were all sizes and colors. Nothing matched.

He noticed that the Doctor did not say any prayer before the meal, and not wanting to embarrass him, he did not bless himself. The women had prepared a delicious supper of roast pork, tender sweet potatoes, string beans along with the inevitable poi. When Dutton first ate poi, it tasted like starch and he did not like it, but he knew now that as he was in the islands, he would have to get used to their dietary staple.

The two men did not talk during the meal. Dutton was waiting for a cue, but the Doctor was silent except to thank the women who served them. When they finished, the Doctor asked Dutton if he would like his dessert now or before bedtime, which is what he preferred. Dutton felt well fed and said that he, too, would have his dessert before bedtime.

When they left the table, Dutton also made a point of thanking the two women although the Doctor had not introduced them. Again he noticed the difference, for Malia was part of Damien's family and had a great deal to say. The two women went about their tasks silently. Dutton followed the Doctor out on to the veranda. A light drizzle was falling, as Caleb had predicted, and the sun had set behind the pali. It cast a golden glow across the waters. Settling comfortably in his chair, Doctor Mouritz said, "This is one of my favorite times, after a long day caring for patients."

"I'm curious, Doctor. Why did you accept this appointment when you had such a good practice on Oahu?"

"That's easy to answer, Brother. I have always been interested in leprosy. Patients were usually sent here as soon as they were diagnosed. I had little chance to follow up with my research on Oahu. I felt once I was here where the patients remained until their deaths, I could study the disease from the beginning to the end.

The rains stopped and Dutton breathed in deeply. He liked the smell of the wet grass. There was silence for a moment, then Mouritz said, "I would offer you a pipe, Brother, but I don't smoke. I know Damien enjoys his."

"I used to smoke, Doctor, but I gave that up with other things when I entered the monastery of the Trappists."

There were a few people walking by on the dirt road who waved to the Doctor. He waved back, then turning his attention to Dutton, said, "I did not know that you were studying for the priesthood."

"I thought I wanted to be a priest but I found out that it was not my calling." He offered nothing further and the Doctor did not pursue the subject.

For the moment only the sound of the surf and the cries of the mynah birds in the trees broke the silence. Darkness fell quickly and with it came the buzz of the mosquitoes.

"I think we will be more comfortable inside and better protected from the insects."

Dutton followed the Doctor inside. The women had finished cleaning up and bade the Doctor good night.

"I would like to show you where I spend a great deal of my time."

Dutton went with the Doctor to the closed door on the other side of the living room. The Doctor took a key from his pocket and opened it. Dutton surmised this was a private place which no one could enter without permission. He was amazed at the gleaming white walls and floors of what looked like a large laboratory and treatment room.

There was a desk piled high with papers, two long tables with several microscopes, neatly arranged slides, and more papers. The white cabinets were filled with instruments. The bookshelves along one wall were stacked with books and on the other wall was a framed copy of the Hippocratic Oath and several framed medical degrees. An examining table at one end was covered with a white sheet and there was an odor of carbolic acid.

Mouritz offered Dutton a seat on one of the several white stools at the table. Sitting opposite him he said, "This is my study where I do most of my research. At times, I bring patients here for examination and I also take photographs."

"I can see why you would be happy in a room such as this, Doctor. It is almost like a sanctuary."

"We know so little about leprosy, Brother, and from now on I'm taking your advice."

"Oh," said Dutton, surprised.

"Remember yesterday, when you told me that it was more important to ask questions than to look for answers?" Mouritz pulled a large pad toward him. "When I came back, I sat down and wrote all my questions pertaining to the disease as they came to mind. You may like to read them." He pushed the tablet across the table. "I haven't had time to put them into any sense of order."

Dutton read the questions the Doctor had posed:

What is leprosy?

What causes it?

Where is it found?

Does it affect one race more than another?

How is it contracted?

What are the symptoms?

Why does one person have the lepromatous type
while another has the neural and yet
another has both?

Why does it spread rapidly in some people while
in others it takes many years before it
does any damage?

What are the forms of treatment?

Why does leprosy manifest itself in some members of the same family while others
seem to be protected?

Is it acquired through sexual transmittal?

Does nutrition play a part in the transmittal, prevention or treatment?

Is climate involved?

Why don't we find leprosy in animals?

Do insects carry the disease?

And the list went on for several pages.

"You can see how easy it is to ask questions," said Dutton, "The difficult part is finding the answers. Have you found any?"

"Yes, we have found some, just partial answers. Each time we find an answer, it raises another question."

"It's no wonder the study of diseases can be fascinating but very time consuming."

"You're right, Brother. It is difficult to be both a practitioner and a researcher. Research takes a great deal of money and unless you have someone to provide that, you need to have other means by which you can live."

"That's why in many professions, even in religion, you have those who think and those who do."

The Doctor looked puzzled.

"For example," Dutton continued, "in some religious orders there are divisions of labor. One group, the educated priests, are relieved from manual tasks so that they can spend most of their time in study and teaching. The manual labor is usually done by other members of the Order, by Brothers and Sisters. Perhaps you remember the story of Martha and Mary. Martha was always working in the kitchen while Mary greeted and entertained the guests. When Martha complained, Jesus told her that they each had important roles to play and both would be rewarded."

"If I had my way, I would prefer to spend all my time doing research," said the Doctor. "Perhaps one day this will happen."

"I was never interested in leprosy before," said Dutton, "until I read about Father Damien. Now I am beginning to ask all these same questions."

"If we find answers, we can share them. There is one exciting development," continued the Doctor. "A Norwegian scientist by the name of Dr. Gerhard Armauer Hansen, has discovered a similar bacillus, a form of bacteria, in his testing of thousands of leprosy patients. He believes this bacillus is the causative agent of leprosy. If so, that opens many doors to further research. Not everyone in the field accepts his theory. One of the difficulties Dr. Hansen has is trying to get this material injected into a healthy animal to see if it would get leprosy. To date, no animal has shown positive results. Of course, that opens the door to using this bacillus on a healthy human."

"That seems an unlikely step," said Dutton. "How would you find anyone willing to take that risk?"

"It is being done," Dr. Mouritz answered. "It is not widely known, but some doctors have been using prisoners in return for their freedom. A few have been willing but there has been no record of any success."

"What answers have you found so far, Doctor?"

"I have yet to do a great deal more research, but from what I have studied, climate does not seem to be a causative factor. Leprosy is found in almost every country including the cold countries like Norway where Hansen did most of his work. In the middle ages many European countries had leprosy patients, but it seems that it was wiped out during the Black Plague which killed so many people. In England, there are several Lazar Houses, even though they are empty."

"Lazar Houses?" questioned Dutton.

"Yes, that is what they called houses where leprosy patients were placed. I imagine the name was based on Lazarus who rose from the dead at Jesus' command or the diseased beggar He comforted."

"Most cases, today," the Doctor went on, "are found in tropical climates. A reason may be they wear less clothing and have more chance of direct skin contact. This could be one method of transmittal. A few questions are being answered in part by logic, but in testing for scientific accuracy there is still a long way to go."

The Doctor was enthusiastic about his subject. "Every patient has different reactions. Some will show signs soon after the bacillus attacks. In others, it takes years from one sign to the next. There are two different types. The neural type usually begins with a rash. It could be red with little white scales in the center or white scales with red spots in the center, but it does not cause itching."

Dutton self-consciously looked at his arms.

"Don't be embarrassed, Brother. When I tell people about this they invariably start to examine themselves. It is only natural. There is no pain but soon they begin to experience a loss of feeling in the area of the rash. By this time, the nerve has been damaged. When this happens, should the patient injure himself, he feels no pain. The impulses from the nerve to the brain are impaired and the brain does not receive them, so the patient does not react properly. If they put their feet in boiling water or walk too close to hot ashes, they could receive extensive burns without knowing it. Often the sense of smell is affected. They cannot smell a fire burning, and as a result they do not escape as fast as they normally would. The nerve is also the trigger to bring essential needs to the part of the body that is injured. When these chemicals are not brought to the damaged area, decay sets in. The bones become infected causing them to wear away or the skin to peel off. This usually happens to the extremities, the fingers and toes. The tendons which allow the patient to make a fist or curl their toes are shortened, giving a claw-like appearance, as in the case of Father Damien's helper, Paul.

"One major consequence of this type of leprosy is damage to the nerve that allows the opening and closing of the eyelid, thus moistening the eyeball. Losing this function can cause the eyeball to dry and blindness to occur. But it is a mystery. Some patients have only minor damage while others have severe results. In the case of Paul, it would seem the damage occurred early and now has stopped.

"There have even been cases where people with leprosy in the later stages suddenly have what they call a miraculous cure. The disease totally disappears. It is not known what happens except that the leprosy is arrested.

"Since so many people in the islands go barefoot, they often injure their feet by walking on rough stone and glass. Since they are not aware of the injury, they develop ulcers, making it very difficult for them to walk or maintain balance. The extremities become susceptible to gangrene and amputations have to be done before it can spread. The neural type also seems to affect the larynx which makes the patient hoarse with difficulty in talking.

"The lepromatous type of leprosy usually begins insidiously. Sometimes it takes many years from when the first symptom appears to the occurrence of debilitating effects. The earliest symptom again is a rash but instead of it being isolated in one area, it will cover most of the body. During this stage, the body tries to fight this infection, and one of the means it does this is to increase the body's temperature, causing the patient to have a very high fever accompanied by chills and shaking. Usually the rash subsides and the patient notices tiny, shiny nodules appearing, starting on the face, the ear lobes and the extremities. The skin thickens, the nose swells, the nostrils dilate, the lips protrude and the lobes of the ears enlarge. Most of the nodules contain pus and when they break open, foul-smelling substance drains out. The eyebrows fall out and again, like the neural type, the voice box can be affected.

"The patient with the neural type can more or less hide his symptoms but there is no way that those with lepromatous leprosy can do so. Since the face becomes distorted they develop what is called a leonine expression, resembling the face of a lion. While they have much discomfort, they are not in constant pain. The pain usually comes whenever the rash appears with the fever. The hands and feet become swollen and walking becomes very difficult. Their fingers cannot grasp utensils. There is really no effective treatment as yet. Salves are applied but they afford only temporary relief. They have no effect on the progress of the disease."

Dr. Mouritz got up from his stool. "You know, Brother, " he said, "anyone with leprosy will grab at any treatment he hears about. There are so many—I call them witch doctors—offering all kinds of remedies and the patients are vulnerable to them. The latest 'new' treatment is the Goto Treatment. You may have heard Father Damien mention this."

"No," said Dutton. "There has hardly been time yet to get into details, even if Father had wanted to discuss them with me."

"Well, this treatment is based on the work of a Japanese Doctor Goto at the Kakaako Hospital in Honolulu. Damien has had it and wants to bring it to Kalawao."

"What is this treatment, Doctor? Is it effective?"

"Dr. Goto claims great success in Japan. The patient is given a series of hot baths in water treated with various salts and herbs which Goto has not revealed, and then a drink made from a mixture of other herbs and salts. The patient feels refreshed after the baths but between you and me, I have seen no evidence of any effect on the disease itself. However I will not deny any patient wanting to try it since I have no alternative to offer. There are medicines made from nuts, herbs and oils. Whatever comes along is tried. It is important to keep up the hopes of the patients by offering them these remedies, but I believe having used all of them, no one knows at the moment if there is a cure."

Dutton shook his head. "I would imagine that is the most devastating feature of the disease. I would hate to think there is no hope of getting rid of it."

"That is why there is such fear, Brother. The only way that the healthy have to protect themselves is to isolate the victim of leprosy preventing any contact with the healthy population."

Dutton could not help himself and tried to stifle a

yawn, but Dr. Mouritz noticed and said, "You must be very tired Brother Joseph. You have had a long day. Perhaps its time now to have that dessert and then off to bed. I have to be up very early myself for some appointments."

Dutton rose from the stool. "Doctor, I'm so grateful that you have told me about leprosy and, more important, taken me into your confidence. You put everything right on the line and I like that."

The Doctor led Dutton to the kitchen. The women had made a dessert of vanilla pudding filled with chunks of pineapple sprinkled with coconut and there were cookies. The dessert had been covered with a cloth to protect it from the many insects crawling about. The Doctor offered to make Dutton some coffee but he said that a glass of milk would be just fine. When they had finished, the Doctor walked Brother Joseph to his bedroom and bade him good night.

After saying his prayers, Dutton just about collapsed on to the bed. He felt so tired and his head was swimming with all that he had learned between Caleb and the Doctor. He had the feeling that instead of only a few days, he had been on Molokai forever!

He knew that he would not sleep if he started to dwell on everything that had been said but over the years he had learned to shut it all out of his mind by reliving some of his childhood. In that way sleep would always come easily. He pictured the snow covered hills of Vermont and before he could get any further, the mantle of sleep descended upon him.

He awoke with the sun shining through the shutters and the smell of strong coffee in the air. He stretched and turned over, then realizing where he was, jumped out of bed. There was a tapping on the door. "Yes?" he called.

"Your bath is ready, sir," came the answer.

Bath? he thought. Then he remembered the tub. He had not brought a change of clothes with him. He put on his pants and jacket and walked barefoot to the bathroom. The tub was filled with warm water and fresh towels were laid out. The Doctor's housekeeper had thought of everything. He took off his clothes and sank into the luxurious warm water, but he knew he could not waste much time. He bathed, toweled off, dressed, and went back to his bedroom, finished dressing, combed his hair and entered the kitchen.

The breakfast was prepared and the housekeeper invited him to sit down. She said, "You will like these eggs, they come from Father Damien's chickens. He gives the Doctor a supply every week. My name is Louise."

"I am Joseph Dutton. Where is your helper?"

"You mean Margaret? She only comes late afternoon, Brother Joseph."

She looked sheepishly at him. "Dr. Mouritz told me to call you that." After serving him she left him alone.

He was very refreshed after the good night's sleep and the warm bath. Rising, he put the dishes in the sink, thought of washing them but then changed his mind. When he went out on to the porch, he saw a young boy holding the reins of his horse.

The boy said, "Good morning, Brother. Dr. Mouritz was sorry he could not wait for you. He had to go to the hospital."

He handed Dutton the letter pouch. Putting his foot in the stirrup, Dutton mounted the horse which was standing patiently. So different from yesterday when he had tried to throw him. The horse now knew the feel of the man on his back and was content to be led. Dutton thanked the lad and cantered off for the two mile ride down the Damien Road.

Nearing Kalawao, the patients waved to him in greeting. It was a big change from the first day he arrived when they hid their faces. He had a warm feeling knowing they had recognized and accepted him.

As he rode up to Damien's house, Paul came out and took the reins.

"Good morning, Paul."

"Good morning to you, Brother."

"Where is Father Damien?"

"You will see him in the back. He's working on your house."

Paul took the bag of mail from him and Dutton walked briskly to the site of his new cabin. He was absolutely flabbergasted when he saw how much had been completed. Damien, hammer in hand, strode beaming toward him.

"Well, what do you think?"

"I can't believe it, Father. How did you finish it so quickly?"

"One of the reasons I wanted you to go to Kalaupapa was to free me so that I could get to work on it. Paul and some of the younger ones helped me." Damien turned and looked at the cabin. "It's not completely finished. Some of the interior has to be smoothed and whitewashed, but in a day or two you will be able to move in."

They both went inside the cabin and Dutton exclaimed, "Father this is exactly the way I wanted it. It's just perfect."

Damien, pleased, asked him if he had had breakfast.

"Yes, Father. The women who work for Dr. Mouritz took good care of me."

"You must tell me all about your trip. Did you bring the mail?"

"Paul took it from me. I think he has taken it into the house."

As they walked toward the house, Dutton said, "I really don't know how you could possibly work so fast, it is remarkable."

"I'm glad you like it. It gave me great pleasure and satisfaction to build it for you. I realize how important it is to be alone at times. Living in my house, you are constantly surrounded by people, day and night."

Entering Damien's house, Dutton went over to the desk and handed the mailbag to Damien.

"It seems heavy, Father. I hope that what you are so anxiously awaiting is in there."

Damien put the bag back on the desk. "Sit down, Brother, and tell me all about your day."

"Father, it was truly unusual. Dr. Mouritz was very kind and helpful. He introduced me to Captain Caleb. Do you know him?"

"That renegade? Of course, and he knows me. I'm sure he had a few words to say about me. He thinks I hound him to change his ways."

"He undoubtedly admires you."

"Go on now, Brother, you certainly can be frank with me. We have had quite a few battles, that old Captain and I."

Dutton laughed. "Well most of what he said was in admiration, but I think he feels that you are out to convert him."

"I know him. I'm aware that he attempts to sneak whiskey into the settlement. But he is a good man who has had a difficult life. Now, I believe, he is content just to lay around and enjoy every minute of what is left to him."

"He is quite educated," said Dutton. "He spent hours talking about the history of the Hawaiian Islands. I gathered a good deal of information from him."

"Oh, yes. Brother. He is a good source of knowledge of all the intrigues and the politics going on."

"I also had a delightful evening with Dr. Mouritz. He has a very comfortable house and showed me his laboratory. He told me a great deal about leprosy."

"All in all, you had a most productive day."

"That I did, Father, but I could not wait to get back here. Kalaupapa is nice but I feel much more comfortable here in Kalawao. This is where I belong."

"I'm glad you said that, for I have been feeling a little guilty. You see, there is a guest house, which the government erected, over by the hospital. Guests can stay there for a few days when they come to visit. I could have put you up there, Brother, but I'm afraid I was selfish and wanted you closer to me."

Dutton was feeling more relaxed with him now

and some of the formality was beginning to fade.

"As I told you, Father, the only reason I came here was to help you. When I read about what you had achieved, I just knew there would be a place for me here. I must confess to you, too, that another purpose I had was to do penance for what I have done in my past."

"Well, now that we have got that off our chests, let us see what the mail has brought."

Damien dumped out the contents of the weather-worn pouch onto the desk. There were at least fifty letters of one sort or another, a few newspapers and some pamphlets. Damien hastily scanned each piece. He's looking for something, Dutton thought.

"Ah, ha! Here it is. I hope it is the answer to my prayers." Damien sat down, opened the thick envelope and read in silence.

Dutton, straightening out the other letters and organizing them into piles, glanced over to see disappointment on Damien's face. "Bad news?" he asked.

"For the moment." Damien answered quietly. "But I am not going to give up hope." He sat back in his chair. "I might as well tell you what I was looking for. Perhaps the Doctor told you about the Japanese baths called the 'Goto Treatment'?"

"Yes, he explained it to me, Father."

"Before I go further, I must give you some background information."

For the next hour or so, Damien filled Dutton in on the troubles he was having with his Superiors. Bishop Hermann Koeckemann, coadjutor to Bishop Maigret, succeeded him as Vicar-Apostolic of the Hawaiian Islands.

Bishop Koeckemann, a German, had spent many years in the Hawaiian chain, and as Bishop Maigret's coadjutor, was aware of all the intrigues facing the Catholic Mission and its precarious position.

Reverend Leonor Fouesnel, a Breton, was elected as Provincial. Damien now had two men of far different temperaments to that of his Superior, Bishop Maigret, who was fond of Damien, and understood his personality. Both of the new men felt that Damien was seeking publicity and was filled with his own self-importance, therefore he was difficult to control. They had no evidence of any direct disobedience, yet they felt their positions were threatened by the adulation bestowed upon Damien from around the world.

Both the Bishop and the Provincial were aware of the many changes taking place within the Hawaiian kingdom with the increasing power of the Protestant Calvinists in the running of the government. They were mindful of what had happened to the Church in the early days when it had been expelled from the islands. Therefore whatever decision they made was based on how it would affect their stature with those in authority.

The Bishop was not trustful of either the King or his Prime Minister, Walter Murray Gibson, whom Bishop Hermann referred to as an enigma and a "sly old fox." No one knew exactly what Gibson's past was since he had told so many lies, but it was certain from his personal writings that he was born in England. His parents moved to North America, first to Canada and then settled in New York City. He had a brilliant mind but was always restless, seeking one adventure after another.

In his early teens Gibson left home, settling for a time in the South where he met a young southern girl who was enamored of his adventuresome spirit. They soon married and she bore him three children, two sons and a daughter. A mere six years later she died leaving him a widower, and he remained a widower for the rest of his life.

During the following years, he was involved in a series of schemes always seeking his fortune and eternally looking for danger. He had joined the California gold rush but soon tired of that, and travelled to Central America. He found himself drawn to those who were fighting the authorities, involving himself with their causes. It lead to many escapades for which he had often been apprehended and jailed.

Later, he learned of the Mormons and their plans to establish a foothold in the Hawaiian Islands. Always the schemer, he converted to Mormonism and offered his services to the Elders of the church. The colony they had chosen was located on the smaller island of Lanai.

Gibson was very instrumental in helping the Mormons by cultivating the land and creating plantations, but he did not adhere to the principles and edicts of their religion. As time went by, the Mormons became disenchanted with the island. They excommunicated Gibson and left Lanai.

Gibson, now in possession of their land and their plantations, ingratiated himself with the Hawaiian people, learned their language and studied their customs. His two sons helped him with his enterprises. But Gibson was restless and moved to Honolulu where he became the publisher of a newspaper which he printed in both English and Hawaiian. To conform to the new life he had begun, he changed his appearance, grew a beard and became an impeccable dresser.

Dutton, interrupting Damien's explanation of events leading up to his expected letter, asked, "How did Gibson assume so much power with the King?"

"Well," Damien replied, "When King Kamehameha V died leaving no heir, his cousin Prince Lumalilo, decided to seek the throne through popular election. Gibson, as the owner of the newspaper wielded a powerful influence on the electorate and helped to get him elected. After this, Gibson decided to try for office himself and moved to Maui where he ran for the Legislature and won easily. When King Lumalilo died, the new king, Kalakaua, recognizing Gibson's power with the people, chose him as Minister of Foreign Affairs, and then as President of the Board of Health, much to the dismay of the businessmen in Honolulu. They knew that Gibson would back King Kalakaua in his efforts to restore more power to the throne."

"That makes it clear," said Dutton. "Now I realize how scheming and crafty Gibson is. He seems to play all sides and when you get caught in the middle you are bound to be squeezed out."

Damien continued his narrative.

Despite his devious ways and mercurial moods, Gibson must be given credit for his interest in the health and welfare of the Hawaiians. He was particularly concerned with the fate of the leprosy patients who had been shipped to Molokai. He had printed many articles in his newspaper and when Damien accepted the assignment to go to Molokai, Gibson wrote of this "heroic priest" willing to sacrifice his life for victims of leprosy.

His newspaper articles did not sit well with the Protestant missionaries, for it could be inferred therefrom that they were reluctant to take care of leprosy patients. In their defense, however, it must be stated that most were married with young children and could not expose their wives and families to the dread disease.

Walter Gibson's stories and reports in his newspaper brought an avalanche of mail and the spotlight now fell on Damien. Gibson did not realize that one day he would regret making Damien a hero.

When the edict was issued banishing leprosy patients to the island of Molokai, all suspects were rounded up and shipped to Kalawao, the isolated spot. Although several were found later not to have leprosy and were returned to the mainland, there was an outcry from the Hawaiians who hated the edict in the first place.

Gibson attempted to solve this problem by setting up a small receiving station in Honolulu where suspected cases would be sent first. After examination by doctors, only those determined to be incurable were sent to Molokai. In those days, it was very difficult to make an accurate diagnosis. The only way it could be determined whether a patient had leprosy was by his physical appearance and since other diseases cause similar symptoms, such as syphilis, it was a hit and miss proposition at best.

When the small receiving station could no longer handle the increase in the number of leprosy suspects,

Gibson decided to build a larger hospital at Kakaako. The site chosen turned out to be a disaster. It was located near a salt marsh, subject to high tides, much flooding and high winds, which caused salt spray to cover everything. A high wall was built around the hospital giving it the appearance of a prison and the Board of Health did little to keep up its maintenance.

In no time the number of patients more than doubled, causing crowding and deplorable sanitary conditions. The staff was poorly trained and inadequate. Once again the patients were expected to care for themselves. Those who escaped were rounded up, returned, and kept in isolation as prisoners.

When conditions reached the stage where mutiny and revolution was a possibility, Gibson decided to try to obtain Catholic Sisters to staff the institution. He knew of the dedication of these women who had no husbands or children to concern themselves with, when taking care of the victims of leprosy. He approached Bishop Koeckemann to help in the search for Catholic Sisters.

Damien had wanted Sisters, ever since the day he arrived at the settlement on Molokai, but his requests were always turned down. Both the Bishop and the Provincial were concerned that if Catholic Sisters were sent to Molokai, it would only further alienate the Protestants who were in power.

After being assured by Gibson that every step would be taken by the government to cover the expenses of transportation and housing of the Sisters, the Bishop agreed, despite his personal dislike for the man. He sent Father Leonor Fouesnel to the United States with an official letter requesting a religious order of Catholic Sisters engaged in hospital work, to accept the assignment.

The letter was sent out to more than fifty Congregations. Nearly all of those approached, turned down the request. One positive response came from Mother Marianne Copp, Provincial Superior of the Franciscan Sisters of Syracuse in New York State.

Father Leonor was ecstatic in finding a Congregation that might be willing to accept the assignment. He was as crafty as Gibson and did not mention in his original negotiations the possibility that the Sisters would be caring for the victims of leprosy. During the early stages of negotiations, he painted a picture of paradise where Sisters would be welcomed and comfortably taken care of. They would have their own convent and chapel and every means of support. He also mentioned that there were several other hospitals in the islands including one at Wailuku on the island of Maui where Sisters might be engaged in hospital work.

Mother Marianne began a series of negotiations with her own Superiors. Once they reached the final stage, Father Leonor had no other alternative but to tell Mother Marianne of the plight of the victims of leprosy in the islands. He was extremely relieved when she showed no fear of the possibility of caring for leprosy patients.

After Mother Marianne had been promised that the conditions she had set down would be met, and with the permission of her own Superiors, she volunteered to head the delegation assigned to the islands.

Father Leonor, returning to Honolulu with the good news, received much praise for his success. Soon after, the Sisters arrived with a great deal of publicity and fanfare. They were met by King Kalakaua and the royal family, and by the high Church officials. The streets were lined with welcoming Hawaiians.

When they had settled in at their new convent, Gibson took Mother Marianne to visit the Kakaako Hospital for the first time. She was appalled at the conditions—there was filth everywhere. She pitied the patients who were living in such a horrible environment but she was not dismayed and accepted the assignment to administer the hospital.

From her experience in the United States, she knew that infection was a major problem. Her first and main priority was for cleanliness. A strict disciplinarian, she set rigid rules for her Sisters. They were forbidden to handle or eat from utensils used by the victims of leprosy and they were not to partake of any food prepared by the patients. One of the Sisters remained in the convent to do all the cooking of meals to be consumed by the Sisters.

Gibson gave Mother Marianne all the necessary materials she needed to start the reorganization of the hospital. While some patients complained about the new rules she instituted, they were grateful for the care that they were receiving for the first time.

As the days and weeks passed and the hospital began to take shape, Gibson became more and more enamored with Mother Marianne. His deep affection for her made him very protective. When suggestions were made that the Sisters might be sent to Molokai, he rejected the idea immediately. He said that Molokai was a hell hole and no fit place for women, yet the conditions at Kakaako were even more horrible than those at Kalawao.

In the years since Father Damien's arrival, order had prevailed at Kalawao, while at Kakaako the odors of rotting food and rotting flesh mingling with the brackish smell of the salt marsh, were overpowering. At Kalawao, there were fresh trade breezes, wide open spaces and most patients lived in their own huts and cottages. The main drawback for Kalawao was that there was no escape. At least at the hospital at Kakaako, the personnel and staff could leave and mingle with the healthy community at the end of an arduous day. At Kalawao, both the patients and those caring for them were confined.

Father Damien fully understood this. He was confronted by the helplessness of the patients. They could not see any progress in the treatment of their disease. The monotony and the boredom often led to debauchery and crime. He did everything within his power and means to create a community. He organized various groups in the Church, encouraged the patients to develop their own gardens and taught them how to maintain and improve their dwellings. His great concern was the children. He said that an idle mind was the devil's workshop.

Gibson, with all his faults, did everything in his power to encourage scientists from around the world to come to Kakaako to experiment and give advice. One such physician was Doctor Masanao Goto of Japan. He claimed his "Goto Treatment" was having great success in his own country.

Once Damien had been declared a victim of leprosy, both the Board of Health, Provincial Father Leonor and Bishop Hermann forbade him ever to leave Kalawao again to come to Honolulu.

This did not bother Damien as much as the fact that he did not have a companion priest to whom he could go to confession. He had to wait until a priest would visit the island on an infrequent basis. When he heard of the Goto treatment he thought this would be an opportunity for him to go to Honolulu to participate in it. More importantly, he would have his confession heard. He also wanted to speak to Mother Marianne about accepting an assignment on Molokai.

When he applied to the Bishop for permission to go to Honolulu, both the Bishop and the Provincial wrote him stinging letters. They told him he would not be able to come, that his presence at the Mission would jeopardize all of them if word spread that a leper was in residence. They further informed him that if he insisted on coming, he could not stay with the Community, he would have to remain in isolation in his room where meals would be served him. More importantly, he would not be able to celebrate Mass as the priests would not feel safe with him handling the vessels necessary for the sacrifice of the Mass.

All of these letters and admonitions hurt Damien deeply and he went into a state of depression. Doctor Mouritz and Mr. Meyers, the superintendent, noticed this and finally persuaded the Bishop to allow Damien to go to the Kakaako hospital to take the Goto Treatment. He arrived there just a few days before Joseph Dutton's arrival on Molokai.

One of the first things Damien did was to go to confession. At the hospital, he was denied the use of the chapel to celebrate Mass. He received many visitors, including the King and began the first Goto treatment. He spent many hours talking with Mother Marianne and tried to encourage her to consider sending some of her Sisters to Molokai.

When Gibson got word of this, he was infuriated. He was possessive of the Sisters and rejected any interference. He visited Damien but found it difficult to disguise his dislike. When Damien asked if he would provide him with the necessary materials to build bath houses at Kalawao for the Goto treatment, Gibson surprised Damien by agreeing to his request.

While Damien had felt refreshed after taking the Goto baths, he was no fool and realized that there was no improvement in his overall condition. He abruptly left the hospital without completing the full course of treatment and returned to Molokai.

Damien again turned his attention to his desk. At that moment Malia entered with a tray on which she had arranged a light lunch. He and Dutton both acknowledged her with a nod.

"You know," said Dutton, "despite all the opposition to you, Father, you continue to have deep concern for your people and still want to carry on your work. I'm afraid I would never have the patience or determination to complete those tasks. I would have given up, knowing there were so many against me."

Damien took a sip of his coffee. "God tests us, Joseph, as well you know. He never gives us a cross to

carry heavier than the one He carried. Though I am nowhere near the perfection of Christ, I remember His
words when He was persecuted. He asked God to forgive
His persecutors, for they did not know what they were
doing."

Joseph picked up his cup of milk and took a deep
swallow. "If you had been in Honolulu when I arrived,
and if you had taken the full course of the Goto treatment, you would not have been here on that day I got off
the steamer."

"God works in strange ways," said Damien.

"Yes, but if you had not been there, I'm sure they
would have sent me back on the same steamer."

"Life is filled with coincidences, Joseph, but I
sometimes wonder if they are coincidences or if they are
plans already set forth by God." He took a bite of the
hard tack biscuit which he relished.

"Now I can tell you about the letter I had been expecting and why I was disappointed. Mr. Gibson wrote
that he could not afford to send me the materials for the
bathhouses but that he would send me a heater for the
water and some herbs and salts. I don't believe he ever
intended to send me the equipment and building materials."

"What will you do?" asked Dutton.

"Simple, Joseph. With your help I will convert
some of the older buildings into bathhouses. My people
can at least say they had the opportunity to try the Goto
treatment."

They lost no time getting to work, and when the
construction of the bathhouses was finished, Damien

himself would occasionally take the treatment. Most of the patients, however, refused to try it as they had a great deal of experience with new gadgets and realized their uselessness. But those who did take the baths, at least were refreshed for a time. The bath houses were soon abandoned. It would not be until the 1940s, long after Damien and Dutton were gone, that the first real breakthrough in the treatment of leprosy came with the introduction of the sulfones.

One night, unable to sleep, Dutton's thoughts were racing. He started to ponder on the many problems facing Damien. He knew he had no power whatsoever to bring about a reconciliation between Damien and his Superiors, nor did he have the power to intercede, on Damien's behalf, with the authorities to provide the necessary supplies needed for him to fulfill his dreams. But, Dutton said to himself, I can provide a channel through which he can communicate all of his frustrations. I suppose in the long run that is what God wants us to do—to listen, to give support, to help him overcome the obstacles he faces. For the first time, Dutton began to worry what would happen to him once Damien was gone, and it was evident he could not last much longer.

Where would I go? thought Dutton. What would I be qualified to do if I had to return to the United States? A feeling of panic began to creep in. I do not want to leave this place, he told himself. God has brought me here and finally I am finding my niche in the scheme of things. When Damien goes, there would no doubt be many changes. Would Damien's successor want me to stay? With the turmoil in the government, what would happen to this place if the monarchy toppled?

The security he had been feeling up to now, suddenly was shattered. He began to pray. He would put it all in the hands of God. God would take care of his future. God would not abandon him. The panic left him. He would face the future one day at a time. Had he only known, he was destined to remain on Molokai until his death, more than forty years after Damien went to his eternal reward.

CHAPTER EIGHT

THE NEXT MORNING after Mass, both Damien and Dutton walked to the new cabin. It had been whitewashed and to Dutton it looked larger than he had originally thought. He measured it and found it was about 10 feet by 17 feet with a window on all four sides allowing a breeze to enter no matter from which direction the wind was blowing.

"Tell me what you need in the way of furniture," said Damien, "and I can lend it to you from my house until I get time to make new pieces."

"There is no hurry, Father, I can wait. I don't need to move in right away."

"Brother, I know only too well how much you want to have a place you can call your own."

"Now that you speak of it Father, yes. I never really had a place of my own. Either it was my parents' home, an Army building, or, after my discharge, rented rooms in other people's homes. This will be the first for me and it is you who has made it possible."

Damien beamed and rubbed his hands together as if anxious to continue with the next phase of building the furniture.

"I will only need a bed and a table or desk and

two or three chairs." Dutton continued.

"I will have Paul and some of the boys bring them from my house," said Damien. "I am not expecting any visitors who would need my guest room, so it would be nice for you to stay in your cabin tonight."

Dutton laughed. "You can't stand me, and you can't wait to get rid of me," he said good humoredly.

"You know better than that, Brother. I feel very comfortable with you in my house but you will never have any real seclusion, staying with me."

"There is one thing I would like," said Dutton. He hesitated. "I wonder if I could have shutters on the windows as Dr. Mouritz has on his house."

"They would be easy to make." Damien's mind was already racing ahead to carpentry. "I should have had them on my own house but I just don't want my people to think I am blocking them out or hiding myself."

"I would also like to paint the interior, Father."

"There's no problem with that. We have cans of paint in the shed and you can pick your own color, although I don't know if there will be enough to cover it all. You must have noticed in the Church that the walls are painted with many colors. I just keep going until the paint runs out and then I open another can irrespective of the color—our congregation seems to like the rainbow effect."

They went back to Damien's house and after breakfast Damien went out to feed his chickens. Malia came into the room to clear away and Dutton said to her, "Everyone here seems to love Father and respect him. He is a very special person."

Looking him squarely in the eye she answered, "He is our Kamiano. No one dare hurt him. We would be upon them like a pack of dogs if they tried. He has been touched by God." She wiped her hands on her apron. "Once in a while he loses his temper and scolds us like any father would, but not long after he hugs us and apologizes."

She hardly paused for a breath. "He took care of my husband. He bathed his sores and sat with him for hours when he was dying. He anointed him and when he died, he washed his body and wrapped him in clean sheets. He made his coffin, dug his grave, celebrated his Mass and buried him. I see him stopping by the grave once in a while to say a prayer." Tears were glistening in her eyes. "How can you not love a man like that? He truly comes from God." She started to sob.

Dutton rose and put his arm around her shoulders. He thought of yesterday when Damien had told him about his Superiors. How could they not know what he means to these people. Could it be jealousy?

Just then Damien came back into the room. Malia tore herself from Dutton and flew out the door. Damien, looking puzzled asked if there were anything wrong.

Dutton, with tears in his own eyes, quickly responded, "Oh, no, Father. I just told her that I would be moving into my new cabin and I thanked her for all she has done for me. But I assured her I would still take my meals here if that would be all right with you."

"I was hoping you would do that," said Damien. "Malia is like all the Hawaiians. They are the most hospitable and generous people in the world and I know she was happy taking care of you. Now I understand why she was so upset at your leaving, even if you are only a few yards away."

Dutton was relieved that he had accepted his explanation. He would not want him to know the real reason for Malia's tears.

This Damien, their Kamiano, was indeed touched by God and how privileged I am, thought Dutton, to be with him for what must be his last days on earth. He was resolved more than ever to assist Damien and like Simon of Cyrene, help him carry his cross. His thoughts were interrupted.

"Well, Brother, have you made any plans for the day?"

"No, Father, but I was hoping to go the hospital to help Dr. Mouritz with the bandaging. I would like to become more adept at that task."

"Good," said Damien, "for I must visit the sick in their houses. Why don't we work out an arrangement where we will alternate our tasks."

"That's fine with me. I always work better when I am organized."

"I would like to set up a routine that could be followed. You probably don't believe that I ever had any organization," said Damien walking over to the desk. "But let me show you something." He opened the middle drawer and pulled out a paper.

"I set up this routine for myself when I first came here. I used to post it on the wall near my bed but things happened so fast, I found it useless. I hope you have better luck with yours."

He handed the paper to Dutton. It read as follows:

```
          FATHER DAMIEN'S RULE OF LIFE
              September 3, 1879

 5 a.m.    Rise and go to the Church as soon
           as possible. Morning prayers,
           Adoration and Meditation.

 6:30      Mass and instruction. Thanks-
           giving until quarter to eight.

 7:45      Take care of various matters for
           the good of the faithful.

 8:00      Breakfast followed by a short
           recreation and domestic affairs.

 9:00      Small hours (on the porch).

 9:30      Spiritual reading followed by
           study and correspondence until
           noon.

12:00      Dinner.
           After dinner visit the sick and
           the Christians in general in such
           a way that each week I may know
           all that goes on in each house in
           my district.
           If I can return by 5 o'clock, say
           vespers and occupy myself with
           domestic affairs.

 6:00      Supper.
           When twilight sets in, Rosary,
           Breviary, Night Prayers.

 9-10      Retire.
```

Dutton was impressed. "I will try to make my schedule fit in with this."

"Good luck!" replied Damien with a wry grin. "And now off I am."

Dutton walked to the hospital. As he approached he saw a long line of patients waiting, some on crutches, others sitting in place on the grass. The line snaked up the front steps and into the building. As he passed he said good morning to many of them. Some returned his greeting, others just stared. He entered the hospital and went into the room where the dressings were done. The female nurse's aide was changing the bandages on a patient. Dutton asked if Dr. Mouritz had arrived.

"No," she said, without looking up. "He went to Honolulu and won't be back for two days."

"I came to help him. Can I help you?"

"It would certainly be of great assistance if you could. The line is so long." She finished bandaging the patient and taking Dutton to the next cubicle, showed him where the bandages and the antiseptic solution were. She gave him a long white gown and told him to put it on over his clothes.

The next patient entered and Dutton told him to get up on to the examining table. He had many sores and as Dutton set about dressing them, he questioned him about his background. At first he was hesitant but then began to respond. He thought how kind this man is and how gentle in washing and bandaging my sores. Finished, the patient hopped off the table and thanked Brother Dutton who shook his hand. The patient was pleased at the gesture, this man is not afraid of me, he thought.

When he left, he passed his impressions to the others.

The line seemed unending. It took more than three hours before the last patient was taken care of. Dutton removed his gown and washed his hands in the carbolic acid solution. The pails were filled with stained bandages.

"What happens to these?" He asked the aide.

"Just leave them there, and they will be taken care of."

"But how are they disposed of?" Asked Dutton.

"Those that cannot be salvaged are taken to a big pit at the foot of the palis where we burn them. Those that can be reused are put in boiling water and then dried out. Thank you for all your help today."

As he left the hospital, Dutton saw some patients sitting on the steps and others standing near the trees. When he passed by some raised their hats and many said, "Thank you, thank you."

He went back to the house. Damien had not returned. However Malia had prepared lunch. She looked sheepish. He went over to her and said, "Don't be embarrassed, Malia, what you did earlier this morning was beautiful. You have been holding all that pain and hurt inside and it is good to get it out."

She asked if Father had said anything.

"I only told him that you were upset because I would be leaving Father's house to live in my own."

She looked grateful. "Thank you, Brother."

After lunch Dutton went to the Boys Home. A few little ones ran to greet him.

Dutton asked one of the boys, "Are there any old

horseshoes lying around?"

"I can get them from the blacksmith."

"See if you can bring me four or five and I will show you a new game."

He had hardly finished speaking when the lad was on his way.

Dutton turned to the other boys telling them he would be right back and not to move away. He hurried to Damien's shed where he found two iron stakes and quickly returning to the Home, sought a level piece of land and pounded one stake into the ground. Then he paced off fifteen feet and pounded in the other. He pulled the grass from around the stakes and when they saw what he was trying to do, some of the boys helped him.

The youngster brought back four horseshoes and Dutton marked each pair a different color. They were puzzled but excited about the new game. Brother explained that the object was to get the shoe around the stake. Two people could play against each other. He gave a pair of horseshoes to two boys, warning the others not to get too close to the stakes for they may get hit by a shoe.

He then showed them how to hold the shoe so that it would spin properly in the air and land around the peg. He tossed the shoe and it missed the stake. They all laughed, but Dutton went on unperturbed.

"Even if you don't get the shoe around the stake, you can get points. If you do get the shoe around the stake, it is called a *ringer*, and you get 6 points. If the shoe lands leaning up against the peg, you call that a *leaner*, and you get 3 points, and the one who lands nearest the stake gets one point. Whoever reaches 21 points first, is the winner. Now, you play the game."

After the boys tossed the shoes toward one stake they tossed them back toward the other. They all wanted to take a turn at tossing and soon found out why it was important to stand away from the stake as some shoes took off in all directions.

"You see," said Brother. "You must never play this unless you have a clear area around the stake, or someone might get seriously hurt."

The boys all understood and were still playing the game when Father Damien came by. Some of the boys ran to him saying, "Look, Father, Brother Dutton is teaching us a new game. It is called horseshoes."

Damien was delighted with the enthusiasm and excitement of the boys. He turned to Dutton. "What is this game, horseshoes?" Dutton explained it to him.

"Ah, ha, and all this time the shoes have been lying around rusting when we could have put them to good use." They both watched for a while and then Damien sought out one of the older boys.

"You are in charge of the game, Thomas. Do not let them play unless you are there to supervise them." Thomas agreed.

Damien turned to Dutton. "It's been a long day for both of us. Let's get back to the house. I'm sure Malia has prepared supper."

When Dutton went into his room in Damien's house, he was startled to see it was empty. All the furniture had been moved. Malia had put a bowl and pitcher of water in the kitchen for him to wash up. They ate their meal in silence.

"I must go to the Church and say some prayers, Brother, I am afraid I neglected them today."

"I will go with you, Father."

They both spent an hour in prayer. As they left the Church, Damien said, "I want to look at your cabin, I am anxious to see how Paul has fixed it up."

They entered and Dutton looked well pleased. The bed was fully made and there was a wooden table, two chairs, and his knapsack.

"It looks rather spare, Brother. You will likely need more furniture."

"I don't need very much, this will do nicely."

On the table was a tin can filled with flowers. Damien said it was a gift from Malia. Dutton asked Damien if he would sit with him for awhile, he wanted to tell him what had happened at the hospital.

"When I got to the hospital, I thought Dr. Mouritz would be there, but the aide told me he had gone to Honolulu for two days."

"That's strange," said Damien. "He usually lets me know when he leaves the settlement. I wonder if there is any trouble!"

Dutton went on with his report. "I bandaged almost a hundred patients today. They did not resent me, in fact I have the feeling that many of them waited until I was free, but perhaps my pride is getting in the way."

"Not at all, Brother. The people are sensitive and they know who accepts them and who does not."

"I am sure, Father, it is because of the way you introduced me to them."

"I noticed, Brother, how wonderful you are with children and I have a question to ask. I don't want to pry and you do not have to answer if you prefer not."

Dutton knew immediately what was about to happen. He knew that this was the perfect time. God was giving him the opportunity to tell Damien about his past.

"You told me," Damien said, "that after spending time with the Trappists, you realized that God was not calling you to the religious life. Seeing you with the children, I just wondered why you did not marry and have children of your own."

"Father, I've been waiting for the right time to tell you about my past sinful life."

Damien took his pipe from his pocket and looked more closely at the quiet figure sitting there, his face flushed, his hands trembling.

"Oh dear," said Damien. "I have tried hard to avoid this moment. Ever since you came I have sensed your anxiety to tell me of your past. I was hoping that time and our frankness with one another would overcome your fears. You are a good man, Joseph, and nothing about your past will shake my confidence or my love for you. I will listen to what you have to tell me, but I don't think it's necessary."

"Father, I appreciate that but I think I want to open that book just once if only to reassure you that God has led me here and here I intend to stay as long as you will allow me. I want to lay the ground for a perfect trust, Father, which means that you really have to know me." He paused.

Damien was consoling. "Sometimes we think we

are the worst of sinners. I know you well enough, Joseph, to understand that whatever happened in the past was not a deliberate act on your part to defy God."

"It is not a pretty picture, Father, but I don't think I'm despondent. I know that God has forgiven me and that is why I want to do penance. I don't even despair over the sordid episodes in my life."

Dutton took a deep breath. "You see, Father, I was married."

Damien leaned forward, his pipe forgotten. "Once again, you don't have to tell me this."

"Yes I must, Father, I cannot spend another day with all this on my mind." Dutton shifted in his seat. "I met a girl at a dance in Nashville, Tennessee, when I was in the army. She was beautiful and I fell in love immediately. I had no experience in these matters and I was vulnerable. She seemed to be very popular as there were many who asked her to dance with them. I won't go into any details except to say that I was smitten and could think of nothing else for days.

"My friends, when they saw what was happening, told me I should forget her, that she would break my heart. It seemed they knew things about her that I did not. I didn't listen to them. I proposed marriage to Eloise and she accepted. I really don't know why she did that. Perhaps it was a chance for her to start a new life and get away from the fast and loose company she had been keeping. I gave her the name of some friends in Alabama with whom she could stay until we were married. Later on she went to Mt. Vernon, Ohio, and as soon as I could, I went there and we were married on New Year's Day in

1866. I thought it was to be a bright, new beginning."

Damien said not a word.

"In less than a year she was gone. Another man had come into her life and promised her more excitement than I could give her. Bills came flooding in. Without saying, she had been using my name to make all kinds of purchases. Eventually she asked for a divorce to which I agreed and when that became final, that was the last I heard from her. Later on I learned that she had died in New York, abandoned and penniless."

There was silence for a moment. The roaring ocean pounding against the unyielding rocks was in harmony with the throbbing in Dutton's head.

"Is that why you turned to alcohol, Brother?"

"I don't want to blame it on her, Father, for I was weak and I didn't know where to turn. Alcohol drowned out most of my problems."

Damien nodded, "Many have turned to that."

"I never let it interfere with my work during the day but the nights were something different and often I would lie in a drunken stupor. This lasted for almost five years until for some reason or another, I got hold of myself. I saw where my future was headed and that it would be bleak. On July 4, I remember that date so well, I made a vow never to drink again and I have never broken that vow. It was then that I began my search for forgiveness."

Damien laid down his now cold pipe.

"You say you have offended God. We have all offended God and continue to offend Him though seldom with malice. I dare say we will continue to offend Him until our dying day. But God knows the heart and He has a very special mercy for us. God has indeed worked in your soul, Brother. Your coming here is a balm for my own soul. I will have you in mind as I finish my breviary tonight."

Damien rose from the chair. "Rest well, for I have many plans for you tomorrow."

"You're not going to ask me to leave Molokai?"

"Whatever made you think that, Brother. Not only are you my helper, but you have become my friend. I know how difficult it was for you to tell me of your past life, but let me tell you something. You must stamp out all those thoughts from your mind. You have done your penance and God has forgiven you. Dwelling on the past will keep you from facing the future."

Damien went over and putting both hands on Dutton's shoulders, said, "Sleep well, Brother, in your new home. I hope you will remain here until God calls you home. When you say your prayers tonight, include me, for I need them now more than ever."

"You are always in my prayers, Father, and you always will be.

Damien left the cabin leaving Dutton sitting on the doorsill looking out at the ocean.

Telling Father had been difficult but now that he had, he felt free as if a huge weight had been lifted from him. Now he had a new lease on life and no matter how he tried, he could not find the right words to thank God.

He got up and went back into the cabin. This is mine, he thought, my refuge, my oasis, and he busied himself rearranging the furniture. Before putting out the oil lamp he looked out each of the windows and it suddenly dawned on him how carefully Damien had picked this particular place to build the cabin. From one of the windows, he could easily see Damien's house. The front door led directly to the Church and a breathtaking view of the ocean at the foot of the pali. Through another window he could see the many graves, a reminder of how little time he had, and there was the giant pandanus tree spreading its leaves in protection of Damien's first abode. All this made sense.

As he lay on the bed, forgetting all about the netting, he mused, how can anyone not believe in God. He is always there to show us He cares.

He drifted off to sleep, in his own cabin under his own roof.

CHAPTER NINE

J OSEPH WAS SEATED at his desk, writing by candlelight.
His letter was to Father Hudson of Notre Dame who had
made arrangements with Damien to administer any funds
given by people in the United States for his work among
the lepers. Father Hudson would purchase anything that
was needed. He had just sent two huge tabernacles built
to Damien's specifications. One was for St. Philomenas in
Kalawao and the other for St. Francis at Kalaupapa.

Dutton had mentioned that he wanted to beautify
the area around the Church and various other spots in Kalawao. Damien had said, "Write to Father Hudson and ask
him to send us some seeds."

Since their side of the peninsula was exposed to
the wind and salt spray from the ocean, very few plants
would grow there. Dutton decided to ask for various
kinds of vegetable seeds, as well as plantings of a tree
named catalpa, a Japanese hybrid. This particular tree
would be well suited to the conditions in Kalawao. Dutton had sent some soil samples to the company, and they
wrote that the tree would withstand heavy winds. He
asked Father Hudson to obtain one hundred plantings,
the cost of which would be about $25.00.

As he was writing his letter, he noticed the wind

173

was picking up and the shutters which he had asked Father Damien to make were banging against the cabin.

He rose from his desk and peered out the window. In the gloom he could see the sky was very dark and menacing. He tightened the shutters and went back to his letter writing.

After a short while, everything calmed down and it was deathly quiet, hot and humid. Suddenly, without warning, a howling wind came raging down from the pali. It was a frightening sound similar to that of an approaching tornado.

There was a knock at his door. He opened it to find Paul standing there shivering.

"Come in, lad. What is happening?"

"It's a kona, Brother."

"A kona?"

"It's a big wind. We get it sometimes and it can blow down many houses."

"Were you in the Boys Home, Paul?"

"Yes. I settled them all down. They are frightened but I have moved them to a safe area."

Just then a large, fiery bolt of lightning lit up the sky followed by a deafening crackle of thunder. Dutton's scalp prickled and Paul let out a yell. The rain quickly followed, beating a loud tattoo on the tin roof. The fierce wind whistled through the corners and crevices of the cabin and even the floor seemed to sway. Fear constricted Dutton's throat. He had lived through a tornado. Paul was terrified.

"Tell me, Paul. I know you didn't come here because of the storm. What is wrong?"

"It's Matthew, Brother. He is gone. I cannot find him."

"Matthew? Which one is he?"

"The little one, Brother. Remember, we buried his grandmother this morning. He lived with her in one of the huts."

"Yes, I remember." Dutton was now shouting to make his voice heard above the noise of the wind.

"Go back to the boys, Paul. I think I may know where to find him."

As Paul was leaving, he warned him, "Be careful. Things might be falling down and you could get hurt."

"Are you sure you don't want me to go with you, Brother?"

"No, Paul, I'll be all right. You go back now, the boys must be frightened to death."

Dutton turned and found a kerosene lantern in the corner of his cabin, put there by some thoughtful person, he surmised. Lighting it, he hurriedly put on a slicker and opened the door. It almost blew off its hinges!

He could not stand upright. He had to get down on his hands and knees and he began to crawl. Branches and debris were blowing all around him. The wind tore the lantern from his hand. He clung to the grass and dug his hands deep in the dirt to give himself traction. He thought he was headed in the direction of the graveyard, and although it seemed like hours, he had been crawling along for only a few minutes. His mind was in a whirl. He feared that perhaps the little boy had been blown off the slippery rocks into the sea.

He remembered what Father Damien had told

him about Matthew's mother. She was in her early teens and unmarried. She and Matthew lived with her mother, Matthew's grandmother, who became infected with leprosy. Matthew soon showed signs of the disease as well, while his young mother did not. When the authorities banished both little Matthew and his grandmother to Kalawao, the mother begged to go with them but the segregation laws had been changed and families were no longer allowed to accompany their loved ones to the leprosy settlement unless they, themselves, had leprosy.

As the grandmother had told Father Damien, the day came when she and Matthew were scheduled to board the boat to Molokai. The mother was on the dock begging and pleading with the authorities to let her go with them. As cruel as it seemed, they knew that if they made one exception it would open the doors to more requests. They took the screaming and struggling boy from his mother's arms and gave him to the grandmother. The poor mother fell to her knees and fainted. The grandmother had all she could do to keep Matthew from jumping from her arms—even the guards were moved and the Captain turned away from the sight.

When they arrived at Kalawao, Damien allowed the grandmother to keep her grandchild with her, rather than put him in the Home with the other children.

The grandmother's disease grew progressively grave. When Damien had entered the hut yesterday, he had found the little boy lying across his grandmother's body frightened and whimpering. His *tu tu* (Hawaiian for grandmother) was dead.

After her burial, Damien took little Matthew to

the Boys Home, and put him in care of the older boys, planning to visit him every day until he became adjusted to his new surroundings.

Dutton inched his way along the ground. Water was pouring off the cliffs sending rocks crashing down to the sea below. The ocean was in an angry frenzy and huge waves dashed against the shore. It was pitch black now and the darkness surrounded him as if he were covered with a blanket. Not a star could be seen in the sky. His hands were bruised and bleeding from the jagged rocks over which he was crawling. When he thought he had come to the end of his strength, a sudden streak of lightning revealed an uneven line of crosses just ahead. Thank God, he had reached the cemetery.

He kept calling, "Matthew, Matthew." He heard no answer. As if in mockery, a roll of thunder rumbled threateningly. Another flash of lightning and he saw the great pandanus tree. He groped his way toward it, breathing deeply.

"Matthew, Matthew," he called again. He was gasping now, his chest heaving from the strenuous effort to make headway. Suddenly, above the noise of the wind and surf, he thought he heard a cry. Another lightning flash followed by an ear splitting crack of thunder, and he saw him! A small, terror stricken child hugging the base of a wooden cross.

In one great effort, Dutton reached him, pulling him from the cross and pressing the shivering little body close to his chest.

"Don't cry, Matthew, everything is all right now."

The boy put his arms around Dutton's neck, holding on and squeezing tightly. "Not too hard, Matthew, you're cutting off my breath," panted Dutton. "Don't be frightened. I have hold of you now."

The boy did not speak, he could do nothing but sob deeply. "Get on my back and hold on tightly," said Dutton, and he began the slow, tortuous crawl back to his cabin. Nearing the Church, they heard a crashing sound. Something large had fallen. Matthew tightened his grip around Dutton's neck in sheer terror.

As they came closer, Dutton saw that the tall steeple of St. Philomenas had fallen to the ground leaving a gaping hole in the roof.

The wind began to slacken almost as suddenly as it had started. As they reached the front door, Matthew fell off Dutton's back, completely exhausted. He picked up the little boy and entered the cabin. There was hardly any damage—the chairs had fallen over and some of his papers were scattered about but the structure had held up well.

He quickly dried off Matthew, wrapped him in a blanket, and brought him some water. The boy gulped it down, his sobs lessening. Dutton placed him on the bed and knelt beside him.

"Don't be frightened, Matthew, I am Brother Dutton and I will take good care of you." He smoothed out the boy's matted hair. "I know that you miss your *tu tu*, and I am sorry, but you are not alone. There are many who want to take care of you."

Matthew said nothing and stared at Dutton with

tear-streaked eyes. The glistening bumps of his disease could be seen easily in the glow of the candle. After a few minutes, the boy stopped sobbing and kept saying over and over again in Hawaiian, "I want my *tu tu*, I want my *tu tu.*"

Suddenly there was a strange calm and the moon broke through the shadowy clouds. It seemed like an eternity but in fact it was less than half an hour since the kona had started. Dutton opened the shutters and saw people with lanterns headed toward the Church. He picked up Matthew in his arms and strode out the door to see the crowd gaping at the sight of the fallen steeple.

Damien was nowhere in sight. Paul appeared and assured Dutton that there was no damage to the Boys Home and that they had all survived the storm quite well.

Dutton gently handed Matthew to Paul. "Take good care of him. I am going to look for Father Damien. Perhaps he has been injured."

Paul looked worried. "I'll come with you."

"No, Paul, you stay here with Matthew. I'm sure everything is all right. Perhaps he is visiting someone in the huts."

Dutton strode quickly to Damien's house. He saw no one around and ran up the stairs. There on the floor of his bedroom slept Father Damien, oblivious to everything. Dutton awakened him. Father was confused at seeing Dutton bending over him.

"What is it, Brother? What has happened."

"You slept through a violent storm, Father. You heard nothing?"

"No. I must have fallen into a deep, deep sleep."

"Paul said we had a kona."

"We had a kona and I slept through it? Something must be wrong with me."

"I'm afraid to tell you, Father, but there has been some damage to the Church."

Damien got up immediately from the floor, put on his cassock and both men hurried downstairs and headed for the Church.

The crowd that had gathered was crying at the sight of the fallen steeple and the hole in the roof. Damien stood there for a moment and then smiled.

"Well," he said, "God has spoken once again."

Puzzled, Dutton asked him what he meant.

"Not long after I came here, I was appalled at the fragile huts that the patients were living in. I knew they would not withstand even a whisper of a wind. The authorities ignored my request for materials to build sturdier shelters. Then one night we had a kona. It blew everything down and the poor patients had no place to go. As a result, the government came to its senses and sent boatloads of lumber. I was then able to build these strong huts which could withstand the violent winds. I felt it was God's answer to my problem."

"But Father, what's that to do with the Church?"

"For too long I have been delaying the enlargement of the Church. I have made plans, then changed them, and have gone back and forth with indecisions, instead of actually working on the building. This is God's message to me to get going."

Damien spoke to all of his people telling them that this was a sign from God to rebuild His Church.

Many volunteered and came forward to help.

"The first thing we must do is repair the hole in the roof. Mass will be at the usual time tomorrow and I would like to see all of you attend so that we can give thanks to God that no one was lost in the storm."

Damien turned to Paul who was holding little Matthew. "And what do we have here?"

Paul answered, "It is Matthew, Father. Brother Joseph is a brave man. Matthew was missing and Brother found him in the cemetery."

Damien gently took Matthew from Paul's arms, "Matthew, Matthew, my little one, why did you go to the cemetery?"

"To be with my *tu tu*," the little boy replied.

Just then Malia arrived. Damien gave Matthew to her and asked if she would let him stay with her until the morning when he would make other arrangements. The boy did not resist. In fact he was basking in all the attention he was receiving.

Dutton went back with Damien to his house, and on entering the kitchen, Dutton set about brewing some tea.

"Well, Brother, tomorrow we will go over our plans again and begin to gather the necessary materials to enlarge the Church. I'm afraid I have put it off too long and I began to doubt that I would be able to complete the work. Now I know what God wants me to do."

"You cannot do it alone, Father. There are many of us willing to help. Together we will make a St. Philomenas that everyone will be proud of."

Damien nodded approval.

"I'm wide awake now, Brother. I'm going to visit the patients to see how they weathered the storm. You get some rest. You have had an exhausting night. What Paul told me makes me very proud of you. It took a lot of bravery to go out in the kona and especially to search for that poor little boy. Once again, Joseph, you have proven to me why God has sent you here."

"What will happen to Matthew, Father? He was so frightened."

"Don't worry too much, Joseph, Malia knows how to handle situations like this. The boy has spent all his young life with his grandmother and is not yet used to other children. Malia will slowly introduce him and before you know it, he will be playing with them. He is young enough to forget, and when he starts to have fun, he will be a bright little boy."

The next morning the two men sat down to discuss the renovation plans for St. Philomenas. Damien wanted it to be a stone church but to incorporate the present structure. He told Dutton there was a professional stonemason among the patients and that he previously found that there was plenty of stone available. It had to be quarried, but he could train some of the men.

"There is the question of the tabernacles," said Dutton.

"When they arrived, I did not realize how tall they were or how heavy. The first thing I must do is rebuild the altar and lay a better foundation to carry the weight. Father Hudson is a marvel. His artisans did a beautiful job on the tabernacles. They even lined the interiors to make them insect-proof so that critters could not get to the Holy Eucharist."

"Of course, as you said, Father, the first thing to do is repair the roof."

"I went up there before Mass this morning."

"You did? Aren't you afraid of falling?"

"No, Joseph, I'm used to heights and I was careful. It will not take much to do temporary repairs which I will make as simple as possible. What I want is a metal roof for the new St. Philomenas, and I always thought the steeple was too small. Now I have the opportunity to erect a larger one with a heavier bell that will be heard throughout the settlement. I also have plans for a balustrade and other refinements."

"That certainly sounds like an ambitious undertaking, Father. Will you have enough money to complete it?"

"Oh yes," answered Damien confidently. "I know there will be some problems but the main one, of course, is my own physical condition. I will not be able to work long hours as I did in the past, and the mason is not too well either; for that matter, neither are the men who have volunteered. There are days when they are too weak and ill to do anything. I only hope God gives me enough time to finish this."

"Will the government help financially, Father?"

"No. And we can't blame them. They will spend no funds on any religious structure. They believe it is up to Church authorities to provide the funds. I know my Bishop will not be able to do much for me, but I have friends throughout the world who have always been most generous and I'm sure they will help."

One such benefactor was a Reverend Hugh Chapman of St. Lukes Anglican Church in London. Once he read of Damien contracting leprosy, he wrote immediately offering financial help. He started a fund, and despite the objections of some of his parishioners, nothing deterred him.

He expanded the fund to include donations from Catholics within his area. He placed no restrictions on the funds and trusted Damien to use them to better the life of the leprosy patients for whom he was caring. He had no objection to Damien using the funds for the spiritual needs of his patients. A major portion of the cost of the new St. Philomenas came from this sympathetic and charitable Anglican priest, half the world away, in the heart of London.

With Christmas but a few months off, Damien worked feverishly to finish building the new altar upon which they placed the beautiful tabernacle. This work of art almost touched the ceiling. It would be used for the first time at Christmas Midnight Mass.

For the time being, he used whatever suitable material was at hand for the temporary new roof. Everyone tried to prevent him, but he insisted on getting up onto the roof to direct the workmen himself.

Despite the many duties laid upon his shoulders, Dutton made sure that each day he would set aside a few hours to be at the Boys Home. He was pleased to see that little Matthew had made a fine adjustment and was now part of a group of older boys who looked after him. Malia stopped by to see him nearly every day.

Using the experience he gained in the army, Dutton organized the boys and created squads, each with a leader who would be given special privileges. He taught them how to make their beds the army way, how to clean around their bunks and hang their clothes neatly. Each boy was treated equally when it came to kitchen duty or part of the cleaning brigade responsible for sweeping up around the grounds.

Damien had taught them farming, and each boy, capable of doing so, had a neat and tidy garden. They grew all sorts of vegetables: cabbages, onions, sweet potatoes, green beans, turnips and more. Not only did they have plenty of food for themselves but they grew enough to sell to others for which they received the money.

Most of the chores were done in the early morning hours before the heat of the day. Some of the older boys were assigned the task of milking the cows, others managed the pigs and tended the horses. The object was to keep them as busy as possible. Dutton gave lessons on close-order drill and calisthenics. Not all were of equal strength and many had deformities preventing them from doing certain things, but lighter chores were found for them. The boys created a disciplinary court which would mete out punishment according to the severity of the offense.

In the afternoons, Damien would teach classes on the catechism, while Dutton took over reading, writing and arithmetic. Before supper, there were games to play and afterwards, lights out.

It was during this time that Dutton began his letter writing campaign to friends and acquaintances. Later in life it would become his principal occupation. His address book eventually contained over 4,000 names of people of every persuasion in all parts of the world. He would write to his friends asking them to contact their friends to send athletic equipment, uniforms for the ball team, checkers and other games, as well as instruments and uniforms for a band. The whole community of Kalawao became involved and life began to take on a different meaning. Before there was apathy. Now many took an interest in all of the activities.

Dutton did not forget the girls and with the help of the women working in the Girls Home, they were organized in the same way as the boys.

In mid-October, Damien and Dutton sat down and prepared a list to be sent to the Sacred Hearts Sisters in Honolulu for Christmas gifts for the children. The list included the name of each boy or girl, age, sizes of clothing, and if possible their special requests. Each gift would be gayly wrapped with a card bearing the child's name. The children would know that the gift had been specially chosen for them. The Sisters were able to use money that had been expressly donated by the people in Honolulu for this purpose.

Several days before Christmas, Damien spent many hours in the confessional. Nearly every Catholic wanted to receive Holy Communion at Midnight Mass. Three Societies had been formed by Damien, one for the men, one for the women and a third for the children. Each Society had its own band, uniforms and banner. One of the bands would play at any major event—even at funerals, and all would take part in the procession for Christmas Mass.

The women's sodality was responsible for the cleanliness of the Church. On the day before Christmas they would wax the floor, polish the pews, and drape the altar in starched linens. And Damien would bring out the beautiful gold chalice, the monstrance and candlesticks which had been given to him by a priest in France. These were used only on special occasions. The Church was decorated with sprays of flowers and hung with ornaments which Damien had received from Belgium many years past. They were old and faded, but useable. When he saw them, Dutton made a note to ask his friends to send new ones for next year.

A creche was built and the figure of the Christ child would be placed on the straw at Midnight Mass. An hour before Mass, several men went through the settlement beating drums and calling out "Merry Christmas, Merry Christmas." It was a beautiful sight to see all of the patients emerging from their huts and cottages, each holding a lighted candle as they walked to St. Philomenas.

The Church was filled to overflowing. Many had to stand outside and look through the windows. Even non-Catholics attended.

Father Hudson had sent a harmonium and one of the patients, who had been an organist in her church before being declared a victim of leprosy, was playing hymns. She had several fingers missing from her right hand. She replaced them by taping three sticks on to the stubs with which she hit the keys.

The procession formed outside the Church. First

was the men's marching band, followed by the women's sodality, and the little girls dressed in white with flowers in their hair. Then came the boys' band and the altar boys in their red cassocks with white surplices. Father Damien followed, robed in beautiful gold vestments which had been sent to him by friends in Belgium.

Dutton and Paul waited in the sacristy.

As Damien entered the Church, the choir sang the entrance hymn, the bands played, and the congregation joined in singing *Adeste Fidelis*. The Church was ablaze with the light of many lamps and candles. Damien celebrated a solemn High Mass in Latin, the choir singing the responses. He preached a moving and beautiful sermon, quite lengthy, which delighted the Hawaiians who loved long speeches. It took some time for Damien to distribute Communion to everyone as they knelt at the railing. The Mass was followed by Benediction, at the end of which, six little girls and boys carried in the replica of the Child Jesus, placing it between Joseph and Mary. The figures of sheep and cattle surrounded the Holy Family.

At the end of the ceremony, the entire congregation, accompanied by the harmonium and the bands, sang "Hark the Herald Angels Sing." The ceremony took nearly three hours, and as the patients left the Church, Damien blessed them, wishing them all a Merry Christmas.

Damien and Dutton returned to their respective houses. They had to get up at 6 o'clock the next morning to go to Kalaupapa to celebrate Christmas Mass at St. Francis for the homesteaders and the government workers. Nearly everyone, Catholic and non-Catholic attended the Mass. It was not as elaborate as the Midnight Mass at Kalawao but the Church was tastefully and elegantly decorated. Following the Mass, Damien greeted all of the congregation personally. They again exchanged Christmas greetings. Paul drove Father Damien and Brother Dutton back to Kalawao where Malia had prepared a hearty breakfast. They were exhausted.

A large crowd of people had gathered along the beach, and smoke was rising from burning fires. A luau was in preparation. At 3 o'clock in the afternoon all was ready and everyone congregated around the fire site. Blankets had been spread on the ground, tables were piled with food; there was raw and cooked fish, octopus, roasted pig, and cold ham. Vegetables had been wrapped in banana leaves and baked in the fire and there were heaps of poi. They sang Christmas carols and Damien and Dutton distributed the gifts. As everyone tore open their packages, there was much excitement because they all wanted to see what each had received. Finally, the remaining food was gathered up and taken to the hospital and to the huts for patients who were not able to come to the luau. Damien and Dutton distributed gifts to the housebound and hospital patients.

Returning to Damien's house they were greeted by Malia, who had prepared coffee and Christmas cookies. They presented her with gifts, a new dress, apron, and a lovely ivory comb and brush set sent by one of Dutton's friends. Malia was overwhelmed with the kindness shown to her and draped each of them with leis she had made.

It was then that Dutton gave Damien his gift, a new pipe and pouches of tobacco. Damien, with tears in his eyes presented Dutton with a beautiful rosary. The beads were made from the seeds of the many plants that grew on the island and each had been perfectly chosen for size and shape. Wishing each other a blessed Christmas they said good night.

When Dutton entered his cabin, he was surprised to see two colorful, wrapped packages on his table. He opened the first, it was from Paul. Inside was a horseshoe painted gold and a note that read, *"This is an old shoe from the horse that I saddled for you. I thought he would throw you but you showed me how wrong I was. Please forgive me. — Paul."*

The other was a long, thin package. He was astonished to see that it was from Caleb. He tore open the wrappings—it was a new fishing pole. Dutton chuckled. That old sea dog thinks he is tough but his heart proves him otherwise. He learned later that Dr. Mouritz had bought the gift on Caleb's behalf and passed it on to Damien to be given to Dutton at Christmas.

He was very tired but did not neglect his night prayers. It was without a doubt his best Christmas ever. He did not miss the snow or the scent of a pine Christmas tree. He had spent too many Christmases alone. Here, he was surrounded by those he loved and who loved him in return. This is the real magic of Christmas, Dutton thought, the love that God gave in sending His Son to us on this beautiful day. Within a matter of seconds he was sound asleep.

CHAPTER TEN

Soon after the first of the year, at the end of a long, hard day, Damien and Dutton were sitting at the dinner table. Damien was unusually silent, hardly speaking a word. Dutton was aware that during the last few weeks there were many changes in Damien's personality. His physical appearance seemed to show the signs of deterioration. When they had finished eating, Damien said he was going up to his study.

Dutton restrained him, putting his hand on his arm.

"Father, could I talk with you for just a few moments. I want to discuss something personal."

Damien nodded and the two men set off to their favorite spot on the rocks overlooking the ocean. When they had settled, Dutton noticed that Father did not light up his pipe which was most unusual. He was quiet and looked very depressed.

"Father, we have become very good friends and I would like to ask you something. If you do not want to answer me I will understand and respect your silence, but I want to offer you my help."

Damien raised his head and looked at Dutton quizzically.

I've observed lately," Dutton went on, "that there are times when you seem to be discouraged."

"I don't know how you could have failed to notice it, Brother. I am at a loss to know what is coming over me. I am experiencing feelings I never had, again doubting that I have not done what God wants."

"I don't know if I can help you, Father, but I want to help if I can."

"Well, for one thing, Brother, I am aware that my health is failing. I was hoping the Goto treatment would be the answer and that I would be cured, but it is evident that my body is not responding. In fact I feel worse than I have ever felt before. I know now that I will not be able to be cured of this disease and that has thrown me into an overwhelming sense of hopelessness. There are times when I begin to feel empty and sorry for myself, something that I would never allow myself to do." Damien's voice was hoarse and shaking.

"Eventually we all reach that stage, Father. We are struggling and we don't know what to do about it. We get panicky. What we need is someone to talk to. It really helps to share this, and I'm here for you."

"I'm not afraid of death, Brother Joseph, in fact, this may sound strange, but I'm looking forward to it. I can't wait to be with God. One of the main reasons for my depression, I know, is the attitude of my Superiors toward me. In one of the latest letters from my Provincial he said, 'When you can no longer function, we will send someone.' That will be too late."

Damien went on to explain that there is more trouble brewing in government circles in Honolulu. The

King, a weak man, is not liked by his people. He has spent so much of their money on his own pomp and vanity, and on the royal palace, as well as his jaunts abroad. There are rumors that the sale of opium is taking place within the palace and with his approval. All this unnerves the businessmen who really run the country.

"One day, mark my words," Damien said, "It will topple the monarchy. The Bishop realizes this, too, and since most of the businessmen are Calvinists, he knows they will have little regard for the Catholic Church should they assume full power. Walter Gibson has seized any opportunity to espouse the cause of Hawaii for Hawaiians, and the King is also trying to restore power to the Hawaiians and the monarchy."

Americans were controlling more and more of the wealth of the country. They did not trust Walter Gibson and wanted to get him out of the way. They agreed among themselves they must be careful of Gibson. One moment you are his friend and the next his enemy. As long as he is in authority, the Sisters will never come to Molokai. It was widely known that he had grown very fond of Mother Marianne, and she had not in the least encouraged him. However, his infatuation regarding her, had made him very protective.

Dutton had been listening attentively to Damien's insight of government affairs.

"If Mother Marianne wanted to come here, would she need Gibson's permission?" He asked.

"Of course. No one can come here without the permission of the Board of Health. Gibson has repeated over and over that he will never allow the Sisters to come, even though they are needed here. Nothing would make him change his mind."

"You would think that the needs of the patients would come first," said Dutton.

"The heart can overrule the head, Joseph. I know that Mother Marianne would come here if she could. My thinking on this matter is another reason why Gibson fights me. He surmises I will interfere with his plans for Mother Marianne."

"I wouldn't despair, Father. I'm sure that one day the Sisters will come here."

"I can only pray that they do, before it becomes too late for me. This is no reflection on you, Brother. What I really need is a companion priest, not only to hear my confession, but to give me the spiritual strength I need now and will need more so as I face my last days."

Dutton was silent.

"But talking to you has raised my spirits. God has never failed to hear my prayers, Joseph, and I know he will not fail me now."

In a gesture of friendship, Dutton reached over and put his hand on Damien's. "I have an overwhelming feeling, Father, that soon you will have your companion priest and the Sisters will be here as well."

"I must do everything in my power to shake off these feelings of depression and loneliness. You are right, talking about it helps. I keep things bottled up inside me until they get the better of me."

Both men arose, the mood brightening, and Dutton was especially relieved when he saw Damien light up his pipe.

As days, weeks and months passed, both Damien and Dutton were busily engaged in many projects. There was never a dull moment. The stone mason began work on St. Philomenas—it was a difficult process. They had no explosives so they had to hand carve the stone out of the quarry. It had to be taken by horse and cart over a great distance to reach the Church. The structure gradually began to take shape with the workers following Damien's drawings. As usual they faced many interruptions. There were days when Damien suffered from severe bouts of fever and could do nothing. And then, confounding everyone, would be up and about, full of pep and energy. With his worsening condition he should be bedridden, but his sheer will and determination overcame his physical disabilities. As the work progressed, all were delighted with the evolving larger edifice, and the workers, too, were inspired with Damien's fire.

To Damien, the spiritual care of his people came first, the manual labor, second. He continued to give instruction in the Faith, celebrate Mass, hear confessions, visit the sick and drive to Kalaupapa to conduct Mass and teach the children.

Dutton, when he was not changing the dressings, was taking care of the boys. He had built a classroom and had obtained money for the materials from his friends abroad. Throughout the settlement the two men were familiar figures. Wherever they went they were greeted warmly. Their hard work was an example to many and encouraged the patients to take on projects to improve their surroundings.

Cottages and huts were whitewashed, and gardens weeded. Shrubs and plants were now flourishing from the seeds Dutton had received from Notre Dame. They took root and grew rapidly. His efforts at beautifying the area aroused the interest of many who were eager to help in the project.

Dutton spent his evenings letter writing, requesting his friends for all kinds of supplies and equipment which they gladly sent. Through regular correspondence his circle of benefactors was increasing, filling the pages of his address book.

On a day in May, 1887, Dutton went to Kalaupapa to pick up the mail and supplies as Damien was too ill. While there, he had a conversation with Dr. Mouritz who did not seem himself. He looked somewhat shaken and distracted. Dutton asked if he were feeling ill. Dr. Mouritz was quick to assure him that all was well and that he was just a little tired and needed a rest.

When Dutton returned to Kalawao he told Damien that he did not think the Doctor was feeling well.

"Oh, it's more than that," said Damien. "As you know, while we are isolated here, we are still a community and rumors reach us by many means. It seems that the crisis over the government is coming to a head. There is a sense that the monarchy will collapse and there will be many changes made in the King's cabinet."

"What is the real cause behind all this," asked Dutton.

"It's simple. There's a power play going on. A large group of businessmen who are at odds with the King, control the purse and are waiting for a moment to oust Walter Gibson. Many think he is the principal obstacle to their efforts in persuading the King to see their problems. I fear Gibson is in jeopardy. His days may be numbered. They are just waiting for the right reason to pounce on him."

"That answers a lot of questions about Dr. Mouritz," said Dutton. "Was he not appointed by Gibson? If anything happens to Gibson it probably will affect Mouritz. That could be the reason I found him so depressed."

"Remember when he went to Honolulu just before Christmas, Brother? He never told us the reason why he had to leave so hurriedly. I'm thinking now that he must have been summoned there by Gibson who alerted him as to what was happening."

"If Gibson is ousted, how will that affect the settlement?" asked Dutton.

"I have thought of that myself and I'm sure the Bishop is concerned. Despite his devious ways, Gibson has done a lot of good and has always been friendly to the Church. A new cabinet may not share the Bishop's concerns, and the Church could be in difficulty once again."

"Would that mean our work would be affected?"

"I doubt that, Brother. I'm sure they will keep the settlement going, in fact, I believe there will be an increase in patients. Have you noticed lately, that the admissions have dropped off? It seems that Gibson is trying to find favor again with the Hawaiians who are backing the King. Sending fewer patients to Kalawao pleases the Hawaiians and they are grateful to him for that."

Dutton muttered to himself, I wonder if "tea" is involved.

"What did you say? Did I hear you say tea?"

Dutton laughed. "Father, I was just thinking of the Boston Tea Party."

"I don't understand."

"Just before the American Revolution, there was a rebellion against the English king who imposed a large tax on tea imported from England. The colonists were up in arms and tossed all the tea into Boston Harbor."

"Sometimes it is necessary to rebel and throw over a corrupt regime," said Damien. "But often there is the possibility of someone worse taking over and we could be affected. The next few weeks should be quite interesting in seeing what happens."

That summer, the businessmen who had been looking for a legitimate reason to challenge the King, found evidence that powerful Chinese merchants were selling opium within the palace, as it had been rumored. This infuriated the Calvinists who abided by a strict religious code. They threatened the King with the overthrow of the monarchy if he did not rid his regime of the cabinet. They were taking particular aim at Gibson who was privy to most of the King's activities. The King gave in to the businessmen.

All members of his cabinet were dismissed including Gibson but he did not strip him of all his powers. This further infuriated the businessmen. With Gibson still on the scene, he would be capable of creating a great deal of turmoil leading to a possible coup, and ousting them from their newly obtained position of power.

Dr. Nathaniel Emerson was appointed President of the Board of Health. He was the son of a Protestant missionary, who had married a Hawaiian, and he had been sent to the United States for his education. Dr. Emerson was very frightened of contracting leprosy and his main goal was to send all those with the disease to Molokai, freeing the mainland from any threat. He had served for a short time as a resident physician at Kalawao but like all of the doctors before him, he had very little direct contact with the patients. He would put their medicine on the top of the fence outside his cottage. Although the patients knew he was part Hawaiian, they scorned him, and after only a few weeks he went back to the mainland.

In the government, the upheavals were called a "revolution" although no shots were fired. Eventually, a band of renegades took matters into their own hands. They seized Gibson, charged him with embezzlement, and put him under house arrest. They wanted to send him to another island but realized that he would be too close. He might encourage Hawaiians to rebel. Putting him under a threat of death, they finally booked passage for him on an ocean liner bound for San Francisco. His health had been failing and immediately on arrival, he went into a hospital. There followed sketchy reports about him and it was said that he had tuberculosis. A few months later he died—an ignominious end for one who had wielded such influence and gained so much political power. Rumor had it that before he died he converted to Catholicism.

With Walter Gibson gone, the rules of segregation were once again strictly enforced and more and more patients were shipped to Kalawao.

CHAPTER ELEVEN

On May 17, 1888, one of Damien's prayers was answered. Father Lambert Conrardy arrived at Kalaupapa. Damien's repeated request for a companion priest had previously gone unheard by both his Bishop and Superiors.

Father Conrardy, while not a member of the Sacred Hearts Fathers, was born in Liege, Belgium. He studied under the Jesuits and was ordained in 1866. After ordination, he was assigned to a parish but that life did not suit him. During the typhus epidemic of 1869 he was a pastor who cared for the sick and the poor, giving away everything he owned, even his bed.

A deeply religious man, he had difficulty conforming. He conducted vespers in French instead of Latin. He said his parishioners did not understand Latin and were bored with it. His Superiors realized that he was a priest of great faith, charity, and bravery, but that parish life was too difficult for him. He had begged the Foreign Mission Society to send him to China. Instead, they sent him to Hindustan. He remained for only a few years, antagonizing the authorities.

In 1874, he was accepted by Archbishop Gross of Oregon to serve in his diocese, located in the Rocky Mountains, caring for the Indians. Aware of Conrardy's personality and unorthodoxy, the Archbishop appointed him to a mission chapel.

The area assigned to him was vast and often it took him several months to visit all of his parishioners. He was a rugged man, well suited to the plains and mountains of the West. Traveling on foot and by horseback in all kinds of weather, facing hostile tribes with courage his only weapon, he served the territory for more than fifteen years. His parishioners for the most part were settlers but he was also highly respected by the Indians. They knew of his bravery from stories that had traveled swiftly throughout the territory.

At one time he was stopped by a band of warrior Indians who threatened to hang him. He calmly removed his watch and gave it to the chief, saying, "Since you are going to hang me, you might as well have my watch."

The chief was perplexed and went into a conference with the other braves. They looked at him with awe. What kind of a man is this who, facing death, calmly gives his possessions to his enemies. They gave him his freedom with their respect. That incident became known among all the tribes and whenever they met him they treated him as a "brave." His Jesuit training taught him to find God in the world.

He enjoyed privations which gave him a chance to exercise his ingenuity. Once, when he did not have all of the equipment with which to celebrate Mass, he used potatoes as candlesticks, making small, round holes and pushing in the candles. After Mass he was hungry, so he ate the potatoes.

He had a keen sense of humor and an ability to

be accepted by people of all persuasions. The Archbishop who had known about Damien and his work and had often corresponded with him, mentioned to Father Conrardy Damien's need for help. The thought went through Father's head like a lightning bolt: I must go to help this heroic priest with his lepers.

Torn between his work with the Indians and a desire to help the victims of leprosy, Conrardy decided to wait until God sent him another sign, but he did write to Damien telling him that he wished to join him.

The sign came soon enough. Rome turned the Oregon territory over to the Society of Jesus, the Jesuits. Conrardy wished to remain free and independent rather than become a member of the Jesuits and was now ready to go to Molokai.

Damien was overjoyed at the prospect of Conrardy's arrival but his Superiors were not. There was much controversy and misunderstanding before he could come. Some say he went to Molokai without permission of the Bishop. His letters disprove this.

In 1887, the Bishop had written to Conrardy telling him that he would be able to obtain permission to work as a secular priest and later enter into the Novitiate and become a member of the Sacred Hearts Fathers.

Following this decision, the Bishop was faced with opposition from the priests at the Honolulu Mission. He wrote to the Father General saying he was sorry for having given in at first but that it was Damien's fault for wanting Conrardy to go directly to Molokai. The Bishop stated that he was now in an awkward position. If he rescinded his decision, it would get into the papers and would again seem as if Father Damien were being denied a priest to help him and that none of the priests were willing to go to Molokai. But in fact, all of them would have gone if ordered by the Bishop.

Father Leonor, not wishing to miss an opportunity to chastise Damien, wrote a scathing rebuke. However, it was too late to do anything, for Conrardy had already arrived on Molokai.

Conrardy was responsible for much of the misunderstanding, for he showed the press some letters that were written to him by Damien. It shed a poor light on the Mission and from then on, Father Conrardy was the subject of scorn by members of the Community. Conrardy had never stated that he would not enter the Order but his wish was to serve for a while at the settlement before entering their Novitiate. He was always willing to obey the Bishop in all matters.

Father Leonor would not let the conflict rest. He wrote constantly not only to Father Damien but to the Father General blaming Damien for the impasse. Members of the Community, even some who had not met Father Conrardy, accused him of being a coarse man, stubborn and unwilling to obey orders. He was a perfect companion to Damien, they said, whom they categorized in the same way although there was never any proof of Damien's disobedience.

The Bishop hoped that there would be a clash between Conrardy and Damien and that Conrardy would leave of his own accord, settling the controversy. They were wrong! The two men got along famously. Conrardy had even accepted to stay in Damien's house. He had been favorably received by the patients—his warm hand-shake, his hugs, along with his wonderful sense of humor were just what they needed. He was strong and able to put in long hours of work, relieving Damien of much of his spiritual overload. Dutton and Conrardy likewise enjoyed each other's company and Conrardy pitched in to help Dutton with the boys. The boys loved him and were especially enthralled when he told stories of his life with the Indians. He described the buffaloes and wolves and how the Indians scalped their enemies.

One evening, after they had finished supper and Damien had gone up to his room, Conrardy beckoned Joseph out on to the veranda. He spoke in a whisper.

"Brother Joseph, I wonder if we could go somewhere, so that I may talk to you. I have a problem."

"Of course, Father, we can go down to the sea. It is my favorite spot and Damien's, too."

They walked in silence until they came to the rock where Dutton often sat with Damien. Conrardy was enchanted with what he saw. "What a perfect place. It would be so easy to meditate here. God's beauty is all around us."

Dutton nodded and waited for Conrardy to speak further.

Finally he said, "I don't know how to say this Joseph, I am really ashamed but I seldom can keep things to myself, I blurt them out and then I'm sorry. But it is my nature and I guess I'm too old to change."

"It's a good trait, Father. I'm the opposite. I keep things contained inside me and then they grow out of all proportion."

"I noticed, Joseph, that you are so at ease with Father at the dinner table. I really find it difficult to eat with him. Not only does the odor from his open wounds nauseate me but so does his physical appearance. Sometimes he looks very grotesque. I try hard not to show signs of disgust on my face yet I'm sure he sees through me. I have a hard time swallowing my food. I should have known what to expect before I came here but I have never had close contact with a leprosy patient although I have been in their presence."

"I understand, Father. I found it troublesome at first, but it soon passed."

"How did you conquer it?"

"I looked into Father Damien's eyes and I imagined I was looking into the eyes of Christ. His eyes would be like Damien's. Then I remembered all the things that Christ did during His life here on earth. Remember when he was to open Lazarus' tomb? The disciples told Him not to do so for the stench would be overwhelming, but Christ opened the tomb and Lazarus came forth. When the lepers touched His garments, He did not shrink but blessed them and then He cured them. If Christ had leprosy I would feel it an honor to eat with Him at His table. I am not aware of Damien's odor nor does his appearance bother me any more."

"You shame me, Brother."

Dutton was quick to respond. "No, Father, please don't say that. I didn't mean to shame you. I only told you how I found an easy way to be with Damien."

"Don't fret, Brother. I like frankness. When people say what they feel, it makes it easier to deal with them. You give good advice—I will certainly take it. "

Father Conrardy looked out to sea, the setting sun sparkled on the crests of the waves. "I want to remain here. I hope I can conquer the few little things that bother me. For one thing, I'm not used to this very hot climate. I spent so many years in the wilderness of Oregon where there are extremes of weather, particularly in winter."

"That, too, shall pass, Father. I guarantee it. Your blood will thin and you will not mind the heat. It can get very cold at night, and we have the cool Trade Winds most of the time. Of course, we never have snow," said Dutton smiling.

"You must think me a weakling but these are just a few of the concerns I have and I knew I had to speak openly to you."

Dutton quickly changed the subject. "Everything at times seems to be a paradox. The word Pacific means peaceful and yet look at the ocean, it is far from peaceful. The restless turbulence of the sea seems to calm me. Perhaps that is why it is called the 'Pacific'."

"You have a way with words, Brother. You would be a good writer."

"I'm afraid that I speak better than I write, although I do enjoy writing letters."

"God has given each of us special talents, Joseph. He only hopes that we spend them wisely."

In the months that followed, working side by side, Dutton's admiration for Conrardy grew and their friendship became stronger. Often in the evening, they would sit outside Dutton's cabin. He never tired of Conrardy's experiences about his life with the Indians, their many customs and tribal rites. Dutton was interested in the similarity between the Indian tribes and the early Hawaiian settlers. They each had their gods, their music, dances, rituals and their unique ability to respect nature and the environment, not abuse it.

"Were the Indians difficult to convert to Christianity?" asked Dutton one evening.

"Oh, yes. All people who have deeply rooted beliefs find it difficult to change. I am a practical man, you know. While I did not join the Jesuit Order I will always admire their way to bring about conversions."

Father Conrardy paused. He seemed to be reliving his days in the Oregon territory. "I was aware that it was difficult for the Indians to give up their beliefs in spirits but I accepted this and never pressed or criticized them. When I found some practicing several of their rituals, I never condemned them. Of course, I was often criticized by my peers for my methods but I have grown used to that and it no longer bothers me."

"I wish I could be like that, Father. I am sensitive and if I am criticized, I go into my shell. I try not to get involved in any controversy which perhaps gives the impression that I am not a fighter."

"I've noticed at times, Brother, how submissive you are. If you don't mind me being honest with you, I believe you are too hard on yourself. You often speak of not being worthy of God's love and are worried about your past. Always remember, unlike us, God both forgives and forgets. Whatever you have done in your past, and that is your business, God has forgiven and forgotten."

"I hope so," said Dutton. "We have had many conversions here, Father, but I have often wondered if the Hawaiians have totally given up their belief in the gods who ruled the lives of their ancestors."

"I've discovered that. I have seen certain signs and symbols when I have visited their huts. It will take several generations and eons of time before their past practices will be completely erased, but it does not make them any less a good Christian or Catholic than you or I."

"The people here love you, Father. I have seen that. Perhaps it is because you are so understanding of their weakness."

Conrardy disagreed. "I'm afraid that not everyone admires me. The Bishop, Father Leonor and other members of the Religious Community would be happy if I left. But I am committed to work with Father Damien and he is the only one that I would listen to. If he asked me to go, I would. I am what I am, Brother, and God will let me know when I displease Him.

As they arose from the doorstep, Conrardy turned to Dutton. "Father Damien speaks so highly of you, Joseph. I wonder if you really know what you mean to him. He has been unjustly accused of so many things by people not worthy to touch the hem of his cassock and yet he fights for his people. He is an example all of us should follow."

"He, too, is why I came here. I want to remain as long as I am useful."

"What will you do when he goes, Brother?"

"Like you, Father, I believe that God will let me know when my work here is finished."

Ever since Conrardy joined Dutton to work with the children, they both discussed how they could keep the boys occupied and out of mischief. Unlike other children, they were afflicted with a long-term illness and at times when they had no energy to do anything, they neglected themselves.

In the course of conversation, Conrardy came up with an idea. "Why not have a campfire cookout?"

This immediately excited Dutton who had been in the Zoaves as a youth and was used to hikes and campfires. "That's wonderful," he said enthusiastically.

"When I was in the wilderness," said Conrardy, "Our parishioners would build a fire and sit around it telling tales. Children especially enjoyed spooky stories."

"We won't hike too far, so that as many as are able can participate," said Dutton, aware of the capacity of each boy. "What kind of food should we prepare for such an outing?"

"Why not have cook prepare a paper bag lunch. She could make sandwiches and perhaps we could ask Malia to bake some cookies and sweets."

"I wish we had marshmallows; we could toast them in the fire," said Dutton wistfully.

"Why not try bananas," said the resourceful Conrardy. "The boys can cut them up, take some twigs, make a sharp point and put banana chunks on each twig. They will roast nicely in the fire."

"I knew you would think of something, Father."

The next day the two men went to scout a site not too far from the boys' dormitory. They found an ideal spot, a small clearing in front of a deep cave at the foot of the pali with a bubbling spring nearby.

On the way back to the settlement Dutton told Father Conrardy that he had mentioned the campfire plans to Father Damien, and he said he, too, wanted to join in. Conrardy suggested that instead of the boys telling the stories, they would each tell of some frightening experience that they had gone through.

The boys were excited when they heard of the plans and couldn't wait for all this to take place. When the day arrived, the three men assembled the boys in the late afternoon and gave each of them a bag containing sandwiches, cookies and a banana. The boys formed a ragged line with Conrardy at the head, Damien in the middle and Dutton bringing up the rear.

As they marched along, singing, some of the villagers came to see them off. It was a happy group, the stronger boys carried the little ones piggyback, others led the blind. It was not long before they reached the campsite. They brought lanterns and candles with them as it was starting to get dark. Conrardy and Dutton cleared a small circle and the boys helped to gather twigs and branches for the fire. They sat down and opened their bags. How delighted they were with what they found inside, especially the cookies and coconut candy.

Dutton had brought some tins in which he placed nuts and roasted them in the embers. He showed them how to toast the banana pieces in the burning ashes, making sure that those who had lost feeling in their fingers did not get too close. They were all surprised at how good the roasted banana tasted. It was turning out better than the three men had ever expected.

After they drank from the spring, Dutton seated them in a semi-circle around the fire. The moon had risen over the pali, casting an eerie glow—a perfect setting for ghost stories.

The boys listened intently as Damien told them about the time when he was a young boy and fell through the ice while skating. He almost drowned but his brother Pamphile who was watching, was able to save him.

Dutton began to tell them about an experience he had when he found himself behind enemy lines during the Civil War. But the boys were growing restless. Where were the ghosts? When Dutton came to telling the boys of the freeing of the slaves, their silence was shattered. Richard, the oldest boy who was going on seventeen, snorted loudly. The boys looked at him apprehensively. They knew something they had kept from Damien and Dutton .

Dutton had been aware of changes in the boy's demeanor in the last few months. Richard had always been outgoing, helpful and obedient. Lately he had turned sullen and aloof. Dutton had heard him muttering under his breath when asked to do chores. He surmised it was the change from boyhood to manhood, yet he had the uneasy feeling that the boy was hiding something.

Conrardy broke up the tension, ordering them to stand up and stretch. When they had settled down again, Richard remained standing.

He started to yell, "Slavery, that is what you white men have made of the Hawaiians. You treat us as slaves. You have taken away our freedom and tossed us into this hell-hole to die."

He shook his fist.

"I hate you all!"

And he tore off, running toward the pali.

Everyone sat transfixed. The boys looked frightened. Dutton was stunned.

He arose and started to go after Richard but Damien stopped him. "Let him go. Let him be alone. He will come out of it. He will find himself."

Just then, the boys were startled by the sound of drum beats. Father Conrardy was wrapped in a blanket with a band around his head into which he had stuck highly colored feathers. He pranced around, beating the drum and singing an Indian war chant. All forgot about Richard and were fascinated by the music and the spectacle of Father dancing and chanting.

Finally, Father sat down.

"For over fifteen years," he said dramatically, "I worked in the wilderness of North America. My congregation consisted of cowboys and Indians. Some of the bad Indians would shake their spears menacingly then take out their sharp knives and scalp you."

The boys shuddered and huddled close together, looking furtively over their shoulders.

"The Indians were living in that territory long before the white man came, just as your ancestors were, here in Hawaii. When the white man started to push farther West, the Indians went back into the deep woods and hid in the mountains. There were many good white men who did the right thing and paid the Indians for the land they took. They lived together without any trouble between them.

Father Conrardy adjusted some of the feathers in his headband.

"Other Indians were savages, hated the white man and always would. When they saw that I was not afraid of them, they left me alone. They called me 'the crazy one'."

The boys broke into laughter.

"One time, when it was snowing, I started out to reach one of my villages. I saddled my horse, strapped on a few spare blankets, and put some dried buffalo meat and spare oats for the horse into my saddle bag. I even took along some kindling wood to start a fire if I should run into trouble. I might have known better, since before long, the gentle snowflakes were turning into a blizzard. It would have made sense if I had waited a day or two but I was restless and anxious. I never carried a gun although I did have a knife in case I wanted to hunt for food."

The boys listened with rapt attention. Only the crackling fire and Conrardy's voice broke the stillness.

"Very few Indians had guns. Their main weapons were the bow and arrow, spears and tomahawk hammers. They had excellent eyesight and could toss a spear for many yards. They aimed their arrows accurately—usually at the heart of their target."

One boy spoke up, "We use spears to catch fish." The others silenced him and turned their attention back to Father Conrardy.

"As I got farther away from my village, headed for the next, the snow fell heavier, piling into deep drifts. The wind was howling now, whipping the snow into my face. My poor horse was almost blinded. There was no way to follow a trail, everything was covered with a thick blanket of snow. It seemed my horse had walked for miles. We must have been going around in circles as I could not make out any landmarks. Suddenly, I had to face it. We were lost!"

The boys gasped, "Oh, no!"

"If we did not keep moving, we would have frozen to death. My fingers were cold and stiff, even though I would constantly blow my warm breath on them. There were icicles hanging from my poor horse's nostrils. I could no longer ride him so I dismounted and held onto the reins as he walked behind me."

The boys could picture this. They were so taken by the story, they did not want to interrupt him with questions.

"My fingers were getting numb with the intense cold and I was beginning to lose all sense of feeling."

Some of the boys looked at their own fingers and nodded.

"I kept saying my rosary, pleading to our Blessed Mother to give me some sign. Suddenly, just ahead of me a line of darkness appeared, and I knew there was a break in the snow. As I came closer, I saw black hills and at the base I could see several openings. Caves, I thought.

"I thanked our Blessed Mother for giving me this sign. I was now able to move forward as rapidly as I could, pulling my exhausted horse. Reaching one of the caves, I noticed a small, rippling brook nearby. It had not frozen over. I dropped to my hands and knees and drank deeply as did my poor horse."

The tension was broken momentarily as the boys, murmuring to each other, sighed with relief.

"The cave was not deep, but deep enough to protect us from the howling wind and blinding snow. I took the saddle off the horse, unrolled my blanket, and covered him with it. Then I started a small fire with twigs from around the mouth of the cave and the kindling that I had shoved into my saddlebag. I was careful not to warm up my hands too quickly as I could lose my fingers."

The boys instinctively looked at their hands again.

"Gathering snow into my tin pot, I added a few pieces of chicory and brewed myself some coffee. It revived me and with the pieces of dried buffalo meat, I was able to get something into my stomach. I gave the horse the bag of oats that I had also stuffed into my saddlebag and he chewed slowly but hungrily.

"Darkness had come on quickly and my fire was going out. I said every prayer that I had been taught. I decided to explore the cave and a miracle happened! I felt ashes on the floor, and deeper back there was a pile of wood. Evidently someone had used the cave and intended to return. With the extra wood I built a larger fire and the cave warmed up. I was afraid I would lose my horse as he was standing near the cave's entrance. He was making funny noises and had trouble breathing. Suddenly, I stood stark still."

Conrardy rose, not speaking and looked off into the distance. The boys were frightened now, thinking there were ghosts over there.

"I heard the sound of hoofs and the splashing of water. Looking out, I could see against the white snow, five huge forms. They were buffalo, drinking from the stream! Snow encrusted their sides and across their backs, vapor was pouring from their nostrils with every breath, their fiery red eyes glowed. Then something must have startled them for they raised their heads, sniffed the air and ran off with a pounding and thrashing noise.

Not long after, beyond the fire, I saw five pairs of yellow eyes like slits, staring at me. I knew by their whimpers they were wolves. They had crept up on the buffalo, hoping to make a kill. They have a wonderful sense of smell, and I could tell they had picked up the scent of my horse but they would have to get past me and the fire to make a kill. I flung a piece of burning wood at them and they scattered but gradually crept back. The leader of the pack started to howl and wail. It is the most frightening sound you will ever hear."

Conrardy had the boys mesmerized as well as Damien and Dutton.

"Have you ever heard the wild howling of wolves?" asked Conrardy.

"No, Father, answered the boys. "Is it like a dog?"

Suddenly, a loud, piercing, howling sound echoed from the cave. The small boys jumped up in sheer terror and ran to Father Damien, screaming. Damien and Dutton jumped as well at the blood-curdling cry.

Just then, Paul emerged from the cave, doubled up with laughter. Conrardy had taught him how to imitate the sounds of the wolf and he had been an apt pupil.

"Enough of this," said Damien. "These boys will not sleep tonight."

That set up a howling of a different kind as the boys begged to hear the rest of the story and Damien gave in.

"There I was," continued Conrardy, "confronted by a pack of wolves. I dare not fall asleep for I was sure they would have got my horse. Wolves do not usually attack humans but you never know since they are wild and when hungry, killing is part of their nature. Several hours passed by before they got tired of stalking and since they could not get beyond the fire, they finally took off.

"By now the snow had stopped and the wind had calmed down. Dawn was approaching and before long the sun peeked over the horizon. I dozed off for a few seconds and when I opened my eyes, there, staring at me was a huge, ferocious cat, a panther! It was hissing and its tail switched back and forth. Cats are not afraid to kill humans and I had only a knife. I knew this would not be sufficient to protect myself. The cat crouched, ready to spring. I was doomed!

"As it sprang in the air, hurtling toward me, there was the sudden whoosh of an arrow. It hit its mark, piercing the cat's heart, spilling its blood all over me. I couldn't believe my eyes when I saw four Indian braves from my village standing before me."

The boys clapped.

"I knew them. They were brothers and belonged to my parish."

Entering the cave they greeted me and asked what I was doing there. They said I really was a crazy man.

"Why did you go out in the blizzard, don't you know how dangerous that was?"

"You just saved this crazy old man's life and how can I thank you for that. It was stupid of me, I know, but I was determined to get to my mission."

"How did you find our secret hiding place?" one of the braves asked.

"The Blessed Mother led me here," Conrardy replied. "She takes good care of me."

The braves looked around but could see no one. They offered me a horse and led me to my mission, assuring me my own horse would be well taken care of.

They saved my life, so when you read stories of savage Indians, remember they can be your friends if you show them respect—a lesson we can all learn."

Father Damien rose. "I know that I speak for all of you when I thank Brother Dutton and Father Conrardy for this wonderful campfire."

The boys clapped vigorously. Brother Dutton and a group of boys put out the fire, cleaned up, and made sure all the embers were extinguished. It was a tired and happy group that hiked back to the dormitories. When they arrived, both Damien and Conrardy blessed them and told them to get right to bed. They didn't need a second bidding.

Conrardy and Damien went back to the house, Dutton said he would join them shortly. He searched the dormitories and grounds looking for Richard but when he did not find him, he went to Damien's house to join the two priests. They went over the events and were well satisfied how the campfire had turned out.

Dutton couldn't wait to change the subject. "Father, I have searched the grounds for Richard and I can't find him anywhere. I'm starting to get worried."

"So am I, Brother, but he can't have gone far. I'm sure he will show up shortly. You mentioned that of late you have noticed some changes in his attitude."

"Yes, Father, I have and I must tell you that I re-member some of the boys had told me that many nights he would be missing for several hours. I just assumed that at his age he wanted to be alone perhaps to explore parts of the village by himself."

"I hope he is not seeing someone or getting into trouble," said Damien. "You should have told me."

"That, I should have, Father, but I did not want to burden you. I thought I could handle this myself."

Damien made no further comment on the matter; instead, he said, "It has been a wonderful evening and for once the boys really enjoyed themselves as a group."

He chuckled, and turned to Father Conrardy. "I always considered myself a brave man but when Paul let out that God-awful wailing and howling in the cave, I nearly jumped out of my skin." They all laughed. "If you do that again, I'll be after you with my stick!"

They had been sitting on the veranda. Damien got up and climbed the stairs to his room. Conrardy went back into the house and Dutton headed for his cabin. Sitting at his table he wrote in his diary all that had happened at the campfire.

In his night prayers he especially mentioned Rich-ard, and asked God to look after him. He awoke several times in the night and was tempted to go to the dormitory to see if Richard had returned but he thought better of it.

It was probably best not to let Richard know he was worried. Children can be a problem, he thought. I never realized until now, how my mother must have worried about me when I stayed out late. It is such a tragedy that these boys do not have their mothers to look after them. It's cruel that children are separated by force from their parents.

The next day, Richard was still missing and word came from the Girls Home that one of the girls, Louise, was also unaccounted for. For the ensuing days and then weeks, they searched everywhere for the two runaways and came to the conclusion that they must have escaped from the island. It was several years later before the mystery was finally to be solved.

CHAPTER TWELVE

I_N HONOLULU, AFTER THE DEATH_ of Walter Gibson, the new
Board of Health was faced with many decisions. They
wished to rid the islands of all active cases of leprosy. To
do this they enforced the law of segregation, sending
more and more patients to Molokai. This brought into
question what to do with the Branch Hospital at Kakaaka. After much discussion, they agreed to close the hospital and replace it with a small receiving station to be located outside the city.

The Branch Hospital had been established originally after the laws of segregation had been in place for
several years. The original function of the Branch Hospital was to serve as a clearing house where leprosy suspects would spend a period of time before being sent to
Molokai. Since Mother Marianne's arrival, and when Gibson was trying to ingratiate himself with the shaky
monarchy and the Hawaiian people, fewer patients were
being sent to Molokai. Then the Branch Hospital became
overcrowded with incurable patients.

With the pending closure of the Branch Hospital
at Kakaaka, Mother Marianne was confronted with the
problem of what would happen to her and her Sisters.
The Board assured her of their need that she would con-

tinue to be a part of their hospital system. It was further decided that the Branch Hospital buildings be dismantled and shipped to Kalawao.

The Board approached Charles Reed Bishop, a wealthy businessman, and requested funds to erect a home for the women and girls at Kalaupapa. He had been married to one of the last members of the Kamehameha dynasty. After her death, he was named the administrator of her large estates. He also owned a vast ranch on top of the pali managed by Rudolph Meyer, superintendent of the leprosy settlement, and had an interest in the problem of leprosy control.

Mr. Bishop liked the plans and was pleased to make the donation. The Board of Health acquired tracts of land at Kalaupapa and construction of the Home began in earnest. Later, however, they decided to move the entire settlement to a more suitable place for the treatment of leprosy patients and they tried to buy as much land as possible from the homesteaders in Kalaupapa. It was many years before all the land could be acquired, as a few home owners refused to sell. The Board of Health hoped Mother Marianne and her Sisters would go to Molokai to staff the new Bishop Home, named after its benefactor.

Before any final decision had been made, rumors began to spread that the Episcopal Sisters would go to Molokai to take care of the girls. Once again Father Damien was blamed for starting this rumor. Those opposed to him claimed he did this in order to have his way in forcing the Catholic Sisters to come to Molokai. This was never proved; in fact, with the pending closing of the Kakaaka Hospital, Mother Marianne was already considering a move to Kalaupapa. Now that Gibson had died, there was no one to prevent her from going. All she needed was an agreement to her terms before she would accept the assignment.

While all this was going on, there were many changes taking place at Kalawao. The increase in patients made it necessary for both Damien and Dutton to assist in the erection of new buildings and patient cottages.

Resentment flared up since so many of the new arrivals had spent a great deal of time at Kakaaka, and never thought they would be shipped to the leprosy settlement at Kalawao. They had difficulty accepting the isolation and the fact that their families could not visit angered them. Everyone felt the tension rising.

Damien was still on the scene and was able to maintain a sense of order, but his condition was deteriorating and he was physically growing weaker. However, he used much of his strength in overseeing the continuing work on the renovation and rebuilding of St. Philomenas.

With the increase in their work, something had to suffer. Father Conrardy was assuming more of Damien's spiritual duties. The new patients squabbled with those who had been there for years and Conrardy was called in to settle many disputes. He could not spend time at the Boys Home, neither could Dutton. The Board of Health did not send health workers to take care of the burgeoning community. Those who were trained worked long hours, often well into the night, to change dressings and take care of the ill. Damien turned to Paul who was sharing more tasks and put him temporarily in charge of the Boys Home. The boys listened to him for the most part, but the older boys tried to take advantage of his lack of experience with children. However with Damien's and Dutton's backing, they knew better than to disobey him. Damien was involved with planning the Bishop Home for Girls but could not take any part in its construction.

Although Dr. Mouritz had been discharged as the resident physician of the settlement, he remained at Molokai for several months. When the day finally arrived for his departure, both Damien and Dutton were on the dock as he left. He and Damien often had many quarrels, but they also shared a great respect for each other. After Mouritz left the settlement, he continued to work with leprosy patients and years later wrote a book, entitled "The Path of the Destroyer." Destroyer was his name for leprosy.

In his book, he praised Damien highly and defended him against charges of having had sexual relations, an attack brought against Damien after his death, by the Reverend Charles Hyde, a Protestant clergyman, which created a furor. Also in his book, Dr. Mouritz lauded Father Damien's organizational and administrative skills in handling many difficult problems, which, along with his love for the patients, made the leprosy settlement one of the best in the world.

Prior to this, another layman had arrived and offered his services to Father Damien. He was James Sinnett who came from Chicago where he had gained a great deal of experience as a nurse. When he wrote to the Board of Health telling of his desire to help, they immediately forwarded him his passage money to Honolulu. It was evident, as with Dutton, that he was seeking to make amends for his past, which he never revealed.

Damien gave the name of Brother James to the newcomer, just as he had called Dutton, Brother Joseph. Sinnett was assigned to help Paul with the older boys in the Boys Home.

Brother James displayed an admirable devotion to the work he had undertaken and he was unreservedly accepted as part of the team. It was not long before he played a more important role in caring for Damien during the last weeks of his life.

Damien, who had spent so many years alone begging for help, was to find, in the waning years of his life, many more ardent workers coming to assist him.

Dutton awoke abruptly and sat up. The moonlight filtered through the shutters. His blanket was on the floor and the sheets were rumpled. He sat there quietly. An eerie feeling crept over him as if he were in another time and place. He heard no strange noises, only the usual sounds of the tropical night. What is wrong, he thought. Why do I have this strange feeling. Was it something I ate. Am I having a heart attack. He felt his pulse—it was beating rapidly but regularly. I must have had a bad dream, but he remembered nothing.

He picked up the blanket, covered himself, and hoped that sleep would return but found himself tossing and turning from side to side. It was no use. Why fight it. He got out of bed, went to the table and poured himself a cup of water. He looked at his watch, the hands were at midnight. Perhaps a walk would calm him.

He dressed and left his cabin, the light of the full moon making it easy for him to find his way. Heading toward the sea, he passed by St. Philomenas Church and noticed a flickering light through the stained glass windows. The Church was never closed and perhaps some patient was inside in prayer. He passed by the door but something told him to stop. What was occurring. Why all these strange feelings as if something terrible were about to take place.

As he approached the open door he peered in. Several candles were lit on the altar and he noticed a figure in the first pew. Whoever it was seemed to be in deep prayer. Not wanting to disturb him, he crept down the aisle and slipped into a pew behind the figure.

It was unmistakably Father Damien. His shoulders were slumped, his head bowed, his chin resting on his chest. In Damien's swollen hands Dutton could see a rosary but the beads were not moving. He could hear no breathing. My God, he thought, Damien is dead!

As he said those words to himself, Damien's head rose and Dutton heard him quietly sobbing. He touched his shoulder.

"Father, is everything all right?"

Damien showed no sign of being startled and his sobs lessened. After a few seconds he spoke in his raspy voice.

"No, Brother. I am all right but God has not answered me."

Dutton rose and moved next to Damien. He put his hand over Damien's disfigured hand and felt the beads beneath his fingers.

"Why do you say that, Father? You know better than I that God never forsakes anyone."

"I have told no one else, Joseph, but for almost a week now I find myself unable to pray. No matter how hard I try, the words just will not come out. I have begged God to speak to me but He is silent."

"He is not silent, Father. He is just waiting. You never had this feeling before?"

"No, never. I have always found it easy to pray. He has always answered me. I am beginning to have doubts that I have lost my vocation. I have such an empty feeling. I just can't describe it and it frightens me."

"I know how you feel. It has happened to me several times."

"Really? What did you do?"

"Whenever I felt abandoned, I sought out someone whom I could trust and who was close to me. I did not keep this to myself. I could not bear it alone."

"I am so ashamed, Joseph, for doubting God. I could never reveal any of my doubts except, of course, to my confessor."

"If you want to talk to me, it might help, Father, if you trust me."

Damien was silent for a moment.

"Perhaps it is my fault," he said. "I have always been arrogant, even with my classmates in the seminary and my own family. I would lecture them if I thought they were neglecting their faith. Maybe for that reason they felt that I would not be able to understand that they had doubts, so they did not confide in me. Since you came,

Joseph, I have told you more than anyone I have ever known I felt uncomfortable about revealing any weaknesses to laymen. I believed that if I let anyone know that I, too, had times of doubt in my faith, I would lose their respect. Now I see how foolish that was."

Dutton said nothing, allowing Damien to talk. He had kept his hand on top of Damien's which now seemed to be much warmer than when he had first touched it.

Finally Dutton said, "Let us pray the rosary together."

"You begin, Joseph."

"Hail Mary, full of grace. . ."

After the first decade, Dutton heard Damien joining in, "The Lord is with you. . . Blessed is the fruit of thy womb Jesus."

With each decade, Damien's voice grew stronger and the words more fervent. At the end, they both remained silent. Tears on Damien's swollen cheeks glistened in the candlelight.

"Thank you, dear Brother, I have found my voice again, and I have heard God's."

Dutton was too overcome to speak. Damien said cheerfully, "What about a cup of coffee?"

"Sounds good to me."

The two men went from the pew, genuflected, and walked up the aisle to the door. There was no one in the Church. They had shared this magical moment together and in the presence of God Himself.

Dutton knew that time was closing in on Damien.

CHAPTER THIRTEEN

IN THE SUMMER OF 1888, negotiations for the Franciscan Sisters to come to Molokai and take charge of the newly completed Bishop Home for girls and women were near finalization. Mother Marianne had previously submitted a series of stipulations to the Board of Health before she would accept the assignment. The Board, anxious to settle, acceded to all her wishes.

In discussions with Bishop Hermann, who was now willing for the Sisters to go to Molokai, she made several requests to the Mission as well, before she would make her final decision. One of her requests was for a priest to be assigned to care for the Sisters' spiritual needs. Father Damien was not acceptable since he had leprosy. Ever protective of her Sisters, she would not allow them to take food from the hands of a victim of leprosy—this included Holy Communion. She rejected Father Conrardy. The stories she had heard about his arrogance and rough ways made him unsuitable. The Bishop, who had constantly turned down requests from Damien to send him a fellow priest, had no alternative but to acquiesce to Mother's request. He assigned a Reverend Wendelin Moellers as chaplain to the Sisters and pastor of St. Francis Church at Kalaupapa.

When Damien was informed of the decisions he was heartsick. For years he had begged for Sisters to come and care for his leprosy children. Now that they were finally convinced, he was being denied to serve as their chaplain. He understood Mother Marianne's reasoning, but nonetheless it hurt.

In the last stages of his disease there were times when he would deny that he had leprosy. It was his only defense against the constant reminder that he was an outcast. He had been told by some of his fellow priests that they would not celebrate Mass with him. They feared contracting leprosy from using any chalice that he used. He was not allowed to live with them in the rectory unless he was isolated, and he could not eat with them.

Now this!

However, there were others like Father Conrardy and Brothers Joseph and James who were not afraid of his disease. He took comfort in remembering that when the lepers touched the garments of Christ, He did not push them away. He embraced them. Damien had carried this heavy cross up to now and would do so until God called him home.

After completing arrangements with the Board of Health and Bishop Hermann, Mother Marianne wrote to her Superiors in Syracuse for final approval. While awaiting word, she decided to make a brief visit to Kalaupapa to see the progress being made at the Bishop Home. She wanted to see for herself the actual site of the Home and the conditions they would meet once they arrived to take residence. She had never been to Molokai and could only imagine what it was like by the photographs and descriptions given to her by others.

In September, she boarded the steamer accompanied by Dr. Emerson and a woman companion. Their stay at Kalaupapa was to be brief as the Captain was concerned about rough weather. After inspecting the Home, which actually consisted of several cottages and a convent on a site chosen by Father Damien and Superintendent Meyers, she was satisfied.

She had been met by the new resident physician, Dr. Sidney Swift, an Irishman, who seemed to be very hyperactive. They had time to visit Kalawao as she wanted to see the orphanage for the boys and the Damien Home for the girls. On the way they met Father Damien who joined them. Dr. Swift stopped at his cottage and invited Mother Marianne for refreshments served by his wife. Damien did not enter the cottage and waited outside until they had finished eating. He knew he was not permitted to eat with them.

After visiting St. Philomenas and the Boys and Girls Homes, Mother Marianne left to return to Honolulu. She did not speak to Father Damien of her impressions of the Homes but later it became known that she was not satisfied with the way the children were being taken care of. Again cleanliness was one of her main concerns and she felt that Brother Joseph was not sufficiently interested in maintaining the cleanliness of the Home or the boys—men were not capable of caring for small children, she stated. She was also horrified to see the children playing among the headstones in the graveyard.

Despite mixed feelings, Damien was overjoyed to know that the Sisters were finally coming to Molokai. At first he resented the appointment of Father Wendelin, thinking the Bishop had planned for Wendelin to replace him as spiritual director of the settlement. He was happy, however, to have a member of his Congregation as a companion. They would be able to confess to one another and recite the vows of the Congregation.

While Father Wendelin did not approve of Damien's recklessness with his own personal self, especially in his contact with the victims of leprosy, he admired him, and the two men would be able to work in harmony. Now there would be three priests on Molokai: Damien, Conrardy and Moellers. At times a visiting priest would arrive, bringing the total to four. After all those years of loneliness, Damien would now have companion priests, the Sisters, Brothers Joseph and James to be with him during the final months of his life.

Negotiations completed and with permission of her Superiors in Syracuse, Mother Marianne with two Sisters arrived in the latter part of November to take up their work at Kalaupapa. On the day of their arrival, Damien, who had been very sick, left his bed to meet them at the dock. He accompanied them to St. Francis where he celebrated Mass. A temporary priest, Father Mathias, sent by the Bishop for a short stay until Father Wendelin Moellers would arrive, distributed Communion. In the months to come more Sisters arrived.

With a priest installed at St. Francis, Damien did not travel to Kalaupapa except on rare occasions. Mother Marianne and her Sisters would visit him at Kalawao. While he was not able to serve as their chaplain, they greatly admired him and recognized the deep spirituality of this holy man, often requesting his blessing.

At first the girls at Kalawao did not wish to be transferred to Kalaupapa, but Damien prevailed, promising them a much better life with the good Sisters.

On one occasion two of the Sisters went over to Kalawao to visit Father Damien. He showed them the progress being made at St. Philomenas. Afterwards he asked them to partake of refreshments. He assured them that the food was prepared by a non-leper. Remembering Mother's rules, they refused. But Damien was so persistent, they were in a quandary and finally gave in.

Later at supper with Dutton, Damien confessed, "Brother, I did something wrong today. I should not have done it."

"What was that, Father?"

"As you know, two of the Sisters came to visit me and we had a very nice time. They were pleased with the work at St. Philomenas, and following, I insisted on giving them refreshments although I knew it was forbidden by Mother Marianne." He shook his head. "I don't know what got into me but I really was so adamant, the poor Sisters were frightened. They took the refreshments and I am sure that when they report this to their Superior they will be chastised. It was my fault."

"You only wanted to be hospitable and I'm sure Mother Marianne will understand."

"I hope so," said Damien. "But she strikes me as a very strong woman at times. On the other hand, she can be warm and congenial."

Damien did not sleep well that night and the next morning he went to Kalaupapa, and kneeling at the feet of Mother Marianne, begged her forgiveness. There were times when the Sisters would see him kneeling in the dirt outside, looking through the window of their little chapel in adoration of the Blessed Sacrament. Sights such as these always moved them to tears.

Life went on at its usual hectic pace. Not all the newcomers adapted easily to the hostile environment—it was an isolated and lonely place for many. With the Sisters now at Kalaupapa, the three men at Kalawao were so busy they found no chance to think of themselves. There was much to be done and so little time. Damien suffered more and more bouts of fever and did not bounce back as quickly as he once had. It was evident he was growing more frail. Brothers Joseph and James as well as Father Conrardy spent more time with him to relieve him of as much work as possible. Damien remained mentally alert and took an active interest in all they were doing. They always asked his advice, never usurping his authority. The patients were well aware of the changes taking place in Damien, their Kamiano, and their concern mounted. They, too, spent more time with him, and naturally, he enjoyed that.

On December 17, 1888, just a few months before his death, Father Damien received a most unusual visitor, Edward Clifford from England. He was not entirely unexpected. He had written to Damien after reading about him in a magazine. He was a philanthropist who had become interested in leprosy and had visited several leprosy colonies in India where an ointment known as "gurjon oil" was widely used. He thought it could become the best treatment for leprosy.

Edward Clifford dabbled in painting and although he was not a great artist, his work was well known. He had many wealthy friends and before he left England for Honolulu, he had obtained several beautiful gifts which he would present to Father Damien for his lepers. He wondered if Damien would accept him, knowing his own strong viewpoints about the Catholic Church. Clifford was a paradox in many ways. Although he was interested in leprosy, he shunned any actual contact with its victims. He had hoped while at Kalawao to get permission to create a painting of Damien.

On the day he was due to arrive, Father Damien sent Father Conrardy to meet him at Kalaupapa, but the seas were unusually rough and they could not land there. The steamer went around to the other side of the peninsula and anchored offshore at Kalawao waiting for a calm break that would permit them to launch a small boat.

Clifford had spent the night on deck and would not allow the leprosy patients on board to touch his possessions. Finally the seas calmed down enough to permit launching the small boat, and Clifford, with his packages of gifts, approached the ragged shore. He was surprised to see on the rocks, Father Damien wearing an old straw hat, surrounded by patients. They were over a mile from the settlement and Damien happened to be walking with some patients when he spotted the steamer. As the small boat approached the rocky ledge, he reached down to grasp Clifford's hand and hoist him up on to the rocks. Clifford, despite his fear, did not hesitate to take Damien's hand. He was grateful to hear Damien say, "Welcome, Edward. I did not expect you to land on this side of the peninsula."

They walked the distance along the lava rocks back to the settlement, Clifford himself carrying his luggage and the gifts. Just as they arrived, Father Conrardy returned from Kalaupapa expecting to tell Damien that the ship was unable to dock. He was shocked and needless to say a bit confused, but happy to see Clifford had arrived safely.

Damien offered Clifford lunch. He did not decline but sat at a separate table with Father Conrardy. He was worried about the food being offered, so confined himself to a few biscuits and pieces of fruit. Damien then escorted Clifford to the guest cottage a few yards from the house. When Damien introduced him to some of the patients, he was most impressed with the friendly and smiling faces that greeted him. In India, he had found abject poverty and depression among the patients. They never smiled or displayed any sense of happiness or contentment. They were emaciated, ill-cared for and seemed lifeless. To him it appeared they were simply surviving until death would claim them. Here at Kalawao, he witnessed a great deal of activity and was amused to see patients on horseback go cantering by.

That evening, joined by Dutton and Conrardy on the veranda, Clifford presented his gifts to Father Damien. They were from some of his wealthy Protestant friends. Damien was most touched and requested their names and addresses so that he could thank them personally.

Among the gifts were prints of the Stations of the Cross, engravings, and items made of silver. The most cherished of all, as far as Damien was concerned, were the gifts for his children. They included a "magic lantern" which projected colored slides pertaining to bible stories, and a hand-grind organ. The instrument could play forty different tunes just by turning the handle. The children were especially delighted with this gift as were the older patients. For the next few days, wherever you went, the sound of the organ would be echoing across the settlement. In addition to all this, there were gifts of money.

Clifford stayed for two weeks. With Damien's permission he set up his easel on Damien's small balcony. Damien would sit patiently for hours on end, usually reading his breviary, while Clifford sketched his outline then painted in oils. There were always curious patients around, some down on the ground looking up at the balcony, others peering over Clifford's shoulder. As he painted, Damien would talk to him about his life in the past, which was of great interest to Clifford.

One of the reasons for his visit, although he did not confide this to Damien, was that he wanted to write a book about this great man. In the evenings Damien often visited Clifford. They would sit on the veranda as Damien never entered the guest cottage. They talked animatedly about religion and Clifford was pleased to find that Damien was not one of those who believed that only Catholics were able to enter the Kingdom of Heaven.

Damien, now near the end of his life, had become very content and mellow. Most of his energy had left him and he did not attempt to tackle new projects. He had an air of resignation about him and was convinced that his work would soon be finished. Yet he was not morbid or morose. He described to Clifford his first days on Molokai. He told him he was happy to have leprosy for it brought him so much closer to his people. If a choice were to be made that he would be cured of leprosy and leave the island, he would not make that choice.

During the painting sessions, Clifford would sing hymns from his church, which pleased Damien. He also attended Christmas Mass and sat with the choir. One evening, just before Clifford was due to leave the settlement, Conrardy came by the guest cottage, followed by Dutton. The men sat on the veranda. The bright moonlight bathing the whitewashed huts reminded Clifford of sepulchers. The artistic, sensitive nature of the man was seen in his expression of everything he saw. There was beauty in the eye of this beholder that others did not see.

During their conversation, Father Conrardy said, "Mr. Clifford, I'm sure you know how much joy you have brought to Father Damien. He seems more at peace these past few days."

"I noticed that, too," said Dutton. "I am curious about the painting, though."

Clifford raised his eyebrows as Dutton continued, "Your painting of Father is in profile and I notice you have softened his features, eliminating much of his disfigurement. He almost looks like a young man."

"Yes, that is true," said Clifford. "It is how I paint him in my mind. I am sure you are both aware he is a most unusual man, who I can see that at one time was both vigorous and handsome. When the painting was finished, I said I would make a print to send to his brother, Pamphile. He was horrified that I would do that. He said, 'What an ugly face you have painted. I did not know my disease had progressed so far. Pamphile would be devastated if he saw me like this.'"

"Nevertheless," said Dutton, "it is a striking painting. I have never seen him so composed. You have captured something. I'm sure all who view your painting will recognize Damien as a very saintly man."

"Well, thank you, Brother, that is really a nice compliment especially coming from someone who works so closely with him. I have heard many stories about how difficult he is to get along with, but I have not found that at all."

Both Dutton and Conrardy smiled.

"You have met him in his calmer moments," said Conrardy. "Just let anyone show animosity toward his people and you will see a different person."

"Even when he flies off into a rage," added Dutton, "after he settles down, he is sorry and always makes apologies. We are both here to help him. It is the main reason I gave up everything to come here."

"I have seen leprosy settlements in India," said Clifford, "and this place is a paradise in comparison. The people here seem to be well cared for, they have smiles on their faces. I have even watched them around their cottages singing, dancing and enjoying themselves."

"It was not like that when Damien first came here," said Dutton. "He has worked miracles and it is due to his great love for his people. They know they have a protector in their Kamiano."

Conrardy agreed. "I have heard many patients in the confessional tell me that it was a blessing they were shipped here as they were now able to save their souls. On the mainland, they said they were living recklessly and in sin. God works in strange ways which we cannot always fathom."

"I am happy to tell you both," said Clifford, "that I have found a friend in him myself. Despite our differences over religion, he has made me feel most welcome."

"As a convert," said Dutton, "I can understand what you are saying. My life was one horror after another, but once I came into his presence, it completely changed. I will never leave him nor, I hope, ever leave here. There is no other place in the world for me."

"I depart tomorrow," said Clifford, "and go with mixed feelings myself. I shall always remember these two weeks with him."

The next day, before they went to Kalaupapa to meet the steamer, Damien wrote in Clifford's bible: "I was sick and you visited me."

A large group of patients, along with Damien, Conrardy and Dutton, saw Clifford board the steamer and watched as it put out to sea. Brother James, who for the most part had stayed in the background during Clifford's visit, served as the conduit. He wrote Clifford often describing the last days of Damien's life.

While in Honolulu during the next few weeks, Edward Clifford did write his little book, entitled, "Father Damien." The power of Damien's influence on him was seen on every page.

Clifford left a large quantity of gurjon oil with

Damien, who showed no interest in it for it had been tried before Clifford's arrival with no effect.

After the steamer had departed with Clifford at the rail, the three men returned to Damien's house in Kalawao.

"It has been a strange and special time for me," said Damien turning to Dutton. "I never thought I would enjoy the company of a man so different from me. Somehow God has shown me as well, the beauty one can witness through artistic eyes. Artists, Brother, are rightfully blessed by God. Their talents bring forth a beatific feeling and a joy to our hearts. I'm sure God has a special place in His kingdom for artists."

In the middle of March it was unmistakable that Damien was failing rapidly. His fingers were very swollen and his sight so poor he could no longer celebrate Mass. His body was now being ravaged by his disease. He suffered severe bouts of diarrhea and his temperature at times reached 105°. His windpipe was closing and he could hardly breathe. He was unable to sleep but for a few minutes at a time. The most remarkable change was his demeanor. He was calmly accepting what was to come. He began to talk about death and how he looked forward to being with God. He hoped he could celebrate Easter with Him in heaven.

Father Wendelin, although assigned to Kalaupapa, spent more and more time visiting Kalawao to be with Damien. He heard his general confession and together they recited their vows.

Around eleven o'clock each night, Damien would say the preparatory prayers prior to receiving Holy Communion. With Brother James leading the way holding a lantern, he and Father Conrardy would go to St. Philomenas and bring back Holy Communion. This was a highlight for the dying priest. There were moments when he would rally slightly. They would then wrap him in a blanket and carry him to a chair beneath the pandanus tree. Here, many of the patients would come to spend time with him. He tried to make them feel joyful, but his flock suffered deeply. He was their Kamiano. They could hardly believe what they saw as he sat there serenely accepting his suffering. No animation, no restlessness, no arguments.

At the end of March, he received the last rites. Mother Marianne and the Sisters visited him. Kneeling at his bedside they asked for his blessing. The entire settlement, knowing that the end was near, was downcast with a hushed silence. Many of the patients were always at his bedside, making it difficult for Brother James to take care of him. Damien wanted his people around him at all times, and everyone respected his wishes.

A message was sent to the Bishop warning him of Damien's impending death. It was hoped he would be able to come to Kalawao to be with Damien and perhaps some of his fellow priests would also come. That never happened.

Dr. Prince Morrow, a specialist from New York City interested in leprosy, visited Molokai and with Damien's permission gave him a physical examination. When it was completed, the Doctor asked Damien to send him his medical history starting from the onset of the disease to the present. Not long after he left, when alone with Dutton, Damien asked him to write down his medical history as he dictated it. Damien spoke slowly so that Brother Joseph could write it word for word in pen and ink.

In simple language he described his recollection of the first symptoms and also reported the medical history of members of his family. Brother Joseph was impressed with the clarity of his mind and his memory, despite his difficulty in talking.

After a time, Damien paused, then spoke the following words, "I have never had sexual intercourse whatsoever." Dutton could hardly believe his ears. His pen wavered but he made no comment and wrote the statement down exactly as Damien had said it. When finished, Damien asked him to read it all back to him. As Dutton came to this sentence, he hesitated a little but then read exactly what was written. Damien signed the completed history as a true document. Dutton knew then that Damien was aware exactly of the words he had spoken; yet he felt troubled.

That evening when he was able to be alone with Father Conrardy, Dutton said, "Father, I have a serious question to ask you."

"What is it, Brother Joseph?"

"This morning Father Damien dictated his medical history to me which I am to send to Doctor Morrow in New York."

"Yes, Brother, I remember the Doctor asking Damien to do that."

Dutton squirmed uncomfortably in his chair. "I

don't know whether I should let you see this as I hate to break Father's confidence in me, but since he wants to send this to Doctor Morrow, I don't suppose he wanted it to be kept strictly secret."

"You seem very disturbed, what did Father say?"

Dutton took a deep breath. "He said 'I have not had any sexual intercourse whatsoever.'"

Conrardy looked up, "Are you sure he said that?"

"Yes," said Dutton, "and when I read it back to him, he signed his name to the statement, verifying to its accuracy. I was shocked, to say the least, that he would make such a statement to me, a layman, rather than to his confessor."

"That proves his great confidence in you," said Father Conrardy. "Do you have any idea why he should make such a statement?"

Dutton answered, "From time to time, there have been rumors that Father contracted leprosy through relations with women, but I never gave any credence to this kind of gossip, and I have no doubts as to the accuracy of the statement he made."

"I would not be troubled, Brother. Seldom do we know a person's motive for saying something like this. When you think about it, it is a tremendously powerful statement."

Brother Dutton made several copies of the medical history, one of which he sent to Bishop Hermann after Damien's death. Perhaps Damien knew that upon his death there would be many accusations against him—and such did happen.

The Reverend Charles Hyde wrote a scathing letter to a friend of his, in which he questioned Damien's morals and his character. He accused him of having relations with women. His friend published the letter which was picked up by the papers around the world causing a fire-storm.

Robert Louis Stevenson, the famed author, visited Molokai after Damien's death and wrote his famous letter in reply to Doctor Hyde. It is considered to be one of Stevenson's masterpieces.

Even in death, Damien was a controversial figure!

During the second week of April, Dr. Sidney Swift, came to Damien's bedside with photographic equipment. He wanted to take a picture of Father Damien in the last stages of his life. Brother Dutton was present to help prop up the semi-conscious Damien in order for the picture to be taken. Dutton knew that if Damien were fully conscious, he would not allow such an indignity to be heaped upon him, but since Dr. Swift was the resident physician, Dutton had to obey his orders. The picture, of which the doctor made many copies, found its way into all the newspapers including the foreign press. Everyone who saw the stark photo of the ravaged Damien taken on the Saturday before Palm Sunday, was shocked.

Father Wendelin who had to go back to Kalaupapa, said goodbye to Damien, not expecting him to die before he could return the two short miles over the Damien Road.

On Saturday morning, the day before Palm Sunday, Brother James asked Dutton if he would spend a little time with Father Damien so that he could get a few hours rest. Brother James was truly an angel of mercy. In the last weeks of Father's life, he hardly left his side. He bathed him, took care of his sores, and handled him with gentleness and compassion during his bouts of fever and severe diarrhea. He gave him sips of water and moistened his cracked lips with ointment. Never once did he lose his patience in spite of always being surrounded by onlookers who would not leave Damien's room.

Brother James was a shining example to all who witnessed his devotion to Damien. He cradled him in his arms when others would shrink from touching him. He had no thought of self or of fear. To him Damien was the dying Christ suffering on the Cross.

Dutton was happy to relieve Brother James and sit with Damien who seemed to be comatose. His breathing was shallow, his eyes closed. Dutton noticed the sores were drying up and scabs were forming. He had seen this happen before to victims of leprosy as they neared death. It seemed the bacillus could not survive in dying flesh.

Dutton, at the bedside, reached out to take Damien's hand in his.

While there were beads of sweat on Damien's cold forehead, his hand felt warm. Dutton searched for Damien's pulse and locating it, found that it was irregular. There would be strong beats then periods of time when no beat could be felt. Malia, coming to the door, saw Dutton sitting at the bedside and quietly moved all the patients out of the room. She knew that this was the moment when two friends should be alone.

Suddenly, Dutton felt movement and Damien's

fingers tightened on his hand. Damien's eyelids fluttered, then opened. He asked, "Is that you, Brother Joseph?"

"Yes, Father, it is Joseph."

Damien then asked, "Are we alone?"

"Yes, Father."

"What day is it, Brother Joseph?"

"It is Saturday, the day before Palm Sunday."

"Oh," said Damien, "Thank God it's not too late."

"Too late for what, Father?"

"You always told me, Joseph, that God would take me on Palm Sunday so that I could spend Easter with my risen Christ. I wanted to speak to you, Joseph, before I died."

"You don't have to say anything, Father, conserve your strength. Words are not necessary."

"Yes they are, Joseph, and you must hear me out. God has been good to me, Brother, far better than I deserve. He blessed me with this heavy cross so that I could suffer with Him. He allowed me to share with Him much of His sufferings while He was here on earth. He was spat upon, crowned with thorns, denied by his friend, Peter, ridiculed, laughed at, suffered pangs of loneliness, even moments of panic when he thought His Father had forsaken Him. There is nothing that could happen to us that Christ did not experience during His short time here. He set an example for all of us."

There was a moment's pause and a smile flickered across Damien's face.

"I'm afraid, though, that He did not give me the patience He showed when He suffered at the hands of His enemies. Your coming here, Joseph, was God's way of helping me to see, after all my years of frustration and loneliness that He was aware of my needs. Then the arrival of Father Conrardy, Brother James and the Sisters, all within the last few months, proved to me that my work would be finished but it would be continued by others. Now I am ready and can die in peace."

Dutton did not interrupt him. He knew it was an effort for Damien to speak, and yet he had to say these things. He brought Damien's hand to his lips, and kissed the swollen fingers.

"I do not know what will happen here when I'm gone. There will be many factions fighting for control. I only hope, Joseph, you will have the forbearance and the will to withstand whatever storm may arrive. Will you promise me that?"

Joseph was filled with emotion. He could hardly speak and his voice wavered as he answered, "Father, I promise."

"I am growing tired, Joseph, but I must tell you one thing more. I know how much you still worry about your past and how many doubts you have that God has forgiven you. You must wipe all those doubts from your mind, Joseph, for God has surely forgiven you. By dwelling on the past, you will never know the real joy of God's embrace. Remember the prodigal son and the great joy that the father expressed when this errant young man returned to his household. That is nowhere near the joy that God gives to a truly repentant sinner."

At that Damien's voice trailed off, his eyes closed and he was back into a deep sleep.

Dutton was exhausted and drained. There was so

much he had wanted to say to Damien but could not find the words. Brother James appeared in the doorway and seeing Brother Dutton weeping with his arms around Damien, stood back and waited until he heard Dutton rise from the chair.

"Thank you, Brother Joseph," he said, "for giving me these few moments of rest."

Dutton did not reply but tore from the room, ran down the stairs, across the veranda into the yard, and headed toward the pandanus tree. He sat down among the gnarled, exposed roots. The trunk was covered with a creeping parasitic vine, draining out what little life was left in the tree. Many of the branches were bare, shorn of their once large, beautiful leaves. Delicate white blossoms sprang from the parasitic vine, exuding a strange odor.

Dutton muttered to himself, 'Even in death there is beauty.' He felt spent and as he pondered, fell into a fitful sleep.

Malia, watching all this happen, came close to Dutton and sat on the ground, waving away the curious onlookers to a safe distance. She knew what it was to lose someone you love. She waited quietly until Dutton awakened, then rose and went back into Damien's house as Dutton walked quickly to his cabin.

Saturday at midnight, Damien took Communion for the last time. The next day, Palm Sunday, he slipped into a deep coma. Brother James stayed at his side as did Malia and a group of patients.

St. Philomenas was crowded with patients. They

spilled out of the doorway, covering the grounds around the church and many were pressed against the windows. Usually Palm Sunday was a festive occasion but today was different. There was hardly a sound except the shuffling of feet. Even the children were silent. Everyone was aware that something terrible was happening.

Dutton began his rounds of patients in the hospital, while Conrardy went back to Damien's house. All during the day, many patients sat outside Damien's house praying the rosary. Occasionally there would be a loud, wailing cry.

Late in the afternoon, Brother James, always watchful, noticed Damien opening his eyes and in a low voice, that Brother James had difficulty hearing, Damien stated that there was a figure standing at the foot of his bed and another at the head. James asked him if he could identify the figures but Damien lapsed back into unconsciousness.

That evening, as Dutton was readying the altar for Vespers, he saw Paul kneeling at the statue of the Blessed Mother. Dutton joined him and Paul turned toward him.

"I don't know what is wrong with me. I have such a strange feeling. It's like when I felt the coming of a kona. I'm frightened."

"I, too, have that feeling, Paul, but we must remember that Father does not want us to mourn for him. He was praying to be with God for Easter."

The next morning, as Dutton was preparing for Mass, he received word to come quickly to Damien's room. He was cradled in Brother James's arms. There was a smile on Damien's face and without the slightest sound or movement, he was gone.

Dutton, on his knees, his voice breaking, said through his tears, "The mighty oak has fallen."

With that, a loud wailing arose from the patients present. It was eerie and made Dutton's blood run cold.

Father Conrardy had sent a messenger to Kalaupapa to let Father Wendelin know that Damien was near death. Wendelin left immediately for Kalawao but was met with another messenger with the news that Damien had died.

It seemed that even Mother Nature was mourning, for the skies were overcast and a chill wind was blowing.

His coffin had been prepared and Mother Marianne came with another Sister bringing silks and cloths of crepe. She lined the casket with beautiful silk and covered the lid with black cloth. James bathed Damien's body and Father Wendelin dressed him in his priestly vestments. They chose white instead of the usual black. They laid him gently in the coffin and carried him into the church, placing him before the high altar which Damien himself had fashioned with his own hands.

Patients, both Catholic and Protestant, together with government workers, streamed through St. Philomenas during the wake which lasted through the night. Everyone remarked how youthful Damien looked. All traces of leprosy had disappeared, and there was a slight smile on his lips.

Bodies could not be kept long in the tropics and the funeral was scheduled for early the next day. All hope of the Bishop coming with members of his Congregation vanished. Everyone spent that night in preparation. The funeral band polished their instruments and the various societies cleaned and prepared their uniforms.

Early in the morning, Mother Marianne returned with two Sisters and a group of girls from the Bishop Home wearing black sashes. The Church was filled with beautiful flowers gathered by the women of the Altar Society. The fragrance was overpowering. It seemed that every available candle was burning.

Father Wendelin Moellers and Father Conrardy celebrated the High Mass assisted by Brother Joseph, Brother James, and Paul. The music was magnificent— everyone was determined to do their very best for their Kamiano.

After Mass, the procession formed. The grave had been prepared as Damien wished, next to St. Philomenas and near his beloved pandanus tree. The long procession wound around the Church to the grave site led by the funeral band. Then came the church societies, eight patients carrying the coffin on their shoulders, followed by the acolytes, the priests, Mother Marianne, the Sisters, the girls from the Home, Brother Joseph, Brother James and all of the boys.

Father Wendelin said the prayers at the grave, sprinkling Damien's coffin with holy water and incense. All joined in the Lords Prayer. Then they filed by dropping flowers on top of the coffin, orchids of every size and color, sprays of honeysuckle, roses, wisteria, and palms. The coffin was placed inside a concrete vault, and shovels of dirt formed a mound on top. With those duties performed, some slowly left but a multitude refused to leave and sat on the ground surrounding the grave. Many remained there for the entire night.

It was fifteen days later that Damien was remembered with a funeral Mass at the Cathedral in Honolulu presided over by the Bishop. By then the whole world knew of his death.

After all the years of struggle and work, all the years of prayer and suffering, all the waiting, the planning, Damien was now gone and life on Molokai would never be the same again.

Dutton spent a restless night after the funeral. It was difficult for him to believe that the man he had come to serve was gone. There was a heavy feeling in his heart. He consoled himself with the thought that Damien was no longer suffering and that he was now at peace.

He arose early and decided to get to St. Philomenas before anyone else. He wanted to spend a few moments alone in the Church that Damien had built. As soon as he stepped outside he saw groups of patients huddled around the grave, lanterns still lit, and some of them asleep on the ground. They had spent the night watching over their Kamiano. He was pleased to see the Church almost full with patients, silently saying their beads. He noticed Paul sitting in the first pew, his head lowered, his shoulders slumped. He did not disturb him and sat in the pew behind.

Soon there was a slight noise in the sacristy and Father Conrardy and Brother James entered. Conrardy looked as though he had not slept much, either. He said the Mass slowly and solemnly. The congregation sang the Hawaiian songs of death.

After Mass, Father Conrardy, Brother Dutton and Brother James went back to Damien's house and sat down at the table. Malia had prepared breakfast. She did not speak and every once in a while would wipe her eyes. Conrardy spoke first.

"We knew that this was coming. We expected it, but we did not really prepare for it. Father Wendelin informed me that several weeks ago he had discussed with the Bishop what would happen when Damien died. He was told that I should carry on in charge of St. Philomenas until arrangements for a successor could be made."

Father Conrardy paused. There was silence at the table.

"Naturally I will remain as long as I am wanted," he added.

"Father Damien asked me to dispose of his few possessions," said Dutton. "I will make an inventory, pack them up and ship them to the Bishop. He did not have much to leave to anyone."

Turning to Brother James, he asked, "Have you made any plans, Brother?"

"No, Brother Joseph, I haven't. Right now I don't know what I will do but until I make up my mind or someone makes it up for me, I will do what Father Damien would want me to do. I'll continue to take care of the boys as best I can."

"I must take care of the chickens," said Dutton as the thought struck him. "Somehow they know that for these past few weeks Father Damien has not been there to feed them. I have tried, and have been able to get fairly close to them but if I make a quick move or stoop to pick one up, they scamper and fly away. On second thought, Paul seems to have a way with them. It might be best if I ask him to take on the feeding chore."

"I've been looking at Paul," said Conrardy. "He seems very depressed. We must keep an eye out for him. I can feel his deep sense of grief for he has lost not only Father Damien but in reality, the only father he has ever known."

Hearing that, Malia let out a deep sobbing cry and fled out of the kitchen.

A noticeable change was coming over the entire settlement. Brother Joseph could feel the undercurrents in some quarters and sensed that there might be mischief afoot among the patients. Now that Damien was gone, they had no fear of reprimand. He knew he had to be more watchful and alert.

Dr. Swift had ridden over from Kalaupapa to assure both Brother Joseph and Brother James that their services would still be needed and that the government would appreciate their continued care of the boys.

There was talk that another wealthy businessman, Henry Baldwin, was interested in providing a new Home for the boys as Mr. Bishop had done for the girls. Mr. Baldwin was hoping that Mother Marianne and her Sisters would take charge. This did not bother Dutton in the least. He did not feel his authority was being usurped for he remembered what Damien had told him about titles. He would continue to do whatever he could to the best of his ability regardless of who was put in charge.

Now that Damien was gone, Dutton turned his attention to keeping the boys active. It was not long before laughter and screams of delight came from the children as they resumed their games. Brother Joseph knew that Father Damien would be delighted with their happiness.

As soon as news of Damien's death reached the outside world, messages poured in. Some contained donations to carry on with Damien's work and Dutton sent these on to the Bishop. For several weeks it was impossible for him not to see Damien wherever he went. Joseph could still hear him say, "Off I am, Brother!"

At dusk one evening, Joseph was sitting on the steps of his cabin. He heard a cooing sound and looking up saw a beautiful white bird flying over his head. It looked like a dove. It circled several times then landed. He had seen mourning doves before, but never a white one. It was just a few feet from him and cocked its head from side to side. Dutton sat still. Suddenly, without warning, with a fluttering of wings, it rose straight up and disappeared over the pali. He never saw it again. To him, it was a sign from Damien, telling him that all was well with him, not to worry, and to remember his promise to take care of his boys.

An overwhelming feeling of peace descended upon Brother Dutton. It was the sign he was looking for, something to tell him that he must stay. He took out his rosary and as his fingers slipped over the beads he whispered his thanks to Our Blessed Lady. He knew it was she who was the intermediary in sending the sign of the dove.

CHAPTER FOURTEEN

SEVERAL WEEKS LATER, Dutton was sitting on the rocky ledge overlooking the ocean. It was the same spot where he and Damien had often spent many hours in conversation. He loved to sit there drinking in the beauty surrounding him, never tiring of the magnificent view— God's gift of nature's beauty.

It was strange that Richard came to mind. It had been several years since he had disappeared from the campfire outing and he didn't know why he thought of him at this moment. The passage of time had almost erased him from his memory. Dutton said a prayer that wherever he was, he would be safe.

He heard a shuffling of footsteps behind him and turning around, he was happy to see Caleb, the old sea captain, coming toward him. Dutton arose and went to him, grabbing him by the shoulders.

"Caleb, you scoundrel, how good to see you!"

Caleb took off his battered captain's hat and with his large, red neckerchief mopped his brow. It was between twilight and dark, the breeze had died down and the air was sticky.

"It's been so long, Caleb, and I have thought of you many times."

"I have been thinking of you, too, Brother. Where have you been? I hoped that on one of my trips I might catch a glimpse of you at Kalaupapa."

"I hardly go to Kalaupapa any more. I am content to stay here with my work."

"Well, as you know, Brother, there are so many changes in Kalaupapa and I am afraid I will not be able to keep my shack. The government is buying up much of the land."

"Come, Caleb, sit down here on the rock beside me. I was just resting here with my companions."

Caleb scratched his head and looked around.

"I told you this place would make you go daft. I don't see any companions."

"Just look over there at the cliffs."

Caleb looked where Dutton was pointing. He was skeptical, but finally at the base of the cliffs saw two figures that had been formed by nature. They looked as if they came from an outcropping of lava and were darker than the area that surrounded them.

"For the moment I could not make out what you are talking about, Brother, but finally I see something. What is it?"

"Well, there is a figure of a girl and opposite her is an animal rearing up on its hind legs. I call them the girl and the dancing bear. They have kept me company many a long evening."

"Isolation can do strange things, Brother, but if you say that's what they are, then I will accept your explanation. Besides, if they give you good company then that is all that matters."

"You should have been in politics, Caleb. You are a smooth talker. But what brings you here?"

"Paul was in Kalaupapa picking up some supplies and asked if I wanted to ride back with him. I told him that would be fine but how would I get home? He said don't worry, I'll get you home. He is a fine young man. What a change in him in the short time since Damien's death."

"Yes," said Dutton. "He has gotten over much of his grieving and we have given him a great deal of work to do. He has more or less adopted me and is my constant companion. I depend a great deal on him."

"Damien! There was a man," said Caleb. "When I passed his grave coming down here I stopped for a moment and believe it or not, I found myself on my knees. I didn't know what to say so I just whispered to him, 'You might get me yet, Father.'"

Dutton had a good laugh. "That was probably one of the best prayers he ever heard. Damien always wins out in the end."

Caleb looked around to make sure no one was watching, then pulled a letter from inside his jacket.

"Don't read this now," he said. "Wait until you are alone and you will know why I came."

Dutton slipped the letter into his pocket without looking at it.

"It's from Richard," said Caleb.

Dutton turned quickly

"Richard? He's alive?"

"Yes, and doing very well. I trust you, Brother, and will tell you what happened, but if you ever repeat this, I will deny that I said anything, even if they make me swear on a stack of bibles."

"I promise you have my confidence, Caleb. I'm very anxious to hear about Richard."

Caleb settled himself on the rocks and said he had heard why they had run away. Not long after in Kalaupapa, he was dozing in his shack when he heard footsteps. He looked out and there was a young boy reeling in a fish that had been caught on his hook. He did not stop him and pretended to be asleep, but guessed it was Richard. He must have been hiding in one of the caves. Over the years, many patients had tried to escape and hid in the caves but they were usually caught, returned and punished.

The young lad came by for several days in a row. Caleb did not stop him, pretending to be asleep, so he grew bolder. The captain began to leave provisions outside the shack, as if he had forgotten to bring them in. One day, Caleb scooted around to the cave and when Richard took the food and was returning, he stepped out from behind the rocks and confronted him. The poor lad let out a cry of fear, dropped the food, and started to run.

The only way he could go was back to Kalaupapa and Caleb knew he would not take that chance. Richard began to sob and begged not be turned in. Caleb put his arms around him and told him not to be fearful, that he personally would see that he was not discovered. He did not see Louise but Richard said she was with him in the cave. He told Caleb he wanted to escape somehow from the island but didn't know how.

Caleb said he felt sorry for him and told Dutton

that in the past, he had helped a few escape. He thought
Damien knew of this and perhaps it was one of the reasons he was always after him.

One night, when Caleb was ready to return to Hawaii, the steamer arrived and Captain Jeffers took him
aboard. Since it was dark, it was easy for Caleb to dis-
tract the captain, and as he did, Richard and Louise
slipped on to the boat. Caleb knew the steamer quite well
and had told them where to hide. He also made arrangements for Captain Jeffers to join him later at his house
for a meal—luring him away from the boat.

When the steamer docked at Honolulu, it was
dark, giving Richard and Louise a chance to leave the
boat unseen. Caleb had told them where to wait, con-
cealed, near a warehouse. After Caleb and the captain
had had supper in his house, he walked the Captain back
to his quarters.

It was around midnight when Caleb went to the
warehouse where the two youngsters were hiding. He
found them trembling with fear, took them to his house
and sheltered them. He knew that if they were caught he
would be arrested and Richard and Louise would be sent
back to Kalawao and put in jail. His old, adventuresome
spirit took hold and he was enjoying the conspiracy.

He kept the two of them safely in his house until
he could make arrangements with a friend, the captain of
a trading ship that plied the waters between Samoa and
Tahiti. Richard didn't look as if he had leprosy and the
girl, except for a few spots, was very beautiful and appeared to be free from the disease. Only Caleb knew they
were infected. He crossed the palm of the captain with a

few pieces of silver and they were smuggled aboard.

Caleb heard of their progress from time to time from the captain of the trader. He had given the boy a job on his boat and found a friend in Tahiti who took in the girl. They were not as strict with segregation as in Hawaii. The couple finally married and had two little boys.

"Richard spends all his time in Tahiti between voyages," said Caleb. "They are accepted by the villagers. Richard told the captain that he wanted to send a letter to you, but was afraid the authorities might trace him and take him back to Molokai."

Dutton patted the pocket of his jacket.

"This is a real treasure for me, Caleb, and my mind is so relieved to know that those two poor young people are safe and happy."

"Then you are not angry with me?"

"Why should I be angry with you?"

Caleb looked at him with astonishment. "Because of what I have just told you."

"The only thing I heard, Caleb, was the fact you might lose your shack at Kalaupapa and not be able to return there."

"You are really something, Brother Joseph. I bet you were a spy during the Civil War. Were you?"

"If I were, I wouldn't tell you," Joseph chortled.

Paul appeared and reminded Caleb that it was getting dark, and they should leave. They walked toward the buggy, and Caleb turned to Dutton.

"This might be the last time, Brother, that we will see each other, unless you come to the big island. I don't want to say goodbye and God forgive me, but I'm going to ask you to keep me in your prayers."

"You will be happy, Caleb, to know how forgiving God is. Damien would be pleased if you would turn over a new leaf."

"You never know, you never know," said Caleb.

Paul helped him up into the buggy and as they drove off. Dutton stood watching them until they disappeared into the darkness. Caleb did not turn around to look back and the two never did meet again.

Dutton could hardly wait to get to his cabin. He lit the lamp, took out the letter and spread it on the table.

His heart leapt with joy.

Dear Brother Joseph,

I know that you will be surprised to hear from me. I want to ask your forgiveness for causing you so much trouble. I constantly pray to Father Damien asking him to forgive me, too. I don't know what got into me but I could not face being alone any more. When I met Louise, she was the answer to all my prayers. I knew they would not let us marry and if we lived together and had any children, they would take them from us and ship them back to the mainland.

You will be happy to know we have two boys. The first I named Damiano and the second, Joseph.

Please, Brother, burn this letter as I am so frightened they will come after me.

Aloha, Richard

With teary eyes, Dutton took the paper and held it to the flame. He watched it catch fire and when it singed his fingers he dropped the ashes into the dish beside him on the table.

It was a few months after, that Dutton learned of Caleb's death. His old drinking companions and sea buddies wrapped his body in a canvas bag, filled it with heavy weights, and took him out to sea. With appropriate prayers and sea chanties, they slipped him into the deep.

When Dutton knelt at his bedside to say his evening prayers, he said a special one for Caleb. God knows how to get the best out of sinners, he thought. I am sure that Damien will welcome him one day and will say to him: "I finally got you, Caleb."

CHAPTER FIFTEEN

Peace, thought Dutton grimly, seemingly peace was buried with Damien. Saint Matthew, the tax collector, had written, "For wheresoever the carcass is, there will the eagles be gathered." No sooner had the last shovel of earth been piled on Damien's grave, when they were swooping around the settlement, waiting to pounce on the first opportunity to take charge. Gone were the comparatively quiet, purposeful days of building and teaching, and there was no end to the avalanche of letters pouring in asking for information, begging for pictures.

The shaky truce between the factions, political, sectarian and hierarchical, had dissolved on Damien's passing. New disputes were fueled by the mounting interest and accolades for Damien which were interpreted by some as personal affronts. It seemed everyone was trying to become Damien's successor. In reality, there could be no true successor to Damien. Damien—priest, physician, nurse, carpenter, keeper of law and order, and digger of graves—was like a diamond with many facets. His true successor would have to be all of these and there was no one available to fit the qualifications. His duties had to be pieced out to various individuals, each vying with the other.

Only the Bishop could appoint a successor priest to care for the spiritual needs of the Catholic residents at the settlement. Bishop Hermann, not willing to make decisions, preferred not to become involved in removing Father Conrardy who was well loved by the patients. His removal at this time would cause an uproar and Conrardy would not go lightly into the night. In addition, Conrardy's relations with the press were always a threat to the stability of the Church. Rather than stir up a hornet's nest, the Bishop permitted Conrardy to remain at Kalawao on a temporary basis to carry on with the spiritual needs of the patients.

Father Wendelin Moellers remained at Kalaupapa as pastor of St. Francis but often visited Kalawao. Mother Marianne and her small community, now established at the Bishop Home in Kalaupapa, was anxious to do something about the Boys Home in Kalawao, especially the younger ones.

Responsibility for the operation of all the facilities for patient care, including the Boys Home, was under the direction of the Board of Health. Since Brother Dutton and Father Conrardy were actively involved in caring for the boys, there was some concern as to how both of them would react to the appointment of Mother Marianne to supervise the Home.

Mr. Meyers, the Superintendent of the settlement, who preferred to live on the top of the pali at his ranch, only came down about four times a year. He visited Mother Marianne who told him of her desire to care for the boys, and Meyers persuaded the Board of Health to appoint her as supervisor of the Home in Kalawao.

Again, the Bishop, not wishing to become engaged
in any decisions that might upset the Protestants on the
Board, left the matter in her hands. The shortage of Sisters made it impossible for Mother Marianne to permit
Sisters to reside at the Home. Two Sisters were assigned
to go to the Home each morning and return to the convent in Kalaupapa in late afternoon. As a result, there was
no supervision by the Sisters between four o'clock in the
afternoon until 10:00 a.m. the next morning. Added to
this problem, they had to travel to the Home by horse and
buggy and there were days when weather conditions did
not permit them to make the trip.

Aware of these difficulties, Mother Marianne
asked Brother Dutton to assume responsibility for the
older boys. They were passing into manhood and were
more difficult to handle. They resented strict rules and
regulations. Dutton accepted the assignment but no one
knows how he really felt about it. He never lost his temper or argued with authorities. His rigid army training, his
vow of penitence, and his conversations with Damien
who had warned him he would meet many challenges
after his death, had steeled him to accept whatever
changes came his way.

He continued to dress the sores of many patients
and seemed to turn more and more to his letter writing.
Whether this was a result of the changes in the operation
of the Home, can only be surmised.

The settlement seemed to be reverting back to its
ways before Damien had arrived. Damien's presence had
kept rebellious forces from erupting into action, but a
small band of malcontents threatened bodily harm to

both Mother Marianne and Father Conrardy and had to be quelled by government security forces.

This was too much for Brother James and he left as mysteriously as he had arrived. He was not heard from again but those few months he spent with Damien were enough to earn him a special place in the eyes of God.

There were many attempts to remove Father Conrardy from the scene and Conrardy knew this, which strengthened his resolve and he refused to leave. In 1892, Bishop Hermann died and was succeeded by Bishop Gulstan.

Henry Baldwin, a wealthy American sugar cane owner and son of an American missionary, had made his fortune on the island of Maui. He finally agreed to finance building the Boys Home. It took several years to complete the Baldwin Home consisting of many buildings, eventually numbering over fifty. The site chosen was at Kalawao across the road from Damien's Church. While the original plans were to move the entire settlement to Kalaupapa, they were changed and it was decided the men and boys were better suited to remain at Kalawao. It was one method of isolating the men from the women as it was still believed by many that leprosy was contracted through intercourse.

During construction, it became more apparent that the supervision of the boys would be better handled by men, a suggestion to which Mother Marianne agreed. Bishop Gulstan enlisted the Sacred Hearts Brothers to take over this task, but the Board of Health was still uneasy about resentment from the Protestants if Catholic Brothers were put in charge. After much deliberation, they came to the conclusion that Brother Dutton would be the logical person to serve as Director of the Baldwin Home, with the Brothers as his assistants.

Initially, a group of four Brothers arrived as did Father Pamphile, Damien's brother. He had agreed to come to Molokai. With Father Pamphile installed at Kalawao, the enemies of Father Conrardy finally had their way and the Board asked him to leave. Dutton, who had worked so well with him, was sorry to see him go but he had no influence with the authorities.

Father Conrardy turned his full attention to the victims of leprosy in China and made that his main goal. Leaving Honolulu, he sailed for China and arrived in the vicinity of Canton. There, he discovered leprosy victims with no one to care for them. They were truly outcasts and often would be put on board ship, taken out to sea and dumped overboard. Conrardy was well suited to this kind of situation. He wanted to take them all to a small island but did not have the money and the Chinese government would not approve his plan unless he was a doctor.

He returned to the United States and at the age of fifty-five took medical courses in Oregon, receiving his Doctor's diploma. He travelled to England where he gave countless talks and begged from door to door for financial help. Finally, he went to Canada and then on to the United States, still begging for money.

In May, 1908, with funds in hand, he returned to China and found a small island outside Canton suitable for his purpose. He bought the land and built shelters for more than seventy patients. Impressed with the work he was doing, the Chinese officials eventually offered to support him. It was not long before he had seven hundred victims of leprosy, and Sisters arrived to help him, along with two more priests.

He was a second Damien except he never contracted leprosy, despite the abandonment of all precautions. The patients adored him. He washed them, bandaged their wounds, and consoled them. One of his fellow priests beseeched him to be more prudent. "Catch leprosy?" Conrardy said. "That would be the most beautiful decoration for me, but I am not worthy of it!"

In 1914 he died of pneumonia and they buried him as he wished, rolled up in a mat between two victims of leprosy. This was a man reviled by many, even by members of the Religious Orders. They rightfully claimed that he was a difficult man to get along with but no one could ever question his piety.

Father Pamphile found the work at Kalawao not to his liking. He was a scholar and a teacher. The daily tasks that confronted him were more than he could mentally or physically handle. He soon left the island and returned to Louvain.

More men and boys were being admitted to the Baldwin Home and Dutton's work was increasing at a rapid pace, but with the arrival of additional Brothers and with his years of training, he knew how to delegate many of his duties. He, personally, never stopped the task of changing the bandages of patients, and he kept a neat and accurate set of ledgers. The Brothers admired him, and willingly helped him perform his duties. The operation of the Home went smoothly.

He moved his cabin across the road to the Baldwin complex and added rooms. The new cabin stood on a small knoll where he erected a flagpole that could be seen from the sea. While Hawaii was still under the control of the shaky monarchy, he raised the Stars and Stripes each morning, lowering it at dusk, with no objection from any of the residents of Kalawao.

An event was to occur that would give the remaining years of his life on Molokai deeper meaning. Sincerely patriotic, he was soon to find himself working for Uncle Sam.

Back on the large island, the downfall of the monarchy was coming to fruition. King Kalakaua died while on a visit to San Francisco. He had named his sister, Princess Liliuokalani as his Regent with the right to succession. She not only became the first reigning Queen of Hawaii but also the last ruler of the kingdom.

The Queen inherited a weak monarchy and a cabinet composed mostly of foreign businessmen. She was well aware that the Americans wanted to overthrow the monarchy and have Hawaii declared a Territory of the United States. She did everything in her power to restore the Constitution—her aim being to take back for the Hawaiians much of the power given away by her brother, King Kalakaua. Unfortunately, by this time the Hawaiian population was decimated and she was unsuccessful. In January of 1893, a small band of American and European businessmen, aided by the United States Marines, toppled the government. Not a drop of blood was spilled in the coup.

Sanford B. Dole, an American born in Hawaii, was named head of the Provisional Government. The sugar planters, anxious to have the islands annexed to the United States in the hope of insuring the profitability of their sugar crops, appealed to Congress. President Grover Cleveland was appalled at the manner in which the monarchy was overthrown. He refused their request. The Provisional Government then declared the Hawaiian Islands a Republic with Dole as President. The Queen was placed under house arrest and was detained for more than five years.

In 1896, Cleveland lost his reelection bid to the Republican, William McKinley. It was evident that other countries had their eyes on Hawaii. The nation was bankrupt and it was a prize for the taking.

In 1898, President McKinley acted, and signed a resolution making Hawaii a possession of the United States of America.

When the news reached Brother Dutton that the islands were now under the control of the United States, he was ecstatic. He rushed into his cottage and opened a cabinet in which he had stored American flags that had been sent to him by friends and even from his old regiment. Choosing the largest, he went to the flagpole and lowered the small American flag which was fluttering in the breeze. His heart was filled with pride as he slowly raised the large Stars and Stripes. He placed his hand over his heart as the wind picked up the folds, unfurling Old Glory against the blue sky. He said aloud, "Now you are flying legitimately." In the past, he had anticipated orders to take it down. At last he could rightfully conduct his flag ceremony which meant so much to him.

There was sadness among the Hawaiians in the

settlement who were not happy that their kingdom had been overthrown. Disillusionment, too, had crept into Dutton's patriotism when he learned the way the United States had handled the whole affair. It rankled him, taking the edge off his swelling pride. This was different from the Civil War in which goals were so well defined: the restoration of a nation being split asunder. Even then, beneath it all, the same evil, greed, was the force behind the conflict. Those in the South did not want to abolish slavery which would result in a great loss to their economy. Likewise, the American sugar cane owners were only interested in their livelihood when they destroyed the Hawaiian monarchy.

Dutton had lived as an alien among the Hawaiians for many years. He understood their language, their culture, and their needs. He knew them to be a loving people. Money—money, or is it power, he cried to himself. Money, he decided, and what money will buy. He stood at the foot of the flagpole with mixed emotions. He was a fair and honest man. He concluded that with the steady decline of the monarchy and the paucity of its options, that annexation was by far the best choice for Hawaii. He was aware that the Americans were generous people and that the patients would be well served under the new government. This was a comfort to him.

In the ensuing days, many more changes were taking place in the settlement. The new Board of Health and a sympathetic Congress sent more equipment and personnel. The Baldwin Home was ultimately completed and the boys were now living in much improved conditions. The old Boys Home was torn down. More Brothers arrived and Dutton set up a daily schedule. He was a stickler for routine—one day was much like the previous day and this was entirely satisfactory to Dutton. There was always enough to keep him busy.

With the increasing years, his hair and full beard were dusted with white. His correspondence increased with each batch of mail arriving from the United States. Inquiries specifically about Damien had abated and were replaced, often as not, with letters from people asking for information on his own past. In addition, others he had long forgotten were starting to correspond, some even asking to join him. As always he tactfully replied, suggesting they first offer to help their neighbor or community. One answer usually resolved most of these requests. He would inform them there were no funds available to pay for their transportation, housing, or living expenses.

As the boys grew into manhood they became difficult to manage. While the girls were located two miles distant, it did not keep the young men from travelling to Kalaupapa, attempting to make contact. It was not easy as the girls were under the watchful eyes of the Sisters.

Brother Dutton set himself up as the arbiter of morals. He was receiving many suggestive magazines sent by well-meaning people. Before he placed them in the reading room, he would cut out pictures or text he deemed unsuitable. He did not realize that the boys, seeing the censored magazines, would paint an even more prurient picture in their minds than would be on the original pages. The Brothers did not interfere with Dutton's instructions and he was leaving it to them how to discipline the boys.

Dutton used the newspapers to obtain names of people holding important positions to whom he would write and inform them of the needs of the patients. These included those in high political office as well as others engaged in business, civic and social activities. It did not matter whether he was writing to a president, a senator, or a head of an organization, his letters contained bits of information about what was going on in the settlement. Whenever he could, he would send small native carvings. His letters were not profound, in fact, they were uncomplicated and friendly. It was the kind of writing he employed as a young man when he wrote a column for his local newspaper. His birthday list grew larger each year, and the celebrant would without fail receive a message or a colorful card.

These ordinary letters and gestures of friendship struck a cord of compassion with the reader resulting in a wider recognition of the work he was doing. He would write far into the night by candlelight or oil lamp. He refused modern conveniences, even a fountain pen. He claimed they leaked and kept to his pen and ink. The close work and long hours of writing in poor light took a toll on his eyes.

Fastidious always, he was a familiar figure as he strode with erect military bearing in his trademark denim suit throughout the settlement. The patients did not fear him, they respected him. While they found his habits old fashioned and his speech peculiar, they were warmed by the sparkle in his eyes and his ever-ready smile. He had a childlike sense of humor which they enjoyed.

The name of Dutton was more widely linked with

that of Damien, bringing resentment from those who accused him of trying to take Damien's place. The accusations hurt him deeply. Daily he visited Damien's grave,
kneeling in prayer. He was hoping that he would be
buried next to Damien. Once, during the renovation of St.
Philomenas, he had shown Damien a place in the base-
ment of the Church which he felt would make a perfect
crypt for him. Damien told him he was certain that the
Church hierarchy would not approve of such a plan.

Although he thought of death, like Damien, death
held no fear for him. The end was a long way off, as it
seemed Dutton would outlast them all.

Changes were taking place at a dizzying pace. Brother
Joseph could not keep up with the comings and goings of
everyone. After the death of Superintendent Meyers,
there was a series of short term resident superintendents,
none of whom was effective in controlling the settlement.
Dutton carefully avoided becoming involved in any of the
politics and kept to his routine and schedule.

Many patients were moved to Kalaupapa leaving
behind their dwellings, storehouses and other buildings.
All that was left was the Baldwin Home, with the boys
and older men under the care of Dutton and the Brothers
of the Sacred Hearts.

Dr. William Goodhue took over as resident physician and remained in that post for twenty-three years. Father Wendelin left and was replaced by Father Maxime
Andre. St. Francis Church was virtually destroyed by fire
and had to be rebuilt. Dutton was glad that Damien had

not lived to see his hard work go up in flames.

Dutton was often visited by Dr. Goodhue who kept him informed of any major changes in the treatment of patients. Goodhue had told him that the United States government was charging the United States Public Health Service, once known as the Marine Hospital Service, to erect a National Leprosy Investigation Station in Kalawao. Many Public Health doctors were expressing an interest in leprosy and wanted a suitable place to carry on research where patients would be available to serve as volunteer subjects for experimentation.

Surveyors scrambled over a large tract of land adjacent to the Baldwin Home. Soon Chinese workmen were imported to take down all the unused buildings and scorch the land in preparation for building the Station. Boatloads of lumber and equipment started to arrive, much to the delight and interest of the patients who lined up daily to watch all the proceedings.

Later, when full plans were made public, Brother Joseph was sure that the idea would meet with failure. The Station was to be surrounded by two fences, one inside the other to control the entry of "clean" and "unclean" persons. There would be strict isolation between staff and patients. All patients would be volunteers but they would have to agree to be set apart from the rest of the settlement and live in separate quarters within the Station Hospital. It reminded Dutton of the old days when the resident physician would have no physical contact with the patients and would leave their medicines on the fence to be picked up. He knew the Hawaiians would never stand for these plans but he kept his thoughts to himself. He was not about to interfere and would let time provide all the answers and solve all the problems.

When the patients asked why the workers were burning the ground, Brother told them it was an easy way to clear the brush. He did not tell them that one of the purposes was to rid the entire area of any possible germs from those who had lived there.

Dutton was notified that the director of the new Station was to be Dr. Walter Brinkerhoff of Harvard University, and the man to oversee the project was Leighton Gibson. Congress had already approved the grant to construct, equip and staff the Station. Everyone was bewildered to see two beautiful houses being built. One was for Dr. Brinkerhoff and his family and the other was for Mr. Gibson, his wife, Emma, and their son. Eventually Brother Joseph would get to know the Gibsons quite well.

The plans for the Station were staggering. Not only would there be the best and most expensive equipment for laboratories, there would be a power house for electricity and an ice plant. In addition there was special housing for laboratory animals. It crossed Dutton's mind when he saw the masses of equipment, how difficult it had been for Damien to obtain a few supplies.

Separate housing was provided for the Chinese workmen who were forbidden to have anything to do with the patients at Kalawao. Once the fences were in place the volunteer patients could not leave the Station nor could any outsider enter.

In January, 1909, most of the buildings were finished. Brother Dutton was sitting on his veranda when he saw the inter-island steamer approaching the shore. This was unusual as most of the time it docked at Kalaupapa. He walked down to the rocky ledge and watched as the steamer launched a small row boat. A woman in a large, billowy skirt climbed into the boat, followed by three men. Several Chinese workers had been assembled on shore with chairs to carry the party over the rocks to the Station. As the row boat came close to shore, it was necessary for the passengers to jump from the boat on to the rocks. Dutton was amused as the young lady, showing no fear, jumped and landed upright on the rocks. The Chinese clapped and howled in glee. They had been sure she would fall into the water.

Dutton muttered, "That is one plucky lady." He gave no greeting, aware of the desire of the newcomers to have no contact with the leprosy patients or those who worked with them. He turned and went back to his cottage. That night he heard the sound of a violin playing tuneful Scottish airs. The strains floated across the Station, permeating his cottage. They must be a fun loving group, he decided.

A few days after the Gibsons arrived, a kona came pouring down the cliffs. Dutton, used to these by now, was sure it must be a frightening experience for the newcomers. After the storm passed, he noticed that some of the newly erected buildings were blown off their foundations—even the hospital. It took a great deal of effort with block and tackle to put the buildings upright.

Another innovation was the installation of a primitive telephone system making it easier to communicate between buildings of the Baldwin Home and Kalaupapa.

Dutton seldom used it. His hearing was failing him and often there was static on the line. Most of all, it afforded no private conversations. When one phone rang, they all rang and everyone could listen in. However, he was tempted to telephone his new neighbors but on second thought, it would be better if they made the first move—and it soon came!

Mrs. Gibson made a frantic telephone call when she was confronted by a group of patients who were at her gate mingling with some of her Chinese servants. They would not listen to her when she tried to make them go away. Brother Dutton told her he would send the police. They came immediately and peace was restored. He sent her a note which began "Dear Next Door Neighbor," and he addressed them as such ever after.

Before coming to Kalawao, Mrs. Gibson had studied the history of the settlement and knew of the work of Father Damien, Brother Dutton and Mother Marianne. Although she had imposed her own strict rules about mingling with those who administered to leprosy patients, she was impressed with Dutton, his neat attire and his military bearing as he strode about the settlement.

With her husband's permission, she invited him to dinner on Thanksgiving Day. He was delighted to accept. Putting on clean clothes, he arrived to be warmly welcomed. He did not offer his hand nor did they. He admired their young son, but from a distance, and made no effort to go near the boy. The family was immediately at ease with his demeanor.

His first glance at the house and its beauty intrigued him. It was luxuriously furnished and so different from his own sparse, but neat, cottage. The floors were painted black to lessen the reflection of the sun. The lanai screen was made of copper to resist the salt air and glassed in with sliding doors. The furniture was made of the finest Hawaiian woods and each room was blocked with glass doors. The stories Dutton had heard from several sources that they had their own dynamo for making electricity were true, as he saw fans everywhere. They also had their own water supply and a large "ice box" powered by a water pump.

The table was set with fine linens and the best china. Lovely flower arrangements were scattered about. Brother Joseph felt out of place but the kind attention and hospitality of the Gibsons relieved him of his strangeness. It was the first Thanksgiving he had celebrated in many years and he savored every minute. The meal was delicious, especially the turkey, and the pumpkin pie topped with ice cream was the perfect end to the festive dinner. Dutton made a mental note to look into obtaining equipment to make ice cream—how his boys would love that.

The Gibsons had their own flock of chickens, several horses and a herd of dairy cows. Mrs. Gibson did not have to cook, clean or do dishes. They had numerous Chinese servants who were courteous, polite, and most willing to please.

What Dutton was interested in was the Post Office they had set up in their home. Their mail did not have go to Kalaupapa post office where it would be sterilized. Instead, every week a worker would ride to the dock to fetch the mail without it having to go through the leprosy settlement. Mrs. Gibson offered Dutton the use of their post office for his mail. He would no longer have to wait for it to be delivered from Kalaupapa. Dutton accepted the offer immediately. There were times when the amount of mail he received would fill two wheelbarrows. Mrs. Gibson was most impressed when this first occurred.

He thought he would like to return the hospitality shown him by inviting them to Mass on Christmas Day at St. Philomenas and sent the invitation:

My dear Friends and Next Door Neighbors,
The Church looks very pretty. Wish you could take a peep or step inside. It cannot, however, be half as pretty as Midnight Mass with the many lights. If you should come this way, I could go over with you. The weather is a little unfavorable though.
Am wondering if you have met the Sisters of the Bishop Home. Would you like to? They are nice. If you wish, I may suggest to the Mother.
—Joseph Dutton

The Gibsons replied that they appreciated the invitation but the rules of the Station prohibited them from entering into the settlement where leprosy patients lived. He was disappointed but was understanding of their fear.

Later, he wrote again and asked if he might bring the Sisters to meet Mrs. Gibson. He said they would be most interested to see their modern, sanitary plumbing. They would hardly believe it worked by merely pressing a button. Mrs. Gibson wrote back that she would love to have the Sisters come but the risk involved was too great. Her small son was in the crawling stage and would be susceptible to any germs they might bring.

Brother Joseph was disappointed and again felt

that with this attitude, their mission would fail. But he kept this opinion to himself. He would visit them occasionally, always aware of his place, and never intruded on their privacy. They invited him for Christmas and he took little gifts he had obtained from friends, always with the assurance that they were not handled by patients. While he enjoyed the days he was with them, he was anxious to get back to his little cottage and the simple life he had chosen to live.

Often Mrs. Gibson asked him about the plantings, the orchards and the attractive bushes surrounding the area. There were papayas, peaches, plums, apples, sour cherries, as well as guavas, bananas, grapes, pineapples and coconuts. Pheasants could be found nesting in the vegetable patches. She especially liked the ginger blossoms with their pungent odor and the hua tree, about the size of a hawthorn. Its blossoms would turn from a lemon color in the morning to pink in the afternoon and an intense red in the evening. He told her of the seeds he had obtained through the largess of Notre Dame University and described to her how bleak it had been when he first arrived and started the beautification.

Finally the day came for the Station to open and receive its first volunteer patients for the research program. Out of 700 patients, only two showed up. It was exactly as Brother Dutton had predicted. All the gleaming, new equipment, the luxurious quarters and the highly qualified technical staff could not compensate for the strict rules set up by the authorities. The workers wore masks, gloves and protective gowns. The patients were isolated in small rooms and were forbidden to make contact with any of the workers. When they left the Station, word spread throughout the settlement that it was a "house of horrors" and they were being used as guinea pigs. The patients preferred to have their freedom, roam without restraint throughout the settlement and communicate with one another. The staff at the Station was baffled. They could not understand why the patients did not want to help them find a cure.

With no volunteers, Washington decided to close down the Station. The buildings were boarded up and some of the expensive equipment was crated and sent to Honolulu. There were no electric lights or other amenities, once the engineer left the Station.

Before they left, Leighton and Emma Gibson had a last farewell dinner with Brother Dutton. He expressed sadness that he was losing his "next door neighbors." They continued to communicate sporadically and in one letter, Mrs. Gibson wrote that Kalawao was the most beautiful spot she had ever seen in all her life.

CHAPTER SIXTEEN

I**N JULY**, 1908, in his 65th year, Brother Joseph received one of the highest honors ever given to anyone. He had read that the Atlantic Fleet, known as the Great White Fleet, was being sent around the world by President Theodore Roosevelt. Teddy, as he was called, had as his motto, "Speak softly but carry a big stick." Sending the fleet around the world was a way of showing the power of the American Armed Forces. Everyone would see this spectacle of might, and it would give second thoughts to those seeking dominance over the United States.

When Dutton read this, his mind was awhirl and he wondered if it would be possible for the fleet to pass by Molokai on its way to Honolulu. He wrote to the Governor of Hawaii and to several influential friends in Washington. Word reached the President who had heard of both Father Damien and Brother Dutton. He wrote that it would be a good idea to let these poor outcasts, now under the flag of the United States, know that they were not forgotten by a sympathetic and compassionate nation.

When the fleet was in San Francisco, Dutton was notified that they would change course and sail past the settlement. He did not discuss this with the boys or anyone else until just before the great event.

Each year, the Grand Army of the Republic composed of Civil War veterans, to which he belonged,
passed a resolution at their annual convention commend-
ing Brother Dutton and sending him a United States flag.
He had saved these flags for special occasions. Early in
the day that the fleet was to pass by, he raised the flag to
the top of the flagpole. He went back to his cottage, sat at
his desk and commenced writing.

Before long he heard a thunder of footsteps running up the winding path. A dozen of the younger boys
were shouting and pounding on the front door.

"Brother Joseph, come out, come on out. They
are coming."

"Who's coming?" he shouted back.

"The ships, Brother, the ships! There are a hundred of them."

He smiled, opening the door as the excited boys
crowded around him.

"All right now boys, take it easy. You mustn't run
so fast."

He tugged at his flowing white beard and with a
twinkle in his bright blue eyes said, "Are you sure there
are a hundred?"

The boys grinned sheepishly.

"We couldn't count but there are many."

"Let's go to the flagpole and we shall salute the
ships as they sail by."

Dutton was surprised to see that the shore was
lined with people, their hands shading their eyes as they
gazed out to sea.

It was a bright, sunny morning but Dutton would not let the boys go down to the rocky ledge for fear that in their excitement they would fall into the water. He had brought his binoculars with him. The boys took turns looking through the glasses. Far off in the distance could be seen the waves as the bows of the long line of ships broke the azure blue and turquoise green of the Pacific.

Gradually the Fleet came into full view and Dutton said to the boys, "When you see me lower the flag as the first ship goes by, I want you all to stand at attention and salute. They have binoculars on board, and can see you, too. This is the United States Great White Atlantic Fleet steaming by to honor us."

The crews on board the ships had been told that they were going to pass by the leper settlement where Father Damien had worked side by side with Brother Dutton and that Brother Dutton, a Civil War veteran, was still living on Molokai. All were to salute him and the patients as the colors were lowered.

The first battleship to come into full view was the flagship, the USS Connecticut. On board was Admiral Charles Stillman Sperry, commander of the Great White Fleet. As the ship passed by, Dutton slowly lowered the Stars and Stripes and raised it again in salute. Looking through his binoculars he could see that the Admiral's flag returned the salute.

The battleships were accompanied by destroyers and cruisers. It was an awesome sight. As each battleship passed by, Dutton called off the name of the State for which it was named. There was the USS Vermont, where he was born, the USS Tennessee, where he was received into the Church, the USS Georgia where he fought in battles to save the Union, the USS Kentucky where he spent time in the monastery at Gethsemane. At one point he swayed and the Brothers in attendance tried to make him sit down, but he refused. For more than two hours he had stood at attention until the last ship passed by.

Everyone kept staring until the entire fleet had disappeared over the horizon. The crowd of patients and staff lining the shore slowly returned to their homes. Dutton, physically and emotionally exhausted went back to his cottage and sank into his chair.

The sail-by had accomplished its purpose. Those who had doubts about the annexation of Hawaii by the United States began to realize how they were protected by a mighty government. More importantly, it was a government that cared even for these who had been abandoned and shunned by others.

Dutton, now at his desk, picked up his pen to write the Admiral of the Fleet a letter of thanks. He wanted to put his thoughts down on paper before they faded. It was a long letter, typical of Brother Dutton, short sentences and simple phrases. It was like a letter one would write to a close friend, not worrying about its correctness or grammar. He started off by addressing the Admiral without using his military title:

My dear Sir:

That splendid fleet of United States battleships coming from San Francisco to Honolulu, turning from the big road, coming down the lane, passing in parade in our front yard along the full extent of the Molokai leper settlement, under the towering rear wall over two thousand feet high, which is flanked by majestic headlands and backed by a reserve of mountains that are much higher! . . .

In another sentence he wrote:

. . . Thus do I express their [the patients] most hearty thanks. Personally it is a gratitude almost beyond expression. As thinking of myself, 'Did anyone ever deserve so little and get so much?' There has been everywhere in the settlement, so far as I have any knowledge, the greatest possible praise. If anything is lacking, it is a new dictionary to supply words for this. . . .

One sentence must have amused the Admiral:

. . . Thus precisely on time and in exact order, with grave and serious movement, not like the 'cute' little steamer that clicks its heels and scatters the dust, but like a powerful warrior in battle array came the sixteen. . . .

When the Admiral read the letter he realized that Dutton was a great patriot and he wrote back:

Dear Sir:

It gives me great pleasure to receive your letter of 'gratitude and goodwill' expressing your appreciation of the visit of the United States Atlantic fleet.

Anticipating the interest and pleasure of the people of the leper settlement in witnessing the unusual spectacle of a fleet of this magnitude parading before them, your suggestion was regarded as a most happy one and there was never any doubt that it would be carried out, if circumstances permitted.

On behalf of the officers and men of the fleet, I extend to you and to those with you in your splendid work, and to the people of the settlement, my best wishes for the prosperity of all.

The island and the settlement were a beautiful sight as we steamed by almost under the shadow of the mountains and I thank you for the photographs of the scenery and of yourself.

It gives me great pleasure to send you herewith a photograph of the Commander-in-Chief as a token of respect and regard.

Both letters were published in the papers in Honolulu and also throughout the United States. The story resulted in another avalanche of mail. It was a day Dutton would never forget. A day in which a nation had shown its gratitude for his patriotism and service. More honors were eventually to come his way, including the naming of a school in Beloit, Wisconsin, as the "Brother Dutton School." He received apostolic blessings from the Pope, and several books were written about his life.

Like Damien, both men had made every effort to avoid any praise for their sacrifices. It was a perfect example of the adage that honors elude those who seek them, but honors will seek those deserving, despite their efforts to remain hidden.

When war was declared on Germany in 1917, Dutton's patriotism flared anew.

He contacted several members of his old regiment asking if it would be feasible for them to join the army with him as a special unit but they were all beyond the age of eligibility. Frustrated, he found ways to assist in the war effort, first by selling war bonds and then by collecting for the Red Cross from the staff and the patients, who in spite of having little money gained from the odd jobs they did around the settlement, were anxious to contribute. It was not enough however—he wanted to do something personally. Spying his binoculars he decided, 'If I can't go, I can send these and part of me will be in the battle.'

He quickly dispatched them to the War Department and was delighted to receive a letter from the Assistant Secretary of the Navy, Franklin D. Roosevelt, assuring him that the binoculars were in use on a battleship. After the war they were returned to him together with a certificate. He was satisfied that he had done his duty for Uncle Sam.

In August, 1918, Mother Marianne, after suffering a serious illness for many months, passed away. Although they had not met recently, Brother Dutton had been in contact with her. He admired her deeply and felt the loss. She was buried not far from the monument erected to Damien in Kalaupapa close to the Damien Road. Mother Marianne's Franciscan Sisters continued to work at Molokai and are there to this very day.

One by one, all of Dutton's companions from the early days were leaving him. The flow of leprosy patients to Molokai slowed down. While new cases were reported, there was nowhere near the epidemic that existed which had brought about the strict law of segregation.

Each year with a generous government, improvements continued to be made at the leprosy settlement. Electricity was installed, although Dutton refused to have it in his cottage. Roads were built for the few automobiles that arrived, mostly for the government workers, yet Dutton refused to ride in one. The patients were receiving news from the outside world with the introduction of radios, but Dutton preferred to use his own hand-cranked Victrola, playing Strauss waltzes which he loved.

The Brothers took over most of his work as he continued with his writing which he still preferred to do by candlelight. He wrote in a bold, firm hand with no sign of a quiver. His abundant correspondence no doubt attributed to an awakened interest and there were many visitors now, from all over the world, who wished to see this model leprosarium.

There was still no breakthrough in the treatment of leprosy. Ineffective as it was, chaulmoogra oil was the only preferred method of treatment. The patients still developed nodules filled with pus and running sores which had to be cleaned constantly and bandaged. Deformities occurred with no reconstructive surgery available.

Dutton bragged about how little sleep he needed, three or four hours a night, but failed to mention the periods of rest he took during the day. His abundant hair was now totally white and he was tanned from long years in the sun. At age eighty-one, he still had his lithe figure and walked erect. He wore steel-rimmed glasses and although the sight in one eye was almost gone, his mind was as alert as ever. Some likened him to a picture of Saint Joseph and it pleased him greatly when anyone mentioned this, for Saint Joseph was his patron saint. He felt contrite and in spite of the pleas of Damien and others to forget his past so-called sinful life, whenever he was interviewed, he would mention those years.

It was necessary to add another room to Brother Joseph's cottage to accommodate the accumulation of correspondence he had saved. The letters were packed in neat bundles, tied with string and stored in boxes which were scattered everywhere. When he entertained visitors, his furnishings were still only two chairs, his battered old desk and a table. There was a small statue of Saint Francis on his desk, a large American flag pinned to one wall and on the other, a map of the world. He preferred to sit with his guests on his veranda overlooking his favorite scene of the blending of the lofty mountains and the surf rolling in below. With his memory still so keen, he would carry on fascinating conversations, and enjoyed talking of his days with Damien. The depth of his love and admiration for Damien grew with each passing year, and he would say that he was hoping he would soon be with him. Those who came to visit, as well as the Brothers, marveled at his recall of names, dates, places and incidences from years past.

Dutton had not been away from Kalawao for thirty-seven years and in that time had read only one book of fiction, "Pigs is Pigs" by Ellis Parker Butler. He never accepted one penny in salary and the small pension he received from his war years was given to charity. All the personal money that came with the correspondence was spent on the boys in the Baldwin Home.

He had been inducted into the Third Order of Saint Francis in 1892. He also belonged to many organizations: Association of the Trappists, the Holy Name Society, the Wisconsin Grand Army of the Republic, the National Council of the Economic League of the United States, the National Association for Constitutional Government, the Academy of Political Science at Columbia University, the Anti-Saloon League, and the Humane Society of Honolulu.

When he reached the age of eighty-seven, he was asked how he maintained his vigorous health. "I think the main reason is plain living. I live an exceedingly simple life here, and always have. I eat simple food and wear simple clothing. I have not a worry in the world—years ago I ceased worrying. In my opinion, worry will kill a person quicker than disease. I do not use tobacco, alcohol, tea or coffee, which I gave up many years past. I get plenty of fresh air, warm sunshine, and exercise. I have regular work to do and I have many good friends to write to and receive letters from." That was Dutton's recipe for longevity.

One of the Brothers asked him if he had ever grown tired of his work on Molokai. Dutton smiled, "No, I never grow tired of my work. One never grows tired in Christ's service, you know. The work here fascinated me from the very beginning. It continues to do so today and as for leaving the island of Molokai, the thought never enters my head. My life work is here on this little peninsula and among these people whom I have come to love. The rest of the world has absolutely no attraction for me." No wonder he had a statue of Saint Francis on his desk—he also lived a life of simplicity.

It was his ardent devotion to the flag that almost brought his death. Each morning and evening he would raise and lower the flag, even if he were not feeling well. The Brothers often remarked that they could set their clocks by this ritual. One evening, he went out into a raging storm to lower the flag. He suddenly became weak and slumped to the ground. Two Brothers who were watching from the Home rushed out to help lift him up.

He was shaking and kept repeating, "The flag, the flag, it must be lowered!"

They tried to move him to his cottage but Dutton resisted until one of the Brothers had lowered the flag. They took off his wet clothes and covered him with blankets for he was shivering and his forehead burning with fever.

"He must have been ill for some time and didn't tell us," said one of the Brothers.

The doctor came and pronounced that Dutton was suffering from pneumonia. They tried to keep him in bed, even threatening to tie him down if he did not listen.

He would say, "What am I doing in bed? Let me up, there is too much work to be done."

But each time he tried, the exertion would cause him to fall back exhausted and he felt his strength was leaving him. Remarkably he recovered but the illness left him very weak. Deep in his heart he realized his days were numbered.

On one of his visits, the doctor brought up the subject of sending him to the hospital in Honolulu for a complete checkup and rest. Dutton made no reply but hunched his shoulders and the doctor, noticing, tried again. There was one angle to which the old man would be vulnerable.

"You would not want to collapse suddenly and be a burden or bedridden for the rest of your life, would you?"

Brother Joseph blinked, the light seemed to hurt his eyes. More than anything else he dreaded to be a burden to anyone and not be able to take care of himself.

"Well, doctor," and his head shook, "I guess you have the old man pinned down. What is it that you think I should do?"

The doctor relaxed, relieved that it had been easier than he thought.

"It is your eyes. With a simple operation we can remove the cataracts and you will be able to see almost as good as new again."

Brother Dutton perked up. "To see again—I could resume my correspondence and take care of myself?"

Assured by the doctor, he brightened and reminded himself, 'Here I have been preaching all these years to the boys to do what the doctor says and old fool that I am, I have been fighting the doctor myself.'

He looked directly at the doctor. "If I have to go to Honolulu, how long will I be there?"

"Not longer than a week or so." But in his heart the doctor knew better. "The trip will do you good and you will be able to talk face to face with many who have written to you."

Dutton was too weak to argue. The decision made, there was no hesitation. The order was given and the old soldier would obey. He had vowed never to leave Molokai. It had been forty-four years since he said good-bye to the land he loved and sailed for Hawaii.

"Could it be," he thought, "that I have not done enough? Was there yet another sacrifice that God was asking of him? Was he to die among strangers?"

More than anything, he wished to die as Damien had, surrounded by his own, his boys.

While he found the parting hard, he was determined not to show it. Almost impatiently he cut the ties that bound him to Kalawao. As the steamer pulled out of the harbor at Kalaupapa bound for Honolulu, the boys' band struck up the *Aloha*. Through tear-dimmed eyes he could just make out the cliffs of Molokai. He did not know it, but he would not see them again. The exile was returning to the world.

It was a dazed old man who came down the gangplank, half carried by his stalwart companions, Brothers Louis and Luger, detailed from the Baldwin Home to accompany him to Honolulu. Brother Joseph was wreathed in leis presented according to custom when the pilot boat met the steamer.

He had spent a restless night on board. The wind screeching and the slap of the waves against the bow of the boat, though different from the pitiful, human wailing sounds of his first voyage, gave him that same feeling of loneliness. He had given up his friends to come to Molokai those long years ago, now he was giving up his friends again on Molokai.

A photographer pressed forward, then a second, and a third. "Look this way, Brother," one of them urged as he focused his camera on the bewildered Dutton. Scores of dignitaries and curious onlookers shouted, "Smile, Brother Dutton, smile!" With his rheumy eyes he gazed from one to the other. What was it all about? The furthest thing from his mind was the thought that there had been anything unusual about himself, neither did it occur to him that he was something of a celebrity. He raised his head, obediently smiled for the cameras, then urged the Brothers to get him away.

"Get on with it," he said somewhat testily. "This is too much attention for an old man." The world was pressing on the very soul of the exile.

An automobile from St. Francis Hospital drove on to the dock. The Brothers pushed a path through the crowd and lifted Brother Joseph into the front seat. They started off with a jerk and Brother Joseph held on to the handle of the door. Everything was a blur to him as they passed along the busy streets of the city lined with stores and office buildings. The old charm of the city that he remembered was lost. Buses and autos honked their horns and Dutton, turning to his companions in the back seat, chuckled, "What a racket! It's a good thing that I am almost deaf for I think I would go crazy with all this hubbub."

On the outskirts of the city at last, the old Honolulu began to appear with all its beauty. The streets were quiet and lined with tall, waving palms. Houses were blanketed in flowers and ferns. The road wound round toward the high, green mountains that served as a backdrop for this 'Pearl of the Pacific.'

Driving up to the entrance of the hospital under a large green and white awning, Brother Louis remarked, "We're here at last."

Brother Dutton was fingering his rosary. "I never thought we would make it." And he sighed in relief.

The Sisters were waiting for him at the entrance, An attendant helped him into a wheelchair and the Sister Administrator came forward holding out her hand and draping him with more flowery leis.

"Welcome to St. Francis, " she said heartily.

He peered up at her smiling face, distinguishing only the outline of the linens around her head and the flowing veil. She was a Franciscan.

"I hope I will not be too much bother to you, Sister."

"A bother? Of course not. We are honored that you are with us. This is your home for as long as necessary. Our dear Mother Marianne had a great regard for you."

She then led the way into the hospital. They had prepared the best room, with a wide veranda overlooking the harbor. In the distance was Diamond Head. Brother Louis prepared Dutton for bed and as soon as his head touched the pillow he gave a sigh and fell into a deep sleep. He was utterly exhausted. Although Brother Louis remained with him, a Sister Antonia was assigned as his personal nurse. That evening when he awakened, she took his temperature.

"What did you say your name was, Sister?" He was almost shouting, the thermometer dropping to the bedspread.

"Sister Antonia, Brother."

"Sister Anthony. That's a nice name."

"No, Brother," and now she was shouting, "Sister Antonia.

"Oh."

"Now I must take your temperature. Please keep your mouth closed."

He mumbled under his breath, "All this fuss. You would think I was sick."

Sister smiled, having heard all about him.

In the days that followed the surgeons removed the cataracts from his eyes. It was not as simple an operation as they had told him. Smart, that doctor in Kalawao, Dutton said to himself after the operation. *If he had told me what it was going to be like, I would never have come here.* He had to keep his head propped rigidly between two sandbags so that hemorrhaging would not occur and he had to be fed through a straw. But despite all this he did not lose his cheerfulness. He awoke at 5 a.m. every morning, singing, and would joke with the Sisters and the attendants. When possible he would be wheeled to the chapel for morning Mass but when he was too weak, the chaplain brought the sacred Host to him in his room.

Word had reached his hundreds of friends and his room was filled with so many flowers he had them distributed to others throughout the hospital. Messages poured in and reporters tried to make appointments for interviews, but the Sisters kept him isolated from the public.

His mind wandered at times. Once he surprised Brother Louis by asking for a radio to listen to the ball game. This was in contrast to the time at the Baldwin Home when they had invited Brother Joseph into the recreation room to listen to the radio. The reception had been extremely bad and it squeaked and howled. He had stomped out with the remark that he would never listen to that 'box full of noise' again.

His heart was slowing down and he had to be supported by pillows as he was no longer able to sit up by himself. He was becoming a wasted old man. The cataract operation was a limited success; however, he was able to see a little clearer. Sister Antonia, thinking he was asleep, tiptoed into the room and took up the chart hanging at the foot of his bed. He watched her and seeing the sudden look of concern on her face, said, "What does it say?"

She did not answer for a moment, then replied brightly, "It says you are doing fine." Quickly she asked the Lord for forgiveness in concealing the truth. "In fact you are so much better than I am, I ought to trade places with you," she added.

She noticed that he had his rosary in his hands. She had not seen him with it before.

"Won't you sit by me for a while, Sister?" His voice was almost a whisper.

"Of course, Brother."

Sister Antonia pulled up a chair beside the bed. She had many pressing duties to attend to but she knew that Brother wanted to talk, she also knew that nursing was more than giving needles and taking temperatures. A good nurse was a good listener, and listening had great healing power. He reached out and she took his hand.

"I don't think these old bones of mine will ever get back to my boys, will they Sister." His voice quavered. "That is my only regret, otherwise I am quite prepared for death. In fact I am looking forward to meeting my old friends, Father Damien and Mother Marianne."

There was nothing she could say to cajole him. He closed his eyes and drank from the fountain of his memories.

"I haven't done enough."

"Brother, you mustn't say that, you have done

more than you can possibly know. What greater work than teaching children, molding their characters and preparing them for the world. The boys who came under your influence were lucky boys. You have taught them things that will make them fine young men. You gave them hope when there was none. You were a father to them. They will never forget you."

"I hope they won't, Sister."

Dutton's eyes fastened on the crucifix hanging on the wall.

"What I meant, Sister, was that I have not suffered enough to merit the salvation of my soul. You and I know what suffering is, don't we. You see it every day here in the hospital and I have seen it on Molokai. It is good to suffer if we offer it all up to God. Otherwise we waste it."

"That is true, and there is prayer. Prayer is the greatest power on earth."

"Yes, Sister." He was drifting off. "Prayer—pray for me."

It was the month of Saint Joseph, March 1931, just a few weeks before his 88th birthday. Saint Joseph was closer to him now than ever before. Brother Dutton felt he was sharing Joseph's flight into Egypt, or did he look at his worn, calloused hands and feel that, as with his carpenter patron, his work was finished.

Two days later, after his talk with Sister Antonia, he received the last Sacraments.

Death came suddenly. Twenty-four hours of unconsciousness and the exile was home.

After a solemn High Mass in the cathedral at Honolulu, celebrated by the Bishop and church dignitaries with the Governor of Hawaii and officials in attendance, his body was carried to the waiting steamer. They placed it on deck and the casket was draped with the American flag. The boat's flag flew at half mast as it steamed slowly toward the cliffs. He was returning to his home at Kalawao.

On the shore at Kalawao, Old Glory dipped in salute and then was raised slowly to half mast. Brother Joseph's friends and co-workers waited with his boys. They would give him more honors; they would give him their love.

Under Damien's pandanus tree a freshly opened grave awaited.

Forty-two years had elapsed since Brother Dutton shaped Damien's grave and vowed to his friend that he would remain and carry on his work. He had kept that promise. He had fulfilled Damien's dreams and more besides. Now his body was back to be buried in soil hallowed by their common sacrifice. Another generation was here now and times were changing.

The respectful crowd, in mourning for Dutton, was in striking contrast to the hopeless outcasts who had marched to Damien's grave. A contrast as sharp as the shadows etched by the rocks on to the glaring sands in the noonday sun.

The prayers in the Church were over and the moment had come. Priests, Sisters, Brothers, doctors and staff—everyone who could walk was there. The young scouts, as Dutton had taught them, filed by as an honor guard, stiff in military stance. The sun glistened on the raised bugle as the leader sounded the first, clear notes of Taps. Those sad, poignant notes rose over the grave, swelling, filling the air. From the cliffs came the echo, 'Farewell, soldier,' they seemed to say, 'Farewell friend.' The listening hearts sobbed. A breeze ruffled a waving palm, settled in silent waiting for the last, sweet note, then silence again. A silence that throbbed and hurt. A silence that choked the throat. The multitudes silently filed by as the Blessed Earth fell on the flower decked coffin. Each mourner left part of himself in the open grave with their teacher, their counselor, their nurse, their Brother. In silence, they turned and left him.

A lone figure remained, standing on crutches with only one leg. It was Paul! He had grown older, the disease deforming him, so that for the most part of the last few years he had to remain bedridden. He stood there for a long time. No one could pull him away until finally he sank to the ground. Two Brothers gently carried him back to the hospital, as he left behind his friends:

Damien, Belgian, priest, martyr of charity;
Dutton, Yankee, patriot, convert-penitent;

and now side by side, together they awaited eternity.

EPILOGUE

For FIVE YEARS the two Josephs lay within a few feet of each other beside St. Philomenas Church. The pandanus tree, finally dead, had been uprooted, its wood cut into small pieces and distributed all over the world as souvenirs.

In 1936, Damien's wish to lie next to his beloved church and Dutton's wish to lie next to Damien was shattered. The people of Belgium wanted Damien's body returned to his homeland and King Leopold III requested the help of President Franklin D. Roosevelt to grant this desire of the Belgian people.

When the Hawaiians found out about this, there was an immediate uproar. Although no patients from Damien's time were still living, he was still known as their Kamiano. The Belgians prevailed and Damien's body was exhumed. It was remarkably preserved and was placed in a new casket made of Koa, a Hawaiian acacia wood that had always been reserved for members of the royal family and high dignitaries.

The mourners surrounding Damien's open grave sent up ear-piercing wails of anguish and chanted old warrior funeral songs. Some were standing on Dutton's grave and said they felt movement beneath their feet which frightened them. They thought Dutton, too, was protesting.

Damien's body was placed aboard a U.S. Navy plane and as it took off, soaring over the cliffs, the entire assembled group sang the heart rending *Aloha oe.*

The song was written by the imprisoned Queen Liliuokalani when the monarchy was overthrown and the United States took control of Hawaii:

> *Farewell to you, farewell to you,*
> *O fragrance in the blue depths*
> *One fond embrace and I leave*
> *To meet again.*

In Honolulu, there were solemn ceremonies in the cathedral, where Damien had been ordained. The highest ranking dignitaries were present, both military, civil and religious. Thousands of people lined the streets. With full military escort he was placed aboard the Army Transport ship *Republic,* headed for San Francisco.

On arrival there, the body was again escorted through crowds lining the streets, and army bombers flew in salute overhead.

Damien was then taken to Panama where the Belgian training ship, *Mercator,* received his body and headed for Antwerp in full sail. At the dock it was met by King Leopold. Another huge crowd had gathered. Cannons boomed and the bells of Antwerp tolled mournfully. A hearse drawn by six white horses with black plumes carried the bier to the cathedral.

At eventide, the hearse commenced the journey through the countryside, past his birthplace at Tremeloo to Louvain. Damien was finally laid to rest in the crypt of St. Joseph's chapel, a shrine dedicated to his patron saint and maintained by the Fathers of the Sacred Hearts.

At Kalawao, dirt had been thrown back into the empty hole but a beautiful white cross, dedicated to Damien's memory remained in place. Just a few feet away, the other Joseph rested under a monument to his memory.

Now there was only one Joseph on Molokai.

The original ceremony of the beatification of Damien had to be postponed due to the illness of Pope John Paul II, but on June 4, 1995, His Holiness conducted the ceremonies of beatification bringing Damien one step closer to sainthood. He would now be known as Blessed Damien.

A delegation of Hawaiians travelled to Belgium to participate in the beatification ceremonies and took with them a Koa case lined with black velvet, to receive the remains of Damien's right hand. This would be carried back to his gravesite in Kalawao where it would be buried with high honors.

It was highly significant that his hand would be chosen as a relic to be returned to Molokai.

It was his hand that had been blessed with holy oils on the day of his ordination; his hand that had baptized so many infants and converts; his hand that had joined so many in matrimony and his hand that anointed the dying. Like Joseph, the carpenter, it was his hand that held the tools that built so many churches, even before he was assigned to Molokai, and his hand that built St. Francis and several churches up on the pali, as well as his beloved St. Philomenas at Kalawao.

It was his hand that held the hammer in building so many dwellings for the victims of leprosy; his hand that held the plane to smooth out the wood for their coffins; his hand that cleansed and bandaged their running sores; that amputated rotting flesh and embraced them in friendship and love; his hand that placed the Body of Christ between their swollen lips; and it was the hand that had reached out and taken Brother Dutton's when he first stepped ashore, on the day Damien had told Paul in the buggy that "it was to be a special day."

And now, once again, there were
Two Josephs on Molokai!

Brother Joseph Dutton

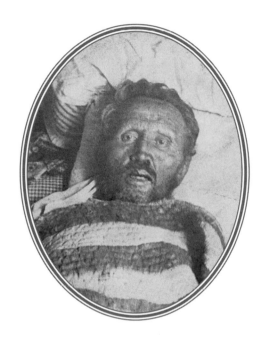

Father Damien

LEPROSY UPDATE

LEPROSY: PATIENT CARE AND RESEARCH
PAST, PRESENT AND PROSPECTS

by

Wayne M. Meyers, M.D., Ph.D.
Registrar for Leprosy and Chief, Mycobacteriology
Armed Forces Institute of Pathology
Washington, District of Columbia
and
Research Affiliate
Tulane Regional Primate Research Center
Tulane University, Covington, Louisiana

INTRODUCTION AND BACKGROUND

The history of the management and control of leprosy is filled with accounts of efforts that often were well-intentioned but went awry. Such were the events that took place in Hawaii. Attempting to halt the epidemic of leprosy sweeping through The Islands, especially among the Hawaiians, King Kamehameha V on January 3, 1865, approved an act to prevent the spread of leprosy to "secure the isolation and seclusion of such leprous persons as . . . may by being at large, cause the spread of leprosy." The place chosen to secure the seclusion was on a peninsula of the island of Molokai surrounded on three sides by rough seas and on the fourth by a high pali (cliff). This peninsula was made up of three sections: Kalaupapa, Kalawao and Makanalua. The first patients landed on January 6, 1866. Arthur Mouritz in his book, *The Path of the Destroyer*, published in 1916, recounts one consequence of this act in what he called "The Leper War on Kauai." This one-time physician to the "Leper Settlement" on Molokai quotes from his personal encounter with Sheriff Hitchcock (known by the sobriquet "The Holy

Terror") as follows: "If leprosy can be stopped by getting all the lepers to Molokai, I propose to keep going after them until I get them all."

Father Damien, undoubtedly the best known figure in the annals of leprosy, in 1886 wrote a poignant report to Walter Gibson, President of the Board of Health in Honolulu. This document occupies eighteen pages of Mouritz' book and is entitled, "A Personal Experience: Thirteen Years Residence and Labor among the Lepers at Kalawao." The social and moral degradation that Damien found in the community of patients and their helpers on his arrival May 10, 1873, is best summarized, as he stated, in Hawaiian, *Aloe kanawai ma keia waki* (in this place there is no law). Thirteen years later in his 1886 report, Damien was able to write, "I am happy to say that . . . my labors here, which seemed to be almost in vain at the beginning, have, thanks to a kind Providence, been greatly crowned with success, as at present, there is very little, if any at all, of the . . . evils committed."

Those who have had the privilege of visiting Kalaupapa and Kalawao will remember vividly the collection of patent medicine bottles retrieved largely from the lava tube caves by Richard Marks, recipient of the Damien-Dutton Award for 1996 and a long-time resident of Kalaupapa. These bottles originally contained the vain hopes of the patients for a cure: a "few physics and their own native medicines" which were all they had available. Damien was, however, a man of vision and stated, "Perchance, in the near future, through the increasing interest and untiring perseverance in the study of the disease by the most intelligent physicians and scientists, a proper specific for the cure of leprosy may be discovered, which to my knowledge has not yet been found." Damien did not live to see the day he envisaged; however, his life so devoted to compassionate care and punctuated by acts of political activism, raised the social conscience of the world toward the stigma of leprosy and its need for mitigation, and his death from complications of leprosy on April 15, 1889, secured his name in the chronicles of the struggle against leprosy.

EARLY RESEARCH

Less than three months before Damien's arrival on Molokai, G. Armauer Hansen in Bergen, Norway, had already begun to pave the way for the modern understanding of leprosy. Hansen was convinced that leprosy was an infectious disease and not, as many of the scientists of the day believed, either hereditary or simply a response to environmental factors. To prove his conviction, Hansen examined numerous specimens of tissue fluid from the skin of leprosy patients, and on February 28, 1873, recorded his belief that the microscopic brownish "sticks" or rods he saw were the cause of leprosy. This landmark in the history of microbiology launched the quest for the scientific understanding of the disease that many years later would lead to the realization of some of Damien's hopes for leprosy sufferers. Hansen's discovery took place nine years before Robert Koch cultivated the tubercule bacillus. The leprosy bacillus *(Mycobacterium leprae)* thus, was the first germ known to cause chronic disease in humans, and was the first of many findings in leprosy research to contribute to biomedical research on other afflictions (e.g., complications of diabetes).

Even though Hansen was unable to grow the leprosy bacillus in test tubes and could not infect animals experimentally, the scientific community accepted his concepts on leprosy as a contagious disease. The Proceedings of the First International Leprosy Congress held in 1897 in Berlin contains reports from many leprosy endemic countries. By then the widely accepted infectious nature of leprosy reinforced measures for isolation of leprosy patients—

"preferably on an island"—in order to control the disease, and it was further recommended that "healthy children should be separated from their leprous parents as soon as possible." Lacking effective chemotherapy, these measures may have reduced the prevalence of leprosy in the more affluent countries but had very little, if any, influence on socioeconomically deprived countries where leprosy was more highly endemic.

MODERN ERA OF LEPROSY CONTROL AND RESEARCH

During 1900 to 1940, commensurate with the modest technological developments in biomedical research, the control and understanding of leprosy progressed little. The 1940s brought a new and exciting era in patient care, ushered in by the work of Guy Faget at Carville, Louisiana, who after careful long-term observations established the efficacy of intravenous sulfone in treating leprosy. By 1947, Dr. Robert Cochrane had shown that an oral and more useful form of sulfone, dapsone or DDS, was highly effective. This drug was inexpensive, withstood harsh tropical climates and was relatively nontoxic. More than a decade would pass before this "miracle drug" was employed widely. Gradually, however, DDS brought revolutionary changes, liberating many patients from both the physical damage and the stigmatizing sequelae of leprosy. Ambulatory treatment programs gradually replaced domiciliary care, markedly diminishing the stigma, and the social dislocation of patients and often their families. Patients could now live at home and visit the medical center periodically, or mobile units could go to satellite clinics along roads or paths. One by one some leprosaria were closed, but more frequently, the leprosaria became reference centers and provided care for the severely disabled. During this same era, pioneering surgical rehabilitation, coupled with injury-preventive measures for insensitive hands and feet, permitted patients to lead happier, more productive lives. The renowned orthopedic surgeon Paul Brand spearheaded this remarkable effort.

Many proactive groups over the years had called for abolition of the term "leper" to help minimize the stigma of leprosy. Improvements in treatment and management of patients helped their cause. One important event in this movement was the following resolution approved by the International Leprosy Association in 1948 in Havana:

> "That the term 'leper' in designation of the patient with leprosy be abandoned, and the person suffering from the disease be designated 'leprosy patient.'"

Others, notably Stanley Stein, Founding Editor of *The Star*, the patients' publication at Carville, preferred the designation "Hansen's disease" or HD for leprosy. Successive staff members of *The Star* have remained faithful to this policy.

Beginning with Hansen in 1873, numerous investigators attempted to grow the leprosy bacillus in the laboratory, without success. John Hanks, for example, spent his long professional career in pursuit of this elusive grail of leprosy research, in laboratories from Culion in the Philippines (1941-1945) to Harvard University and finally Johns Hopkins University.

Failure to achieve cultivation of the bacillus obstructed studies aimed at understanding the organism, and made it all the more important to develop models of the disease in animals. Based on observations by Chapman Binford in the late 1950s, leprosy infections were established in experimental animals during the next two decades. Infections in mice became the standard for testing chemotherapeutic agents and revealed the important discovery that leprosy bacilli were becoming resistant to DDS. In the early 1970s, Storrs, Walsh and others at Gulf South Research Institute in

Louisiana, found the armadillo to be highly susceptible to leprosy. This salient discovery opened up new avenues of leprosy research by providing large numbers of leprosy bacilli for an amazing array of leprosy-related scientific studies in, for example, diagnostic reagents, pathogenesis, epidemiology, chemotherapy, immunology, vaccines, and molecular biology.

For what many view as unfortunate missed opportunities, research on the pathogenesis and treatment of experimental leprosy in the armadillo was never sufficiently funded to reach its enormous research potential. Nevertheless, as a spin-off, the armadillo opened new vistas in the epidemiology of leprosy: newly captured animals often already had leprosy, indicating that there were nonhuman sources from which humans could contract the disease (see page 323).

PRESENT STATUS OF LEPROSY AND PROSPECTIVES

With the above background we now proceed to several topics of current interest in the battle to control leprosy. Some of the subjects are controversial; while the views expressed here are often shared by others, unless otherwise indicated any opinion that appears to be polemic is my responsibility.

Chemotherapy with Multidrug Regimens

The result of sulfone-resistant leprosy in 1964, and the subsequent discovery that such resistance was virtually universal, made therapeutic alternatives imperative and urgent. While several other antileprosy drugs were already in use, combined regimens were not employed. The pioneer multidrug therapeutic trial was undertaken in 1973 by Depasquale and Freerksen in Malta. Their regimen contained dapsone, prothionamide, isoniazid and rifampin, and proved to be effective.

In 1982, the World Health Organization (WHO) issued their recommendations for Multidrug Therapy (MDT). These recommendations were based on carefully considered but empirical judgments of efficacy, applicability in field programs, and cost. Goals were to

1. Treat patients,
2. Prevent bacterial resistance,
3. Interrupt transmission.

The primary drugs employed were dapsone, clofazimine and rifampin, administered for fixed periods of six or 24 months depending on the form of leprosy. Treatment was then stopped and the patient removed from official registries as a leprosy patient, whether or not there were sequelae such as deformity and/or disability. Cooperation between WHO, voluntary agencies, and the governments of endemic countries was excellent. Based on the above criteria, in 1991 WHO reported that the number of leprosy patients worldwide dropped from an estimated 10-20 million to 5.5 million. These statistics prompted WHO to approve a resolution in May 1991 to ". . . attain the global elimination of leprosy as a public health problem by the year 2000." Elimination as a public health problem was arbitrarily set at one patient or less per 10,000 population, by country. WHO data in 1997 indicated that, compared to 1981, the prevalence of leprosy was reduced by 85%. Currently the global prevalence of leprosy is 1.6 per 10,000 population and 91% of the patients live in 16 major endemic countries. Prevalence in these 16 major countries currently stands at 4.3 per 10,000 population. Countries with higher prevalences include India, Brazil, Myanmar, Indonesia, Nigeria, Bangladesh and the Philippines. WHO sets the total global number of leprosy patients today at approximately 850,000.

Many observers expect that WHO will announce in

the year 2000 that the goal of elimination of leprosy as a public health problem has been achieved. To help achieve this goal over the approximately two years that remain, WHO is establishing special strategies:

1. Elimination campaigns to reach hidden cases,
2. Action programs to reach patients in all readily accessible areas,
3. Provision of MDT to every general health facility. At the same time there are attempts to reduce the maximum duration of treatment to one year, or even one month. If such reduced treatment programs become acceptable, prevalence rates will approach the number of new patients "successfully" treated.

The impact that the stated accomplishments to date of the WHO's "elimination of leprosy as a public health problem" program is having, is already alarming, let alone to envisage what effect the announcement of the success of the program would have: leprosy research today is meagerly funded, if at all, in most research institutes; treatment programs are now being increasingly integrated into general health services that do not possess the special expertise in diagnosis and treatment required for leprosy, and the public as well as the medical community are beginning to view leprosy as a solved problem. One little known risk of a summary approach to the management of leprosy is the potential for misdiagnosis. To economize resources and personnel, clinicians are not being encouraged to take skin smears or biopsy specimens to help establish diagnoses or to guide clinical treatment. Our files in the Leprosy Registry of the Armed Forces Institute of Pathology contain many specimens that represent recent misdiagnoses by clinicians. A cavalier approach to the diagnosis of leprosy is never good medical practice.

There is little question that there are fewer leprosy patients now than several decades ago, and that for most patients the quality of life is significantly improved. Much of this can be attributed to the concerted effort to reach more patients with effective drugs. That is most laudable. In view of our present knowledge, however, are we yet in possession of sufficient accurate data to suppose that by 2000 A.D. the goal set by WHO can be reached? Many individuals and some agencies deeply involved in the care of people affected by leprosy believe this possibility is remote. For example, do the reported national prevalences of leprosy represent the real prevalences? Valid data on this question are difficult for most endemic countries to generate. The number of new patients each year (incidence) has declined very little, even in most regions where MDT has been rigidly applied for many years, and remains at about 600,000 new cases each year worldwide. Thus, the goal of the interruption of transmission of leprosy has not been reached. Also, there is insufficient data to assume that there will not be a significant number of relapses following MDT treatment, especially if the period of therapy is reduced to one year or less.

Given the relative vacuum of hard data that would withstand rigorous critical analysis, those who proclaim the "elimination of leprosy as a public health problem" must consider their decision very carefully. When "success" is announced, support will be withdrawn by WHO, national programs will be diminished, and voluntary agencies will experience further reductions in resources to support care of leprosy patients—both active patients and the millions of individuals who remain disabled by the disease. Are those in authority to do so, willing to take this step as soon as approximately two years from now? I hope not, or only if they possess compelling hard data to answer the questions that more and more critics are raising on this issue. Premature reductions in the struggle against leprosy for the sake of a calendar deadline may well spell disaster, and leave our posterity with an enormous health problem, as similar concepts did for tuberculosis.

Eradication of Leprosy

The motto of the XV International Leprosy Congress in Beijing in 1998 was wisely phrased, "Toward the Eradication of Leprosy." This wording was chosen with the belief that eradication is probably a long way off. There are many unknowns. For example, are there significant nonhuman sources of leprosy? What are the most important modes of transmission? Is a vaccine feasible? Can the presumed current trend of reduction of patients be sustained with diminishing resources? Are there modes of control of leprosy other than chemotherapy?

In consideration of the latter question there are two significant historic correlatives: 1) endemic leprosy disappeared from northern Europe long before specific chemotherapeutic agents became available, and 2) no infectious disease so far has been eradicated by chemotherapy. The beginning of the disappearance of leprosy in northern Europe coincided with quantum improvements in housing and other socioeconomic factors in the Renaissance period. Today, socioeconomic status and prevalence of leprosy in most regions are inversely proportional, suggesting that improved housing and other living conditions will reduce or even eradicate leprosy. Further, if the most important route of transmission is the nasorespiratory passages, as most authorities believe, then more spacious dwellings would reduce contagion.

We now know that there are nonhuman sources of leprosy bacilli. A high percentage of armadillos in the southern United States are naturally infected with leprosy bacilli. Some wild nonhuman primates (monkeys, chimpanzees and possibly baboons) in West Africa and the Philippines have leprosy. These animals may serve as reservoirs that could perpetuate endemic leprosy, in spite of all efforts to eradicate the disease in humans. Some investigators believe that the leprosy bacillus may survive in soil, but this is not widely accepted. At any rate, the role that nonhuman sources of leprosy may play in efforts to eradicate leprosy in humans has been investigated only superficially.

Candidate vaccines for leprosy have long been tested in large field trials, and found wanting. Repeated BCG vaccination confers significant protection against leprosy and may have use in high risk individuals. The effect, however, is insufficient to consider BCG as part of a leprosy eradication program.

In conclusion, the struggle against leprosy must go on until all people affected by the disease can live happy and productive lives. Today there are insufficient valid data to decide that the present infrastructure of leprosy control and management programs can be abolished, and such data will be a long time in coming.

The job is far from completed.